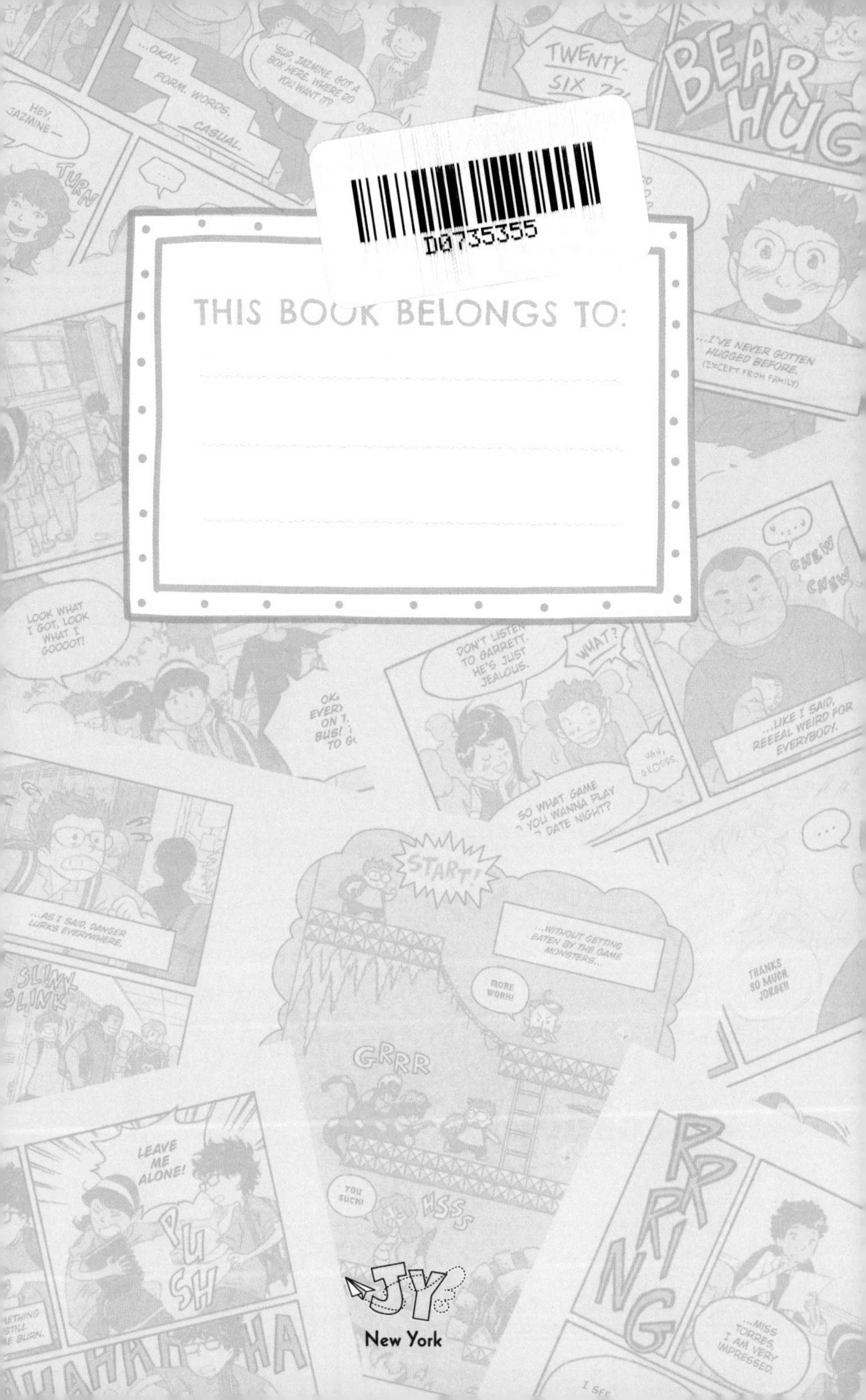
HEY, JAZMINE—
TURN
...OKAY.
FORM. WORDS.
CASUAL.
'SUP, JAZMINE. GOT A BOX HERE. WHERE DO YOU WANT IT?
TWENTY-SIX
BEAR HUG
...I'VE NEVER GOTTEN HUGGED BEFORE. (EXCEPT FROM FAMILY)
CHEW CHEW
LOOK WHAT I GOT, LOOK WHAT I GOOOOT!
DON'T LISTEN TO GARRETT. HE'S JUST JEALOUS.
WHAT?
UGH, GROSSS.
...LIKE I SAID, REEEAL WEIRD FOR EVERYBODY.
...AS I SAID, DANGER LURKS EVERYWHERE.
SLINK SLINK
START!
...WITHOUT GETTING EATEN BY THE GAME MONSTERS...
MORE WORK!
THANKS SO MUCH, JORGE!!
GRRR
LEAVE ME ALONE!
PUSH
YOU SUCK!
HSSS
RRRING
...MISS TORRES, I AM VERY IMPRESSED.

THIS BOOK BELONGS TO:

JY
New York

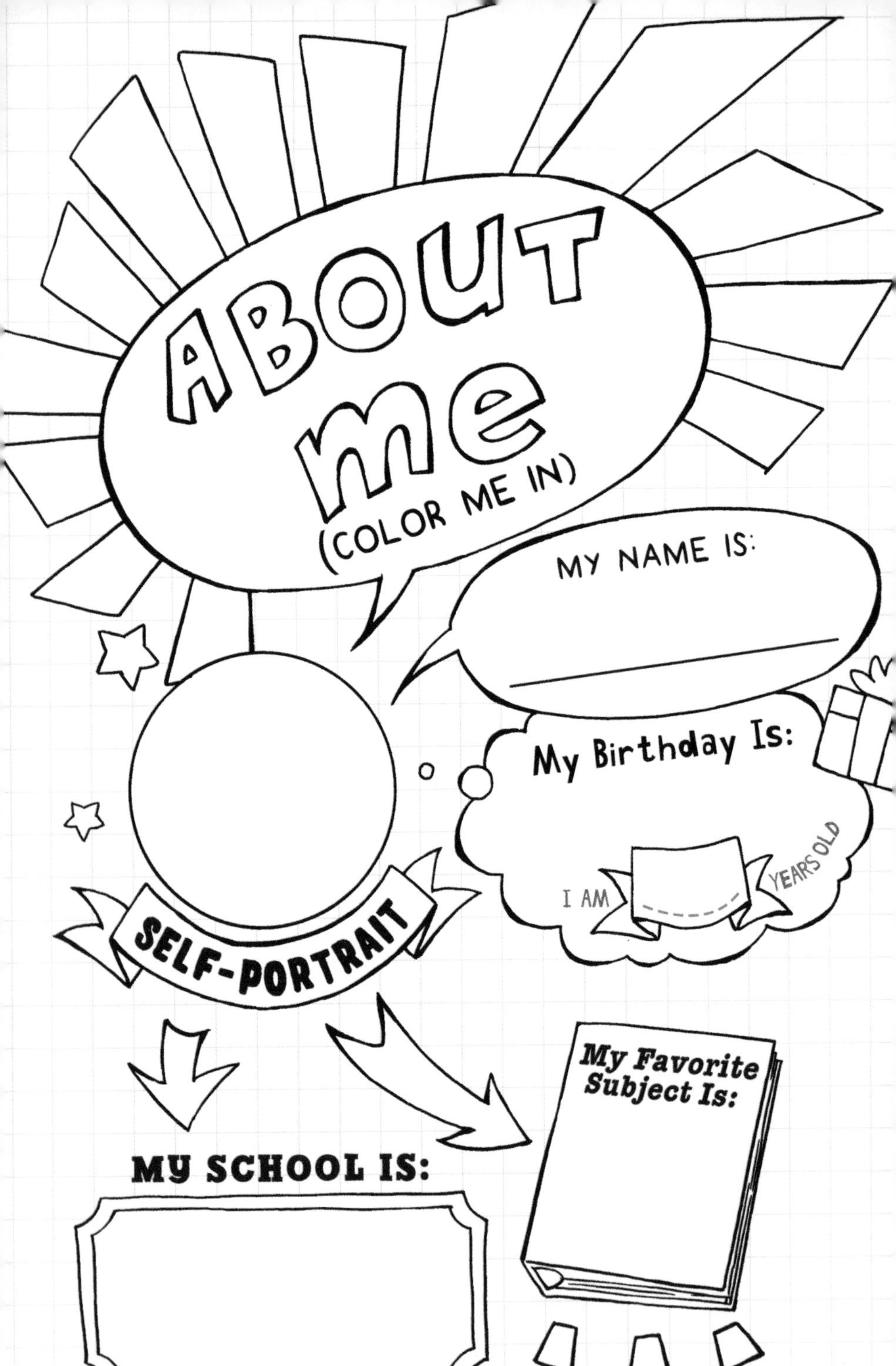
ABOUT me
(COLOR ME IN)
MY NAME IS:
My Birthday Is:
I AM
YEARS OLD
SELF-PORTRAIT
My Favorite Subject Is:
MY SCHOOL IS:

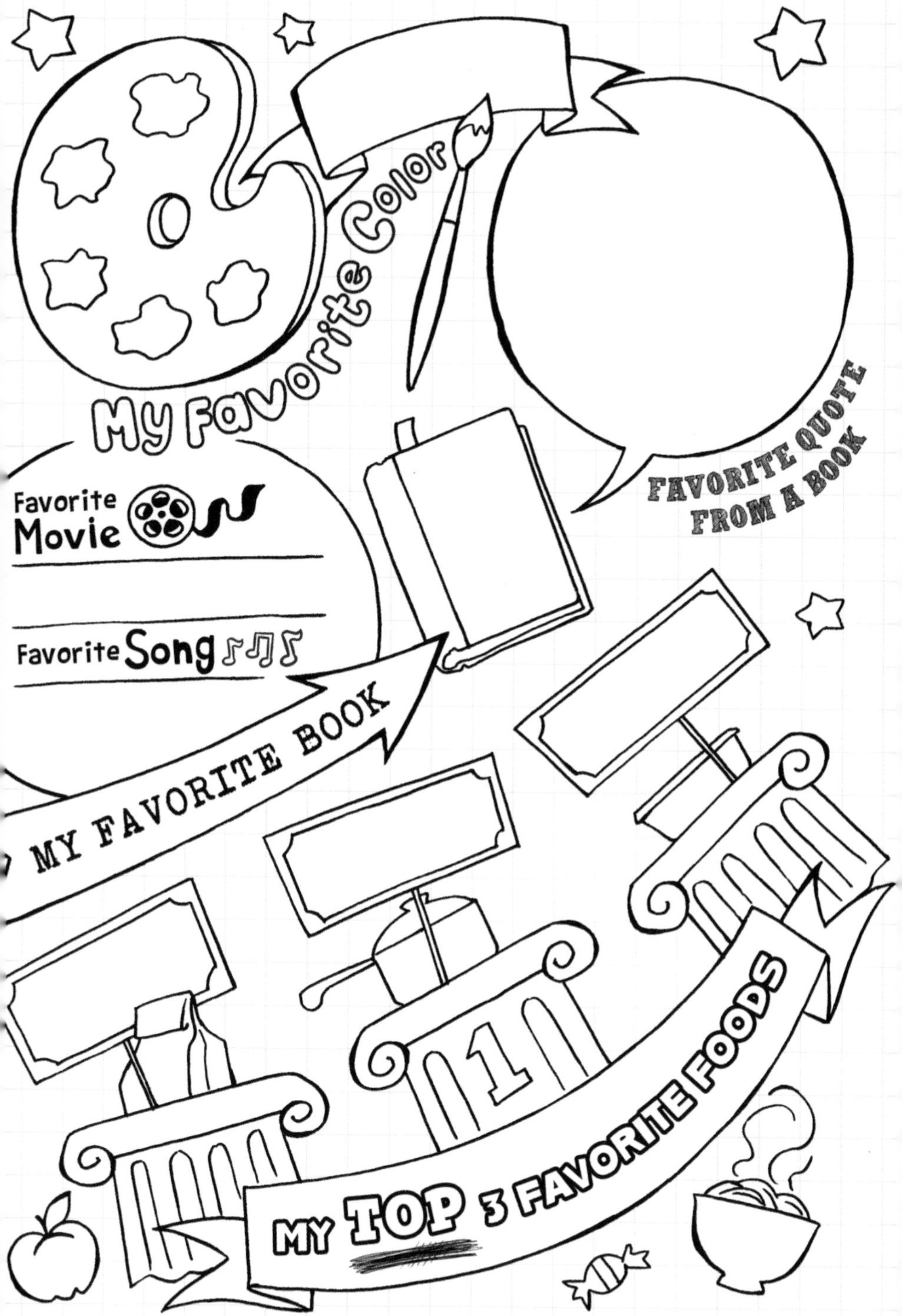

My Favorite Color
FAVORITE QUOTE FROM A BOOK
Favorite Movie
Favorite Song
MY FAVORITE BOOK
1
MY TOP 3 FAVORITE FOODS

01 JAN

HOLIDAYS

New Year's Day

Spaghetti Day

Trivia Day

Bird Day

Bubble Bath Day

Appreciate a Dragon Day

Thesaurus Day

Popcorn Day

Penguin Awareness Day

Martin Luther King Jr. Day

Squirrel Appreciation Day

Handwriting Day

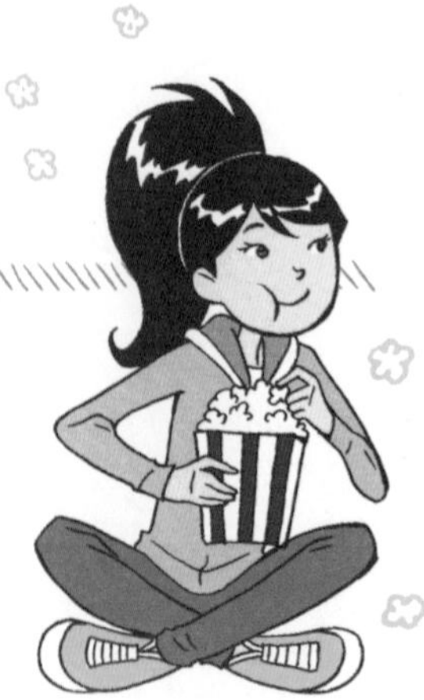

SUNDAY	MONDAY	TUESDAY

WEDNESDAY	THURSDAY	FRIDAY	SATURDAY

02 FEB

SUNDAY	MONDAY	TUESDAY

HOLIDAYS

- Groundhog Day
- Eat Ice Cream for Breakfast Day
- Thank a Mail Carrier Day
- Chopsticks Day
- Pizza Day
- Make a Friend Day
- Abraham Lincoln's Birthday
- Valentine's Day
- Susan B. Anthony Day
- Random Acts of Kindness Day
- George Washington's Birthday

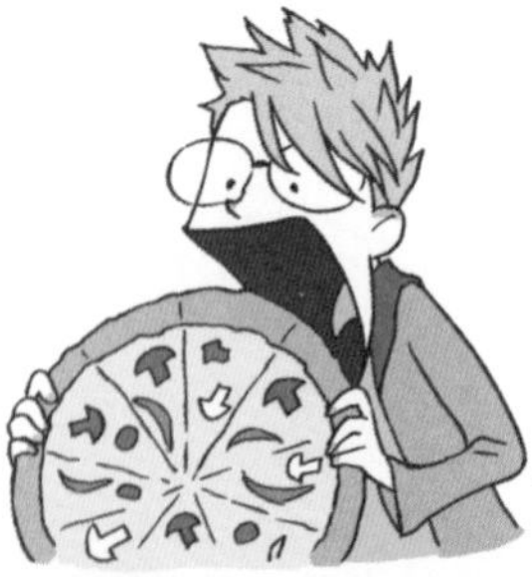

WEDNESDAY	THURSDAY	FRIDAY	SATURDAY

03
MAR

SUNDAY	MONDAY	TUESDAY

HOLIDAYS

International Women's Day

Daylight Savings Time Begins (U.S.)

Saint Patrick's Day

Spring Equinox

Waffle Day

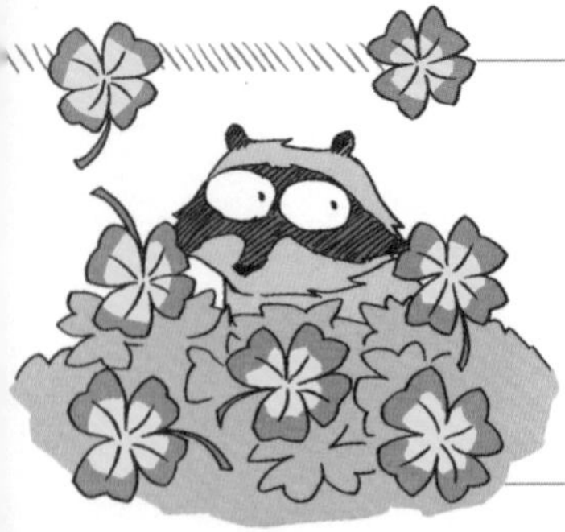

WEDNESDAY	THURSDAY	FRIDAY	SATURDAY

04 APR

SUNDAY	MONDAY	TUESDAY
		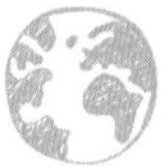
		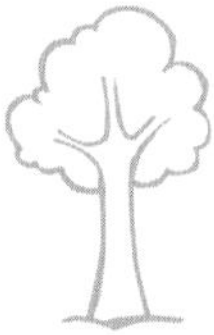

HOLIDAYS

April Fools' Day

Peanut Butter & Jelly Day

World Party Day

Burrito Day

World Health Day

Siblings Day

Easter

Grilled Cheese Sandwich Day

Garlic Day

Earth Day

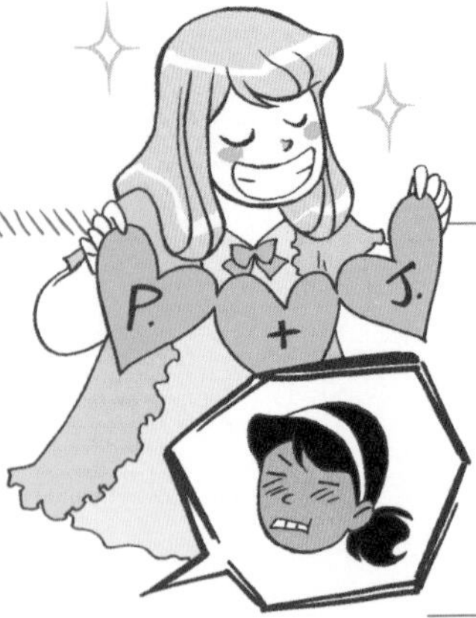
P.
+
J.

WEDNESDAY	THURSDAY	FRIDAY	SATURDAY

05

MAY

HOLIDAYS

Cinco de Mayo

Teacher Day

No Socks Day

Clean Up Your Room Day

Mother's Day

Dance Like a Chicken Day

World Sleep Day

Victoria Day (Canada)

Memorial Day (U.S.)

Hamburger Day

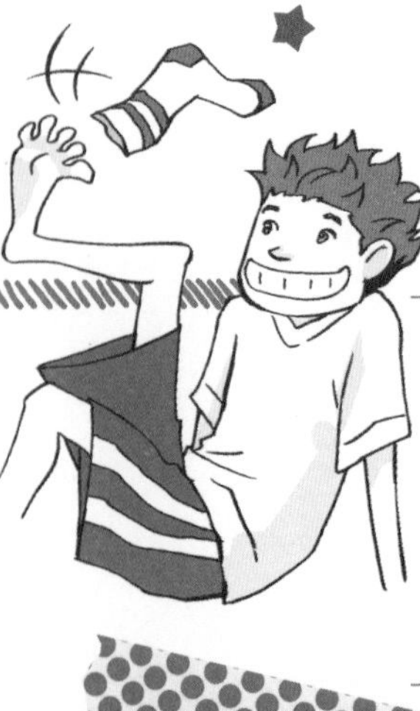

SUNDAY	MONDAY	TUESDAY

WEDNESDAY	THURSDAY	FRIDAY	SATURDAY

06
JUNE

SUNDAY	MONDAY	TUESDAY
		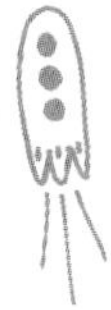

HOLIDAYS

World Environment Day

World Oceans Day

Iced Tea Day

Corn on the Cob Day

Father's Day

Summer Solstice

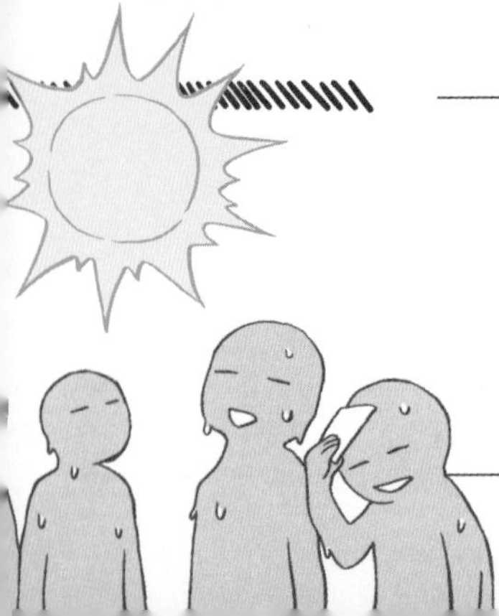

WEDNESDAY	THURSDAY	FRIDAY	SATURDAY

SUNDAY	MONDAY	TUESDAY 

07
JUL

HOLIDAYS

Canada Day

International Joke Day

World UFO Day

Independence Day (U.S.)

Sidewalk Egg Frying Day

Fried Chicken Day

International Chocolate Day

Video Games Day

Global Hug Your Kids Day

Hot Dog Day

Milk Chocolate Day

Parent's Day (U.S.)

International Day of Friendship

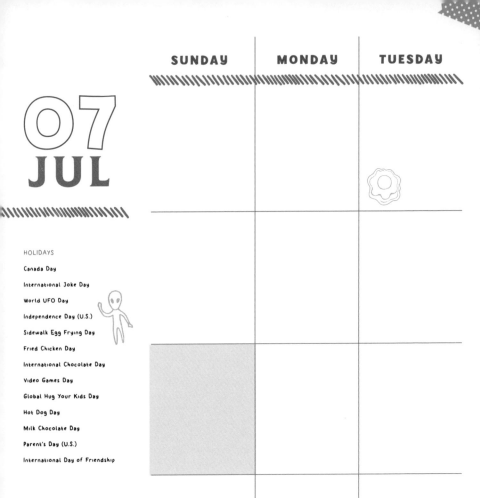

WEDNESDAY	THURSDAY	FRIDAY	SATURDAY

08
AUG

HOLIDAYS

Campfire Day

Ice Cream Sandwich Day

Sister's Day

Watermelon Day

Chocolate Chip Cookie Day

Underwear Day

Book Lovers Day

Lazy Day

S'mores Day

Middle Child's Day

International Left Handers Day

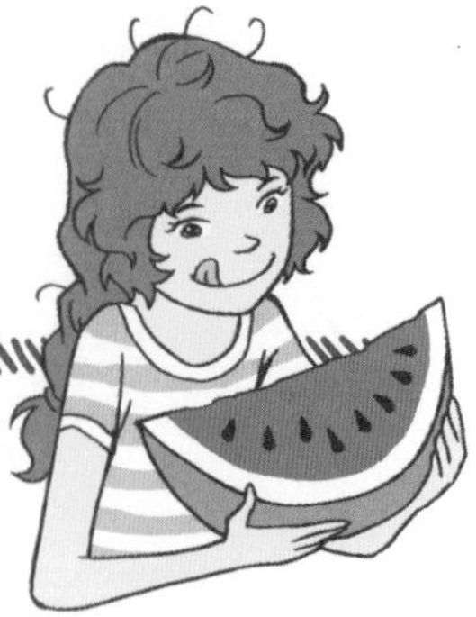

SUNDAY	MONDAY	TUESDAY

WEDNESDAY	THURSDAY	FRIDAY	SATURDAY

09
SEPT

HOLIDAYS

Read a Book Day
Labor Day (U.S.)
Grandparents Day (U.S.)
International Literacy Day
Teddy Bear Day
Patriot Day (U.S.)
Chocolate Milkshake Day
Fortune Cookie Day
Mid-Autumn Festival
Rosh Hashanah
Mexican Independence Day
Constitution Day (U.S.)
Cheeseburger Day
Women's Friendship Day
International Peace Day
Autumn Equinox
Comic Book Day
Native American Day

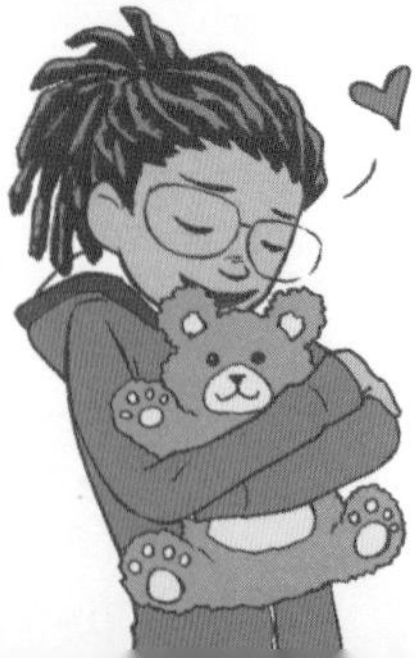

SUNDAY	MONDAY	TUESDAY

WEDNESDAY	THURSDAY	FRIDAY	SATURDAY

10
OCT

HOLIDAYS

Hair Day
World Smile Day
Poetry Day
Taco Day
Do Something Nice Day
World Teachers' Day
Child Health Day
Walk to School Day
World Cerebral Palsy Day
World Mental Health Day
Columbus Day
Halloween

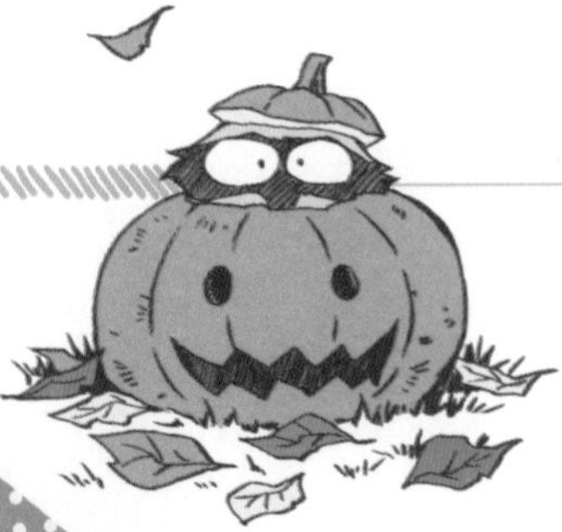

SUNDAY	MONDAY	TUESDAY

WEDNESDAY	THURSDAY	FRIDAY	SATURDAY

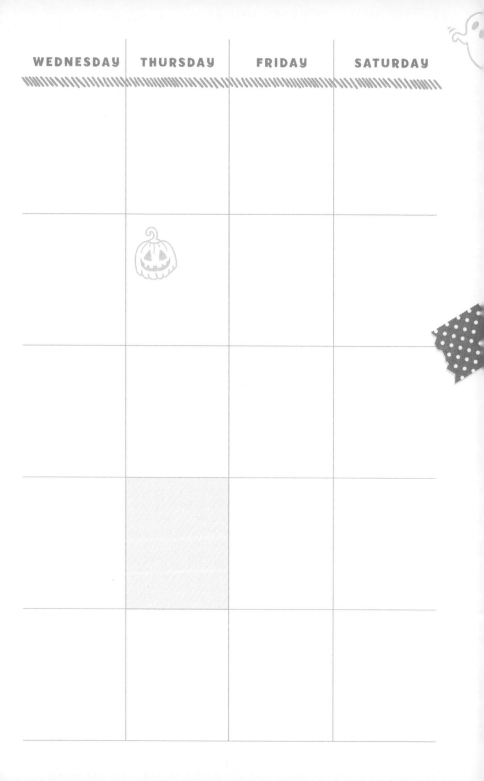

11
NOV

SUNDAY	MONDAY	TUESDAY

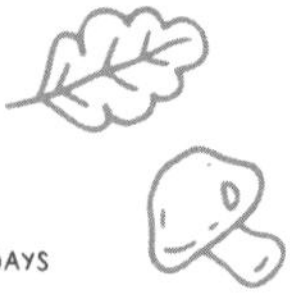

HOLIDAYS

Daylight Savings Time Ends (U.S.)

Election Day (U.S.)

Book Lovers Day

Young Readers Day

Veteran's Day (U.S.)

Chicken Soup for the Soul Day

World Kindness Day

America Recycles Day

Evolution Day

Parfait Day

Shopping Reminder Day

Thanksgiving

French Toast Day

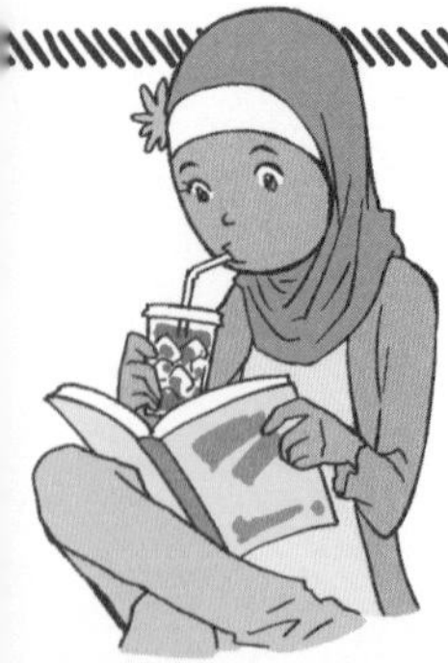

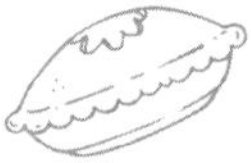

WEDNESDAY	THURSDAY	FRIDAY	SATURDAY

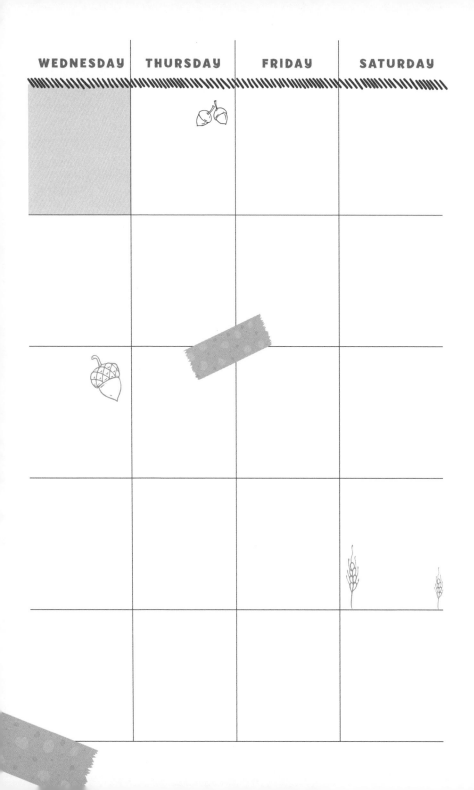

12
DEC

HOLIDAYS

Eat a Red Apple Day
Saint Nicholas Day
Pearl Harbor Remembrance Day
Brownie Day
Human Rights Day
Chanukah
Bill of Rights Day (U.S.)
Bake Cookies Day
Winter Solstice
Christmas
Boxing Day
Bacon Day
New Year's Eve

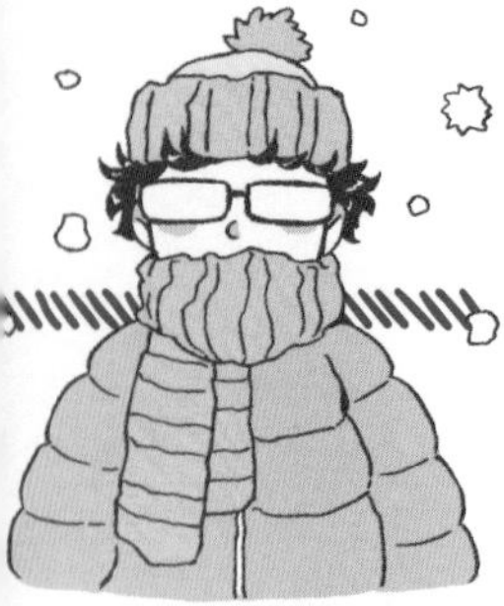

SUNDAY	MONDAY	TUESDAY

WEDNESDAY	THURSDAY	FRIDAY	SATURDAY

01 JAN

HOLIDAYS

New Year's Day

Clean off Your Desk Day

Bagel Day

Martin Luther King Jr. Day

Pie Day

Peanut Butter Day

Croissant Day

Hot Chocolate Day

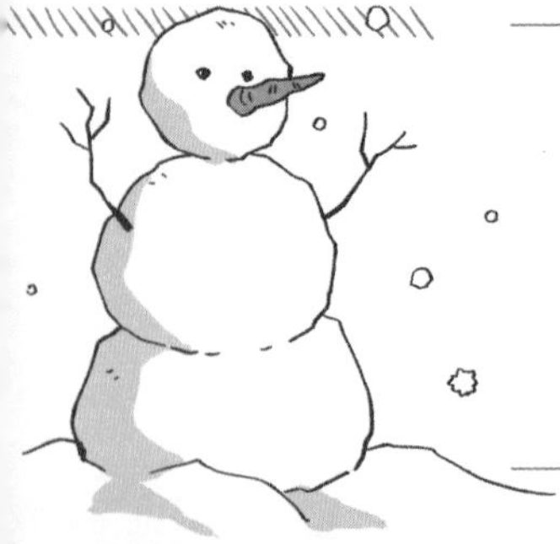

SUNDAY	MONDAY	TUESDAY

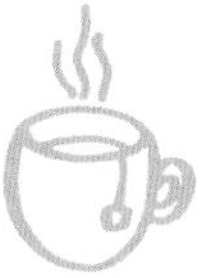

WEDNESDAY	THURSDAY	FRIDAY	SATURDAY

02
FEB

HOLIDAYS

Black History Month

Groundhog Day

Bubble Gum Day

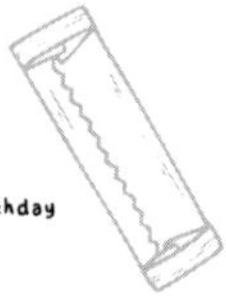

Umbrella Day

White Shirt Day

Abraham Lincoln's Birthday

Ferris Wheel Day

Valentine's Day

Susan B. Anthony Day

George Washington's Birthday

Be Humble Day

Tell a Fairy Tale Day

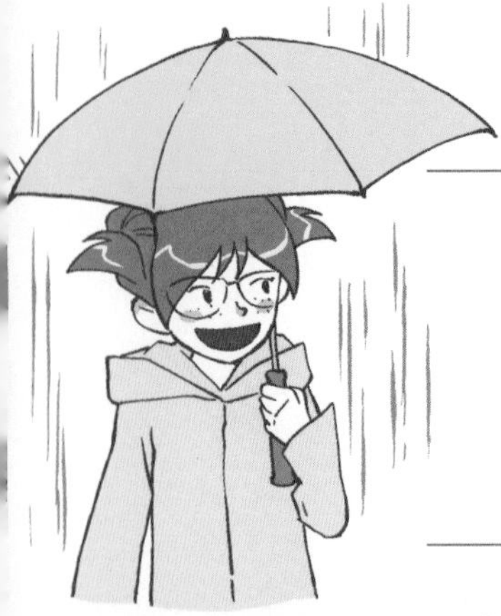

SUNDAY	MONDAY	TUESDAY

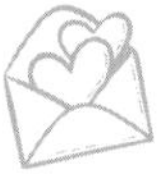

WEDNESDAY	THURSDAY	FRIDAY	SATURDAY
			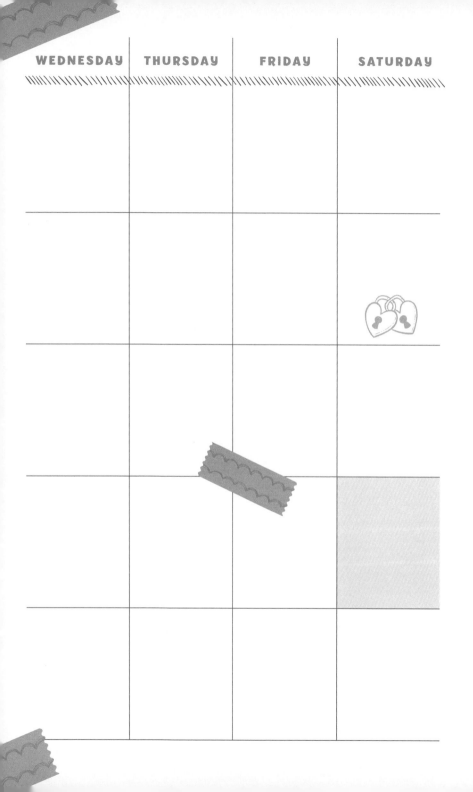

03
MAR

HOLIDAYS

National Women's History Month

Read Across America Day

International Women's Day

Daylight Savings Time Begins (U.S.)

Saint Patrick's Day

Spring Equinox

World Poetry Day

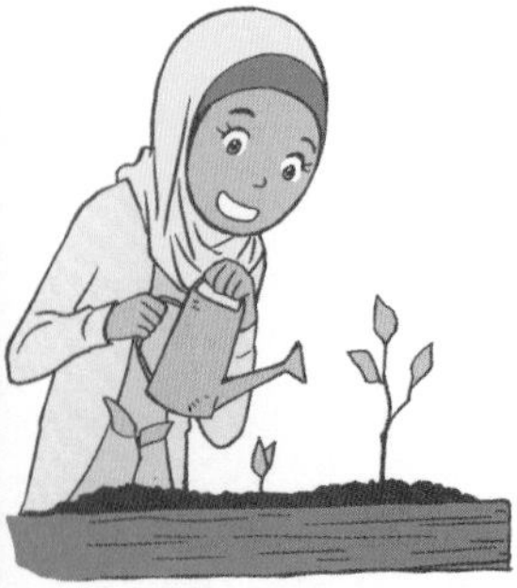

SUNDAY	MONDAY	TUESDAY
	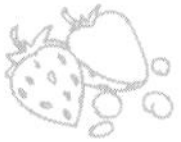	
	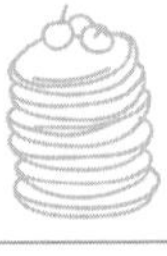	

WEDNESDAY	THURSDAY	FRIDAY	SATURDAY
	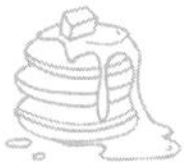		

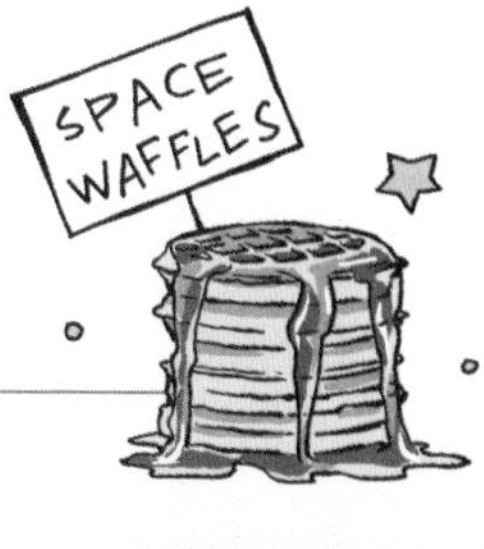
SPACE WAFFLES

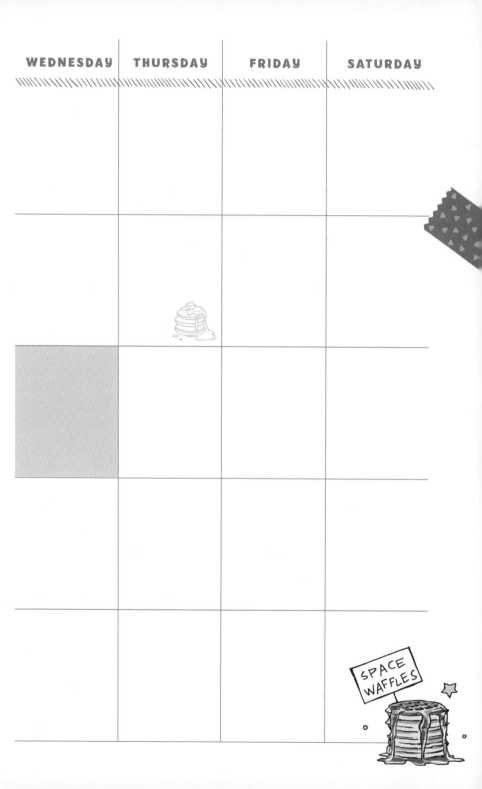

04
APR

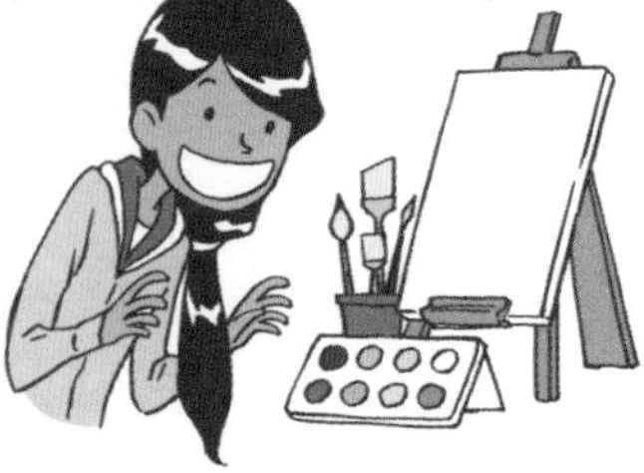

HOLIDAYS

April Fools' Day

Internartional Children's Book Day

School Librarian Day

Easter

Pet day

Rubber Eraser Day

World Art Day

Earth Day

Pretzel Day

Morse Code Day

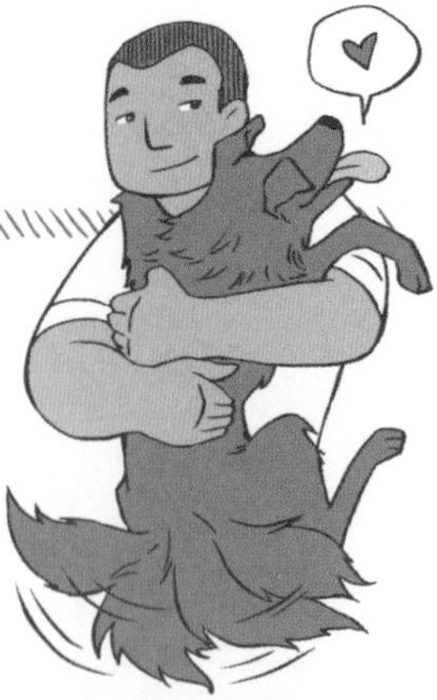

SUNDAY	MONDAY	TUESDAY
		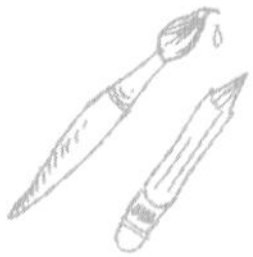
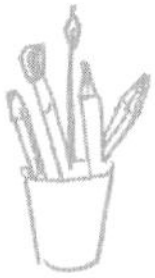		

WEDNESDAY	THURSDAY	FRIDAY	SATURDAY

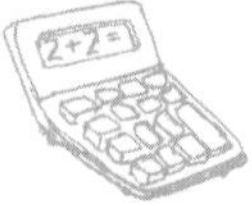

05
MAY

HOLIDAYS

Asian American and Pacific Islander Heritage Month

Free Comic Book Day

Cinco de Mayo

Teacher Day

Mother's Day

Armed Forces Day (U.S.)

Pizza Party Day

Endangered Species Day

Victoria Day (Canada)

Memorial Day (U.S.)

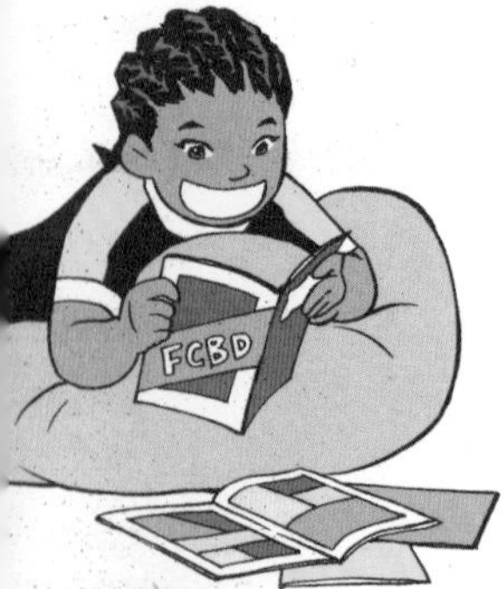
FCBD

SUNDAY	MONDAY	TUESDAY

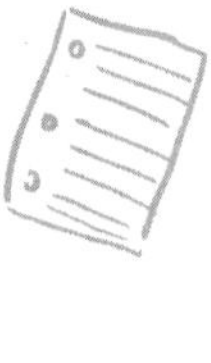

WEDNESDAY	THURSDAY	FRIDAY	SATURDAY

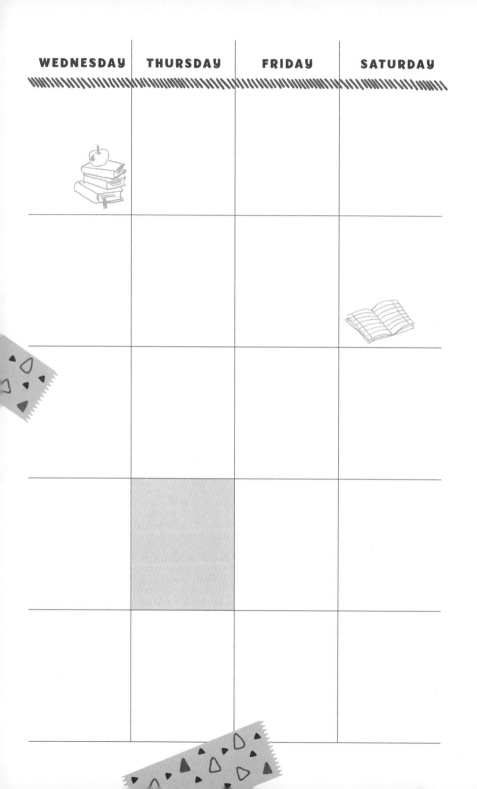

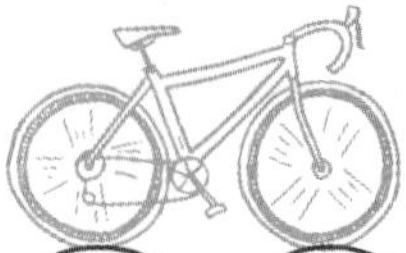

06

JUNE

HOLIDAYS

World Bicycle Day

Donut Day

World Environment Day

Best Friends Day

Flag Day (U.S.)

Father's Day

Summer Solstice

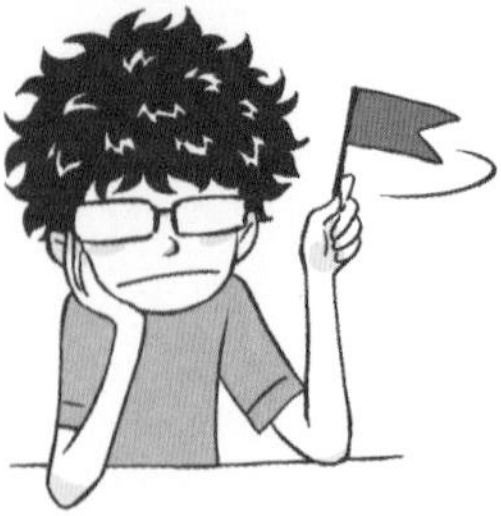

SUNDAY	MONDAY	TUESDAY
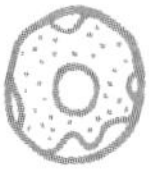		

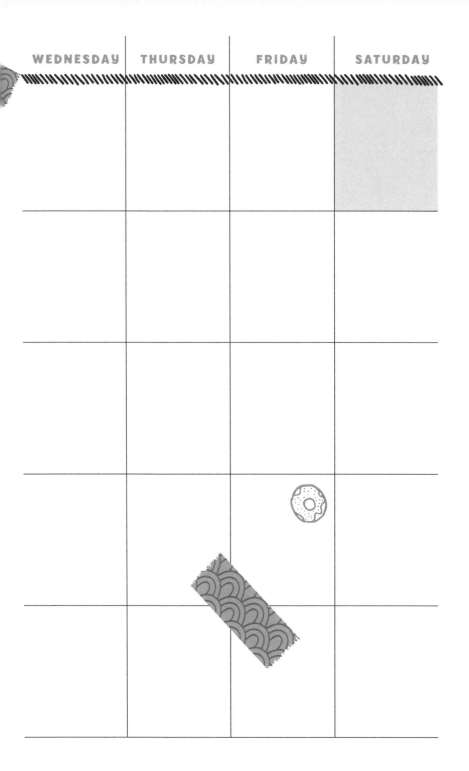

WEDNESDAY	THURSDAY	FRIDAY	SATURDAY

TIME CAPSULE

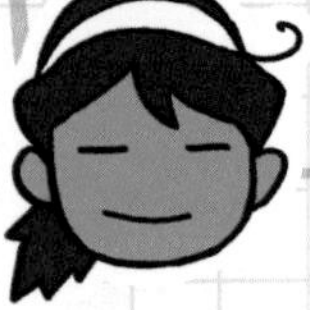

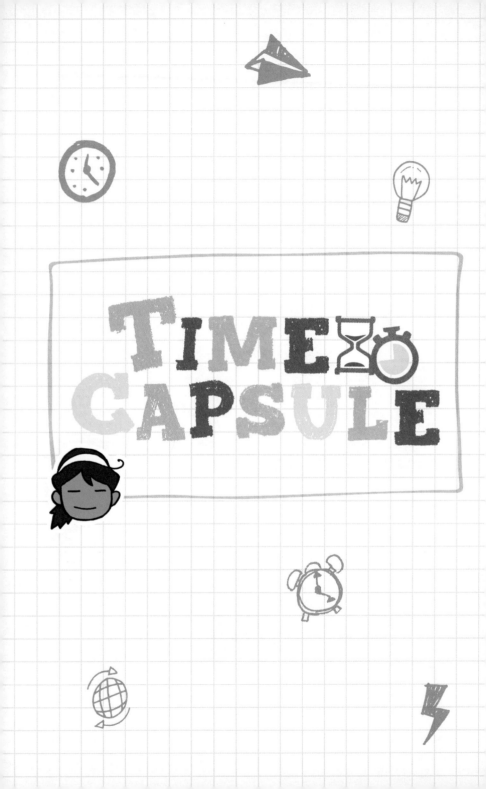

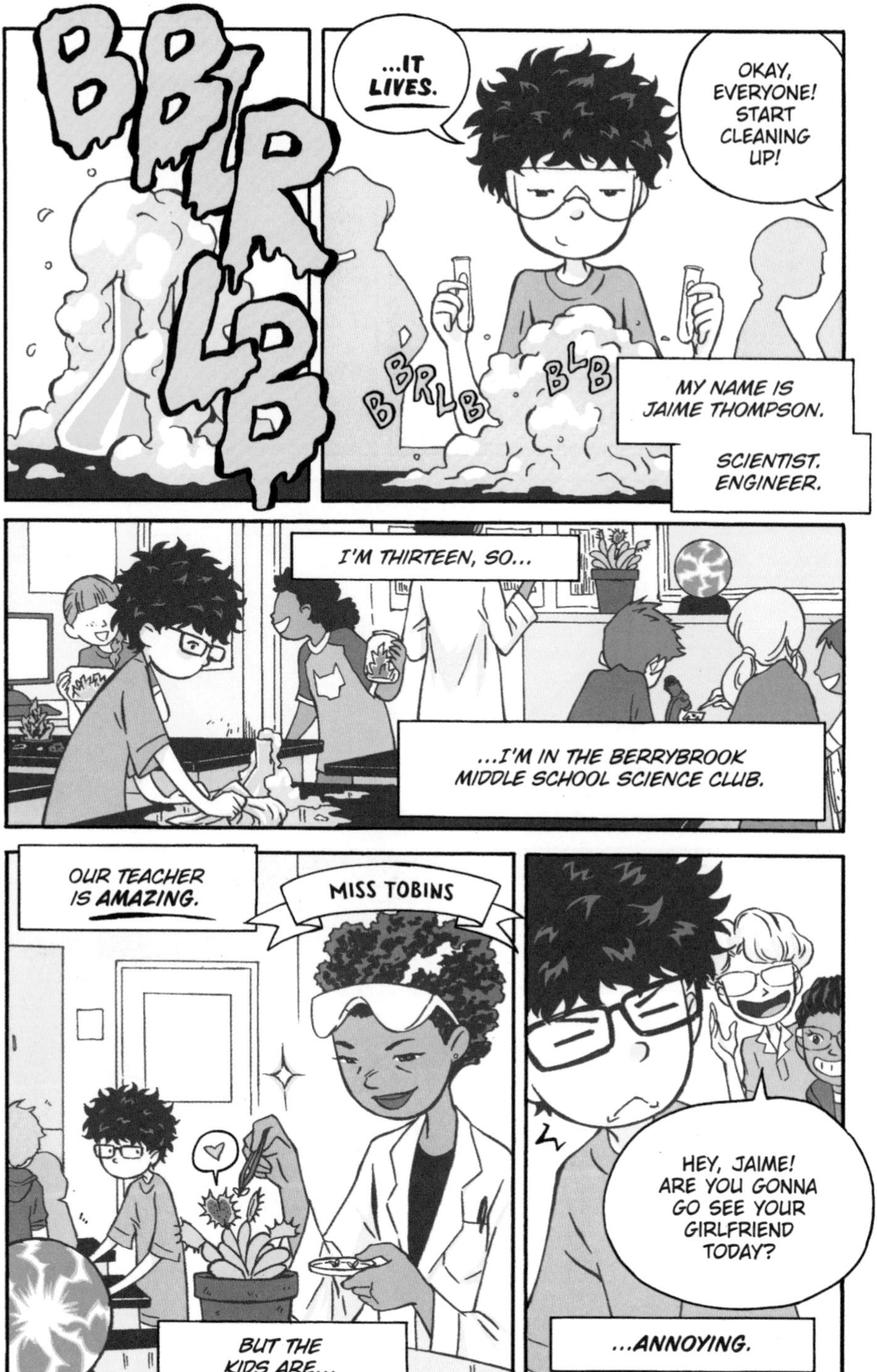
BBRLBD
...IT LIVES.
OKAY, EVERYONE! START CLEANING UP!
BBRLB BLB
MY NAME IS JAIME THOMPSON.
SCIENTIST. ENGINEER.
I'M THIRTEEN, SO...
...I'M IN THE BERRYBROOK MIDDLE SCHOOL SCIENCE CLUB.
OUR TEACHER IS AMAZING.
MISS TOBINS
BUT THE KIDS ARE...
HEY, JAIME! ARE YOU GONNA GO SEE YOUR GIRLFRIEND TODAY?
...ANNOYING.

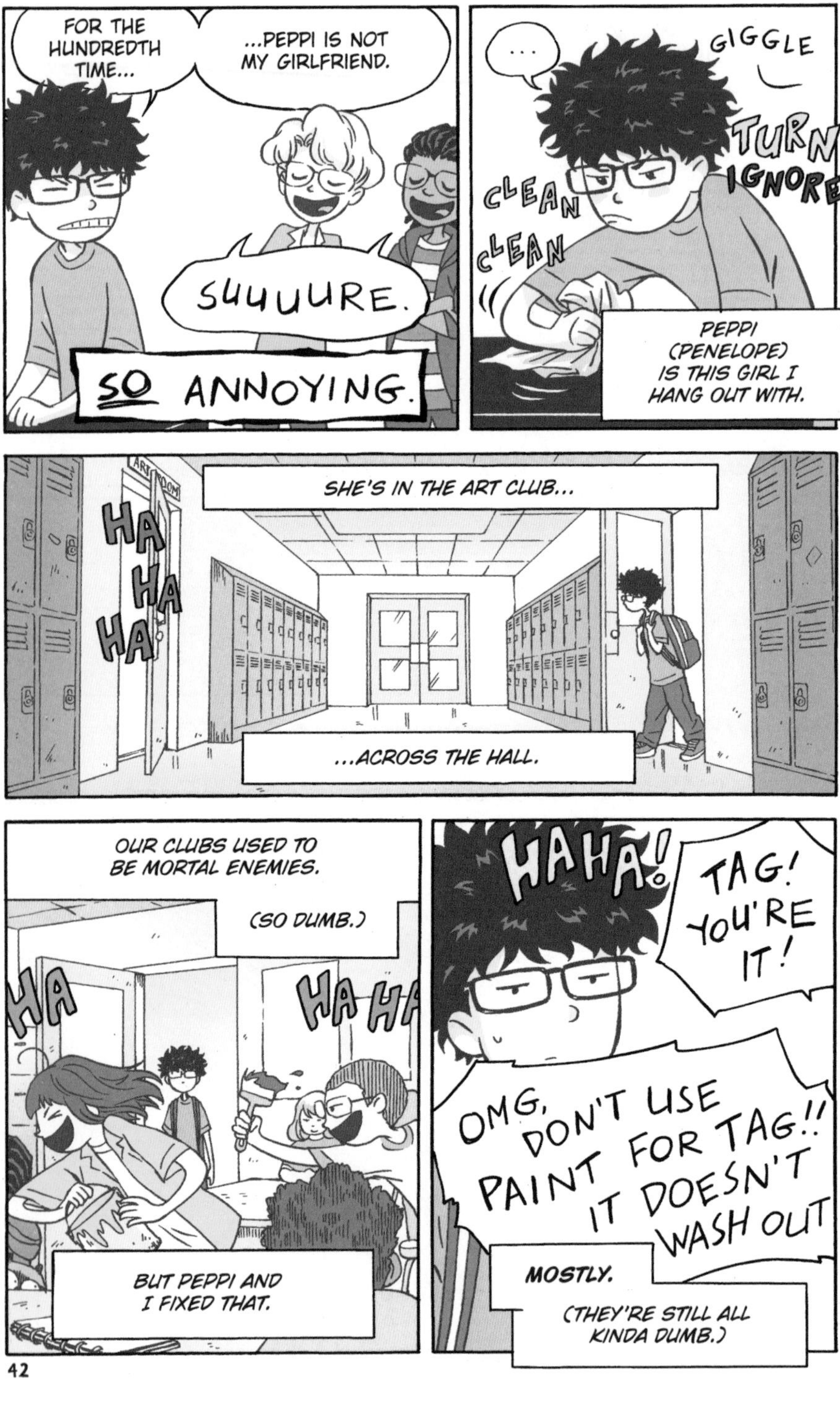
FOR THE HUNDREDTH TIME...
...PEPPI IS NOT MY GIRLFRIEND.
SUUUURE.
SO ANNOYING.
...
GIGGLE
TURN
IGNORE
CLEAN
CLEAN
PEPPI (PENELOPE) IS THIS GIRL I HANG OUT WITH.
SHE'S IN THE ART CLUB...
HA HA HA
...ACROSS THE HALL.
OUR CLUBS USED TO BE MORTAL ENEMIES.
(SO DUMB.)
HA
HA HA
BUT PEPPI AND I FIXED THAT.
HAHA!
TAG! YOU'RE IT!
OMG, DON'T USE PAINT FOR TAG!! IT DOESN'T WASH OUT
MOSTLY.
(THEY'RE STILL ALL KINDA DUMB.)

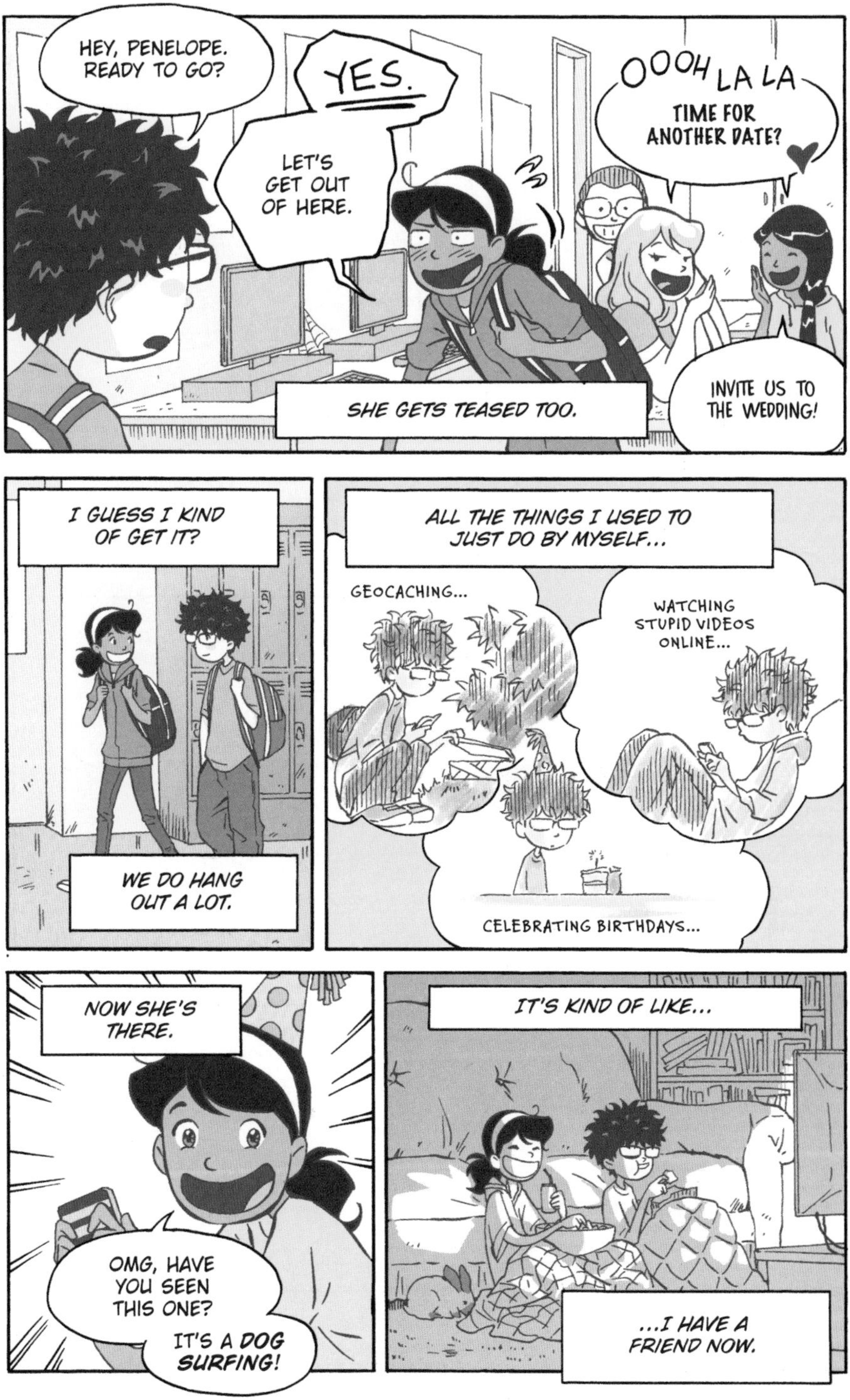
HEY, PENELOPE. READY TO GO?
YES.
LET'S GET OUT OF HERE.
OOOH LA LA
TIME FOR ANOTHER DATE?
SHE GETS TEASED TOO.
INVITE US TO THE WEDDING!
I GUESS I KIND OF GET IT?
WE DO HANG OUT A LOT.
ALL THE THINGS I USED TO JUST DO BY MYSELF...
GEOCACHING...
WATCHING STUPID VIDEOS ONLINE...
CELEBRATING BIRTHDAYS...
NOW SHE'S THERE.
OMG, HAVE YOU SEEN THIS ONE?
IT'S A DOG SURFING!
IT'S KIND OF LIKE...
...I HAVE A FRIEND NOW.

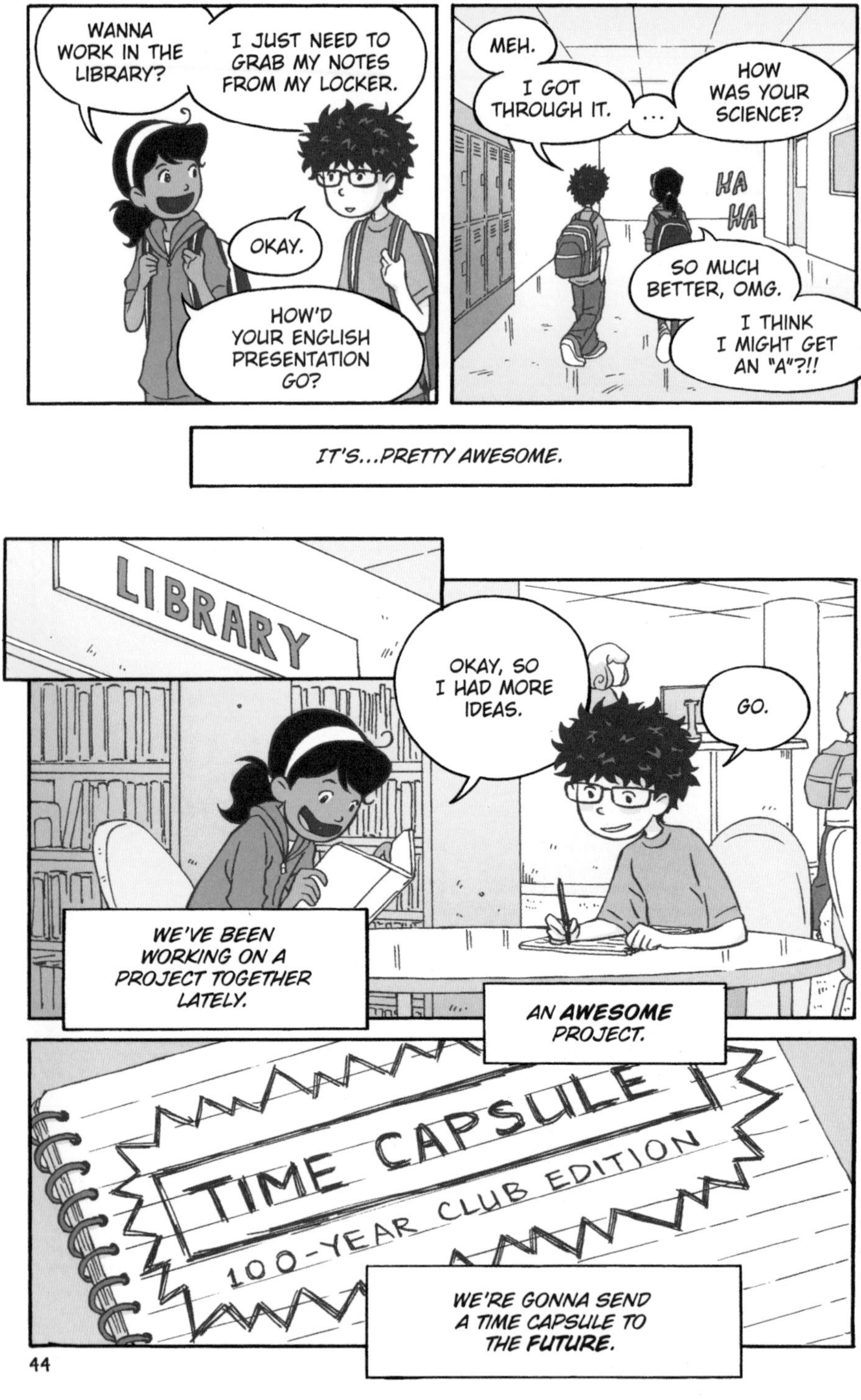
WANNA WORK IN THE LIBRARY?
I JUST NEED TO GRAB MY NOTES FROM MY LOCKER.
OKAY.
HOW'D YOUR ENGLISH PRESENTATION GO?
MEH.
I GOT THROUGH IT.
...
HOW WAS YOUR SCIENCE?
HA HA
SO MUCH BETTER, OMG.
I THINK I MIGHT GET AN "A"?!!
IT'S...PRETTY AWESOME.
LIBRARY
OKAY, SO I HAD MORE IDEAS.
GO.
WE'VE BEEN WORKING ON A PROJECT TOGETHER LATELY.
AN AWESOME PROJECT.
TIME CAPSULE
100-YEAR CLUB EDITION
WE'RE GONNA SEND A TIME CAPSULE TO THE FUTURE.

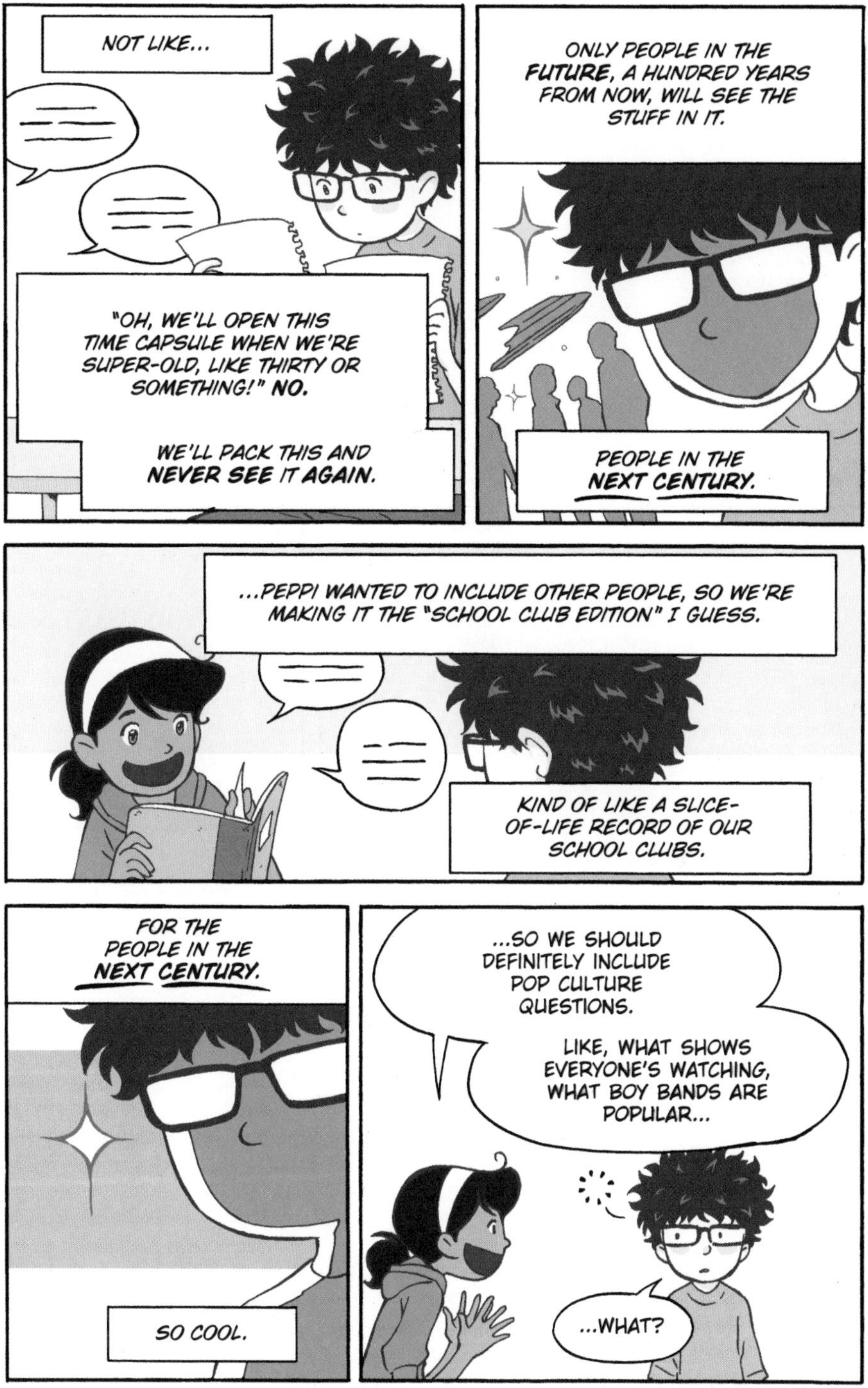
NOT LIKE...
"OH, WE'LL OPEN THIS TIME CAPSULE WHEN WE'RE SUPER-OLD, LIKE THIRTY OR SOMETHING!" NO.
WE'LL PACK THIS AND NEVER SEE IT AGAIN.
ONLY PEOPLE IN THE FUTURE, A HUNDRED YEARS FROM NOW, WILL SEE THE STUFF IN IT.
PEOPLE IN THE NEXT CENTURY.
...PEPPI WANTED TO INCLUDE OTHER PEOPLE, SO WE'RE MAKING IT THE "SCHOOL CLUB EDITION" I GUESS.
KIND OF LIKE A SLICE-OF-LIFE RECORD OF OUR SCHOOL CLUBS.
FOR THE PEOPLE IN THE NEXT CENTURY.
SO COOL.
...SO WE SHOULD DEFINITELY INCLUDE POP CULTURE QUESTIONS.
LIKE, WHAT SHOWS EVERYONE'S WATCHING, WHAT BOY BANDS ARE POPULAR...
...WHAT?

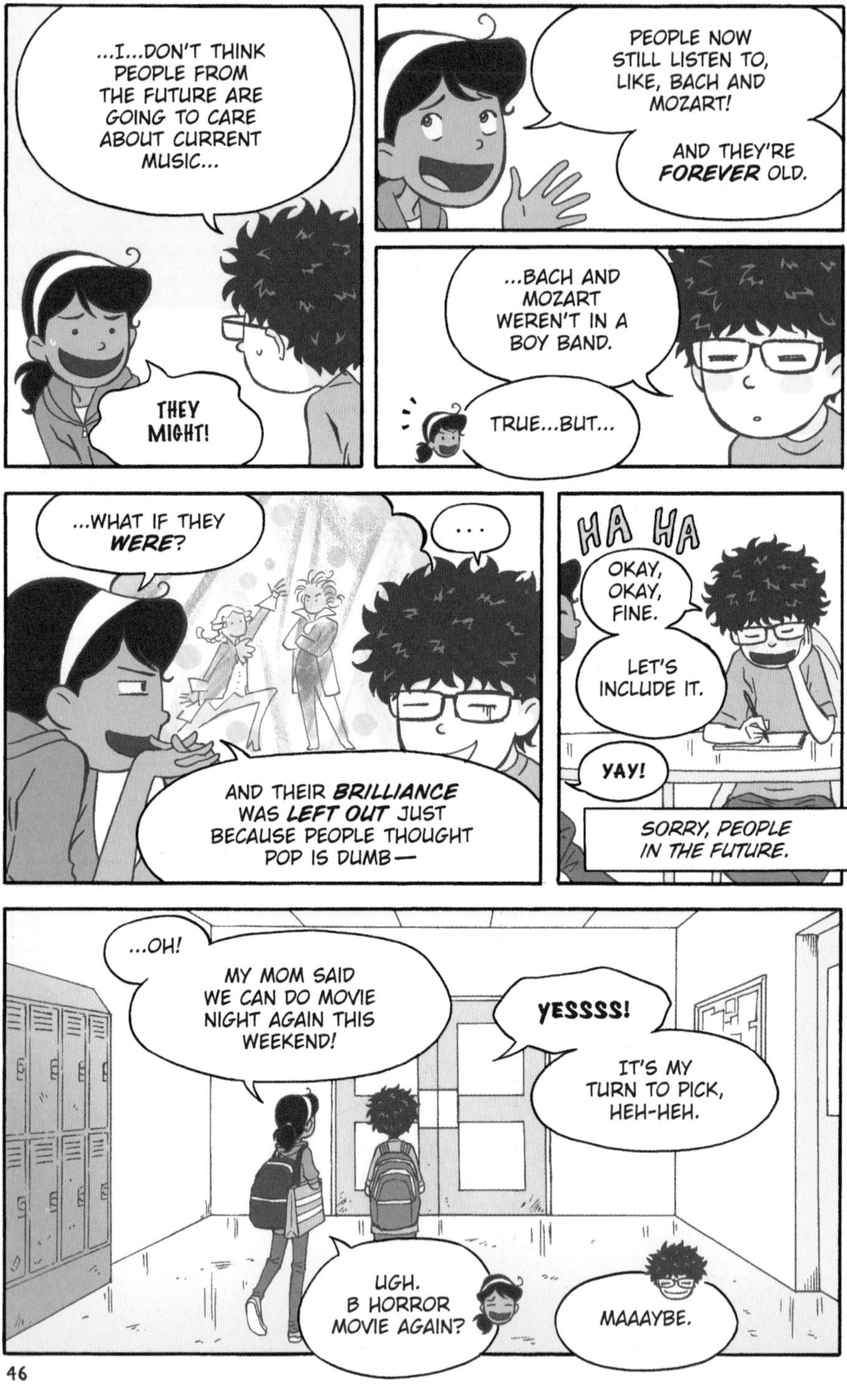

...I...DON'T THINK PEOPLE FROM THE FUTURE ARE GOING TO CARE ABOUT CURRENT MUSIC...
THEY MIGHT!
PEOPLE NOW STILL LISTEN TO, LIKE, BACH AND MOZART!
AND THEY'RE FOREVER OLD.
...BACH AND MOZART WEREN'T IN A BOY BAND.
TRUE...BUT...
...WHAT IF THEY WERE?
. . .
AND THEIR BRILLIANCE WAS LEFT OUT JUST BECAUSE PEOPLE THOUGHT POP IS DUMB—
HA HA
OKAY, OKAY, FINE.
LET'S INCLUDE IT.
YAY!
SORRY, PEOPLE IN THE FUTURE.
...OH!
MY MOM SAID WE CAN DO MOVIE NIGHT AGAIN THIS WEEKEND!
YESSSS!
IT'S MY TURN TO PICK, HEH-HEH.
UGH. B HORROR MOVIE AGAIN?
MAAAYBE.

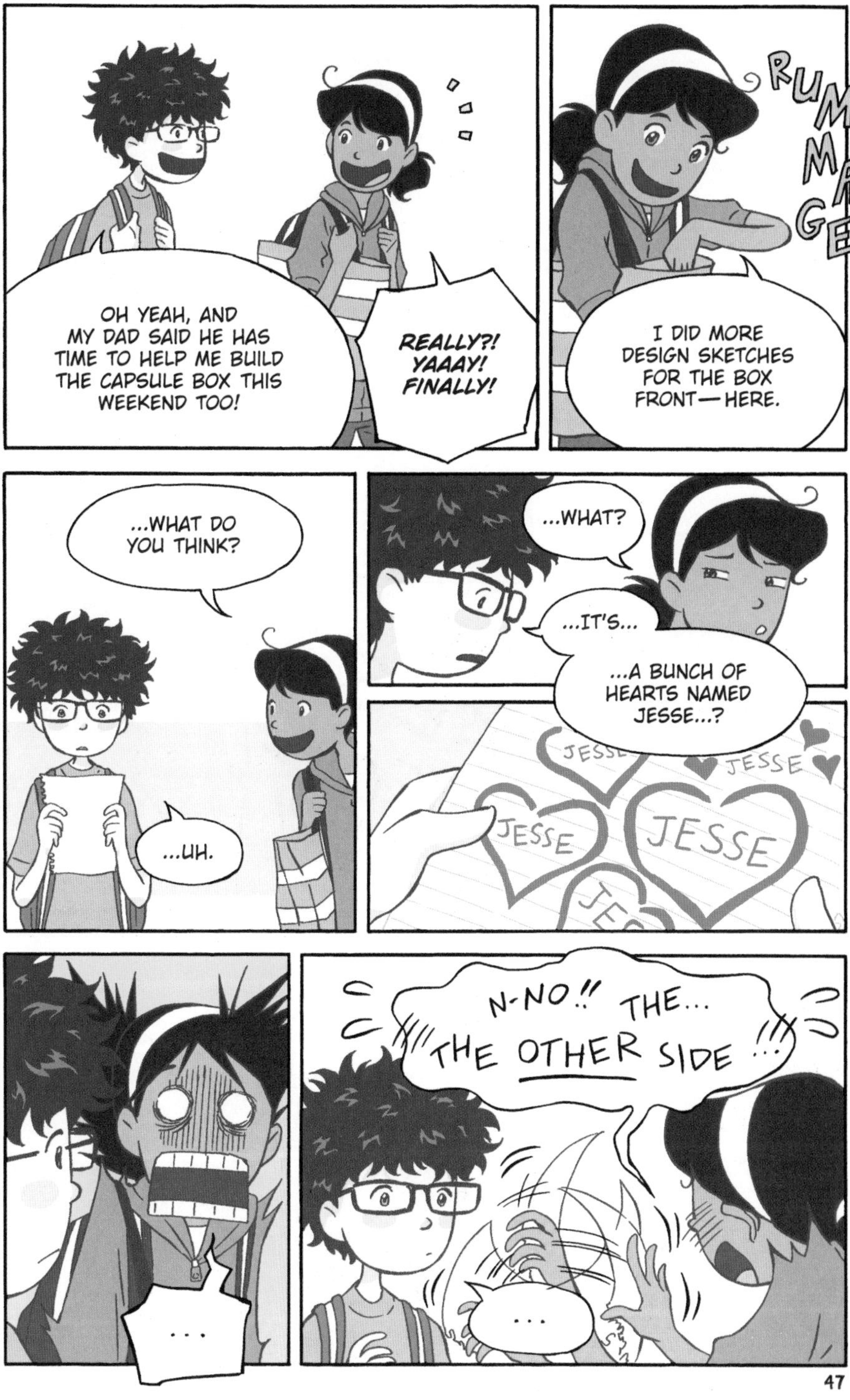
OH YEAH, AND MY DAD SAID HE HAS TIME TO HELP ME BUILD THE CAPSULE BOX THIS WEEKEND TOO!
REALLY?! YAAAY! FINALLY!
RUMMAGE
I DID MORE DESIGN SKETCHES FOR THE BOX FRONT—HERE.
...WHAT DO YOU THINK?
...UH.
...WHAT?
...IT'S...
...A BUNCH OF HEARTS NAMED JESSE...?
JESSE
JESSE
JESSE
JESSE
...
N-NO!! THE... THE OTHER SIDE !!!
...

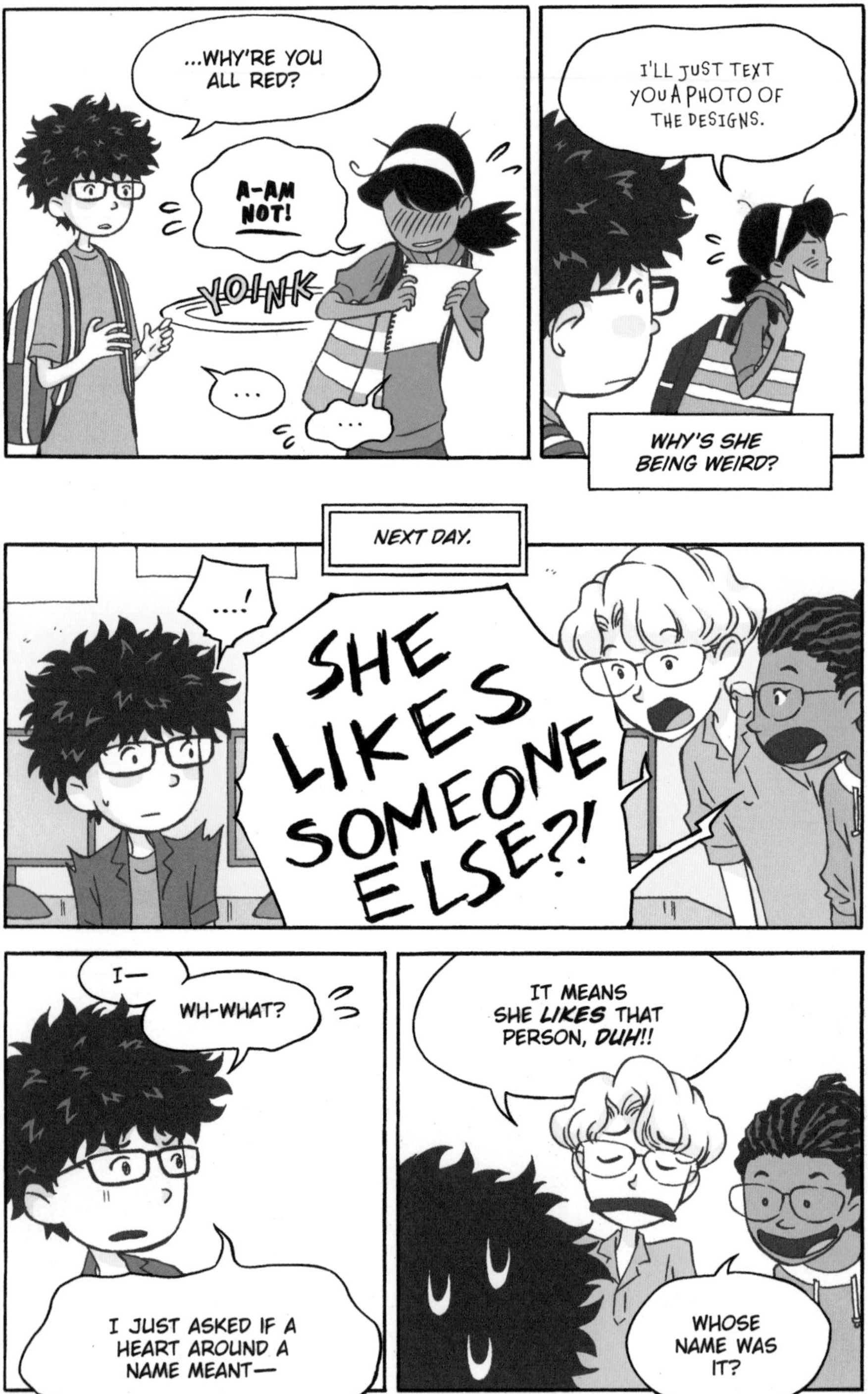
...WHY'RE YOU ALL RED?
A-AM NOT!
YOINK
...
...
I'LL JUST TEXT YOU A PHOTO OF THE DESIGNS.
WHY'S SHE BEING WEIRD?
NEXT DAY.
....!
SHE LIKES SOMEONE ELSE?!
I—
WH-WHAT?
I JUST ASKED IF A HEART AROUND A NAME MEANT—
IT MEANS SHE LIKES THAT PERSON, DUH!!
WHOSE NAME WAS IT?

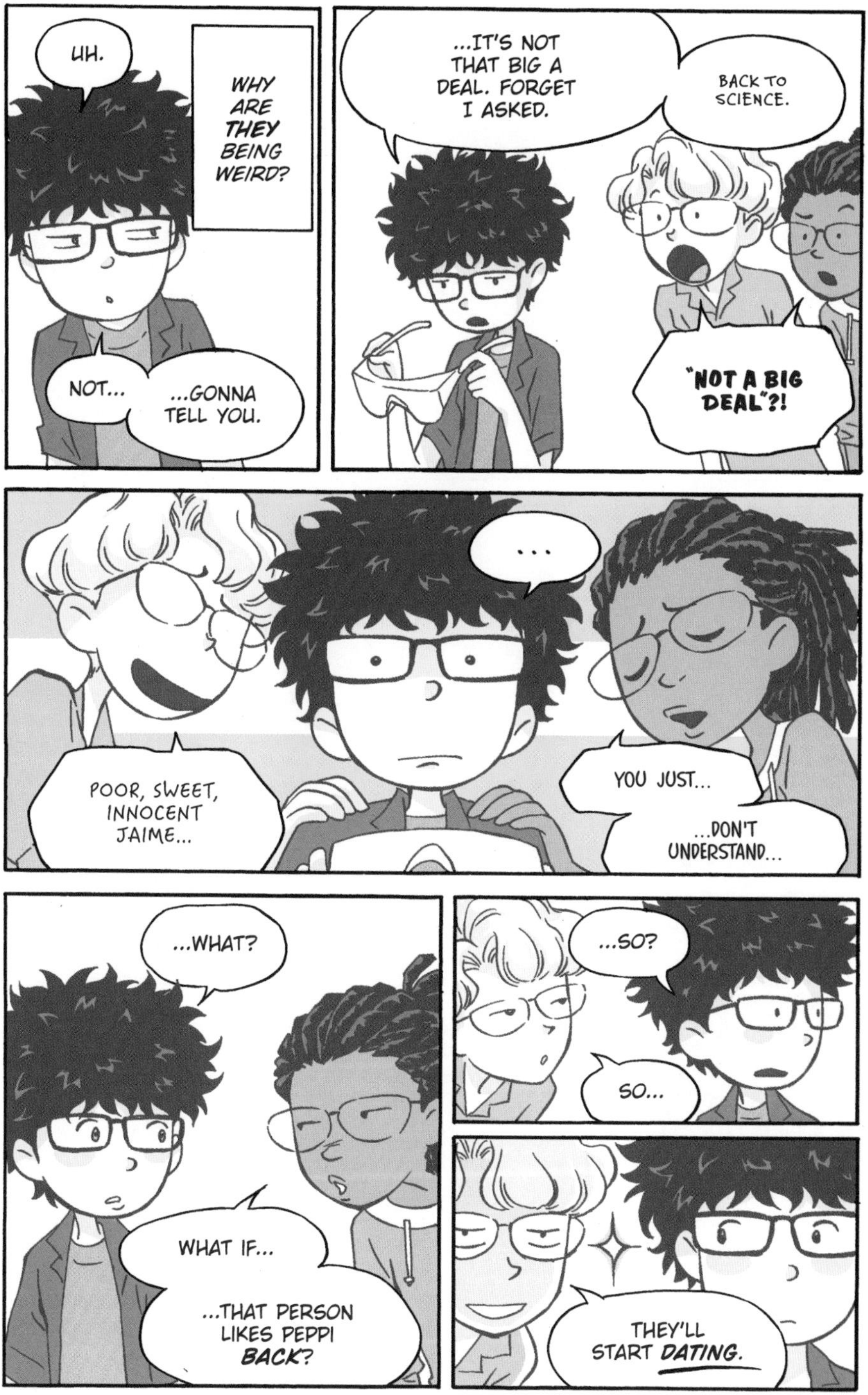
UH.
WHY ARE THEY BEING WEIRD?
NOT...
...GONNA TELL YOU.
...IT'S NOT THAT BIG A DEAL. FORGET I ASKED.
BACK TO SCIENCE.
"NOT A BIG DEAL"?!
...
POOR, SWEET, INNOCENT JAIME...
YOU JUST...
...DON'T UNDERSTAND...
...WHAT?
WHAT IF...
...THAT PERSON LIKES PEPPI BACK?
...SO?
SO...
THEY'LL START DATING.

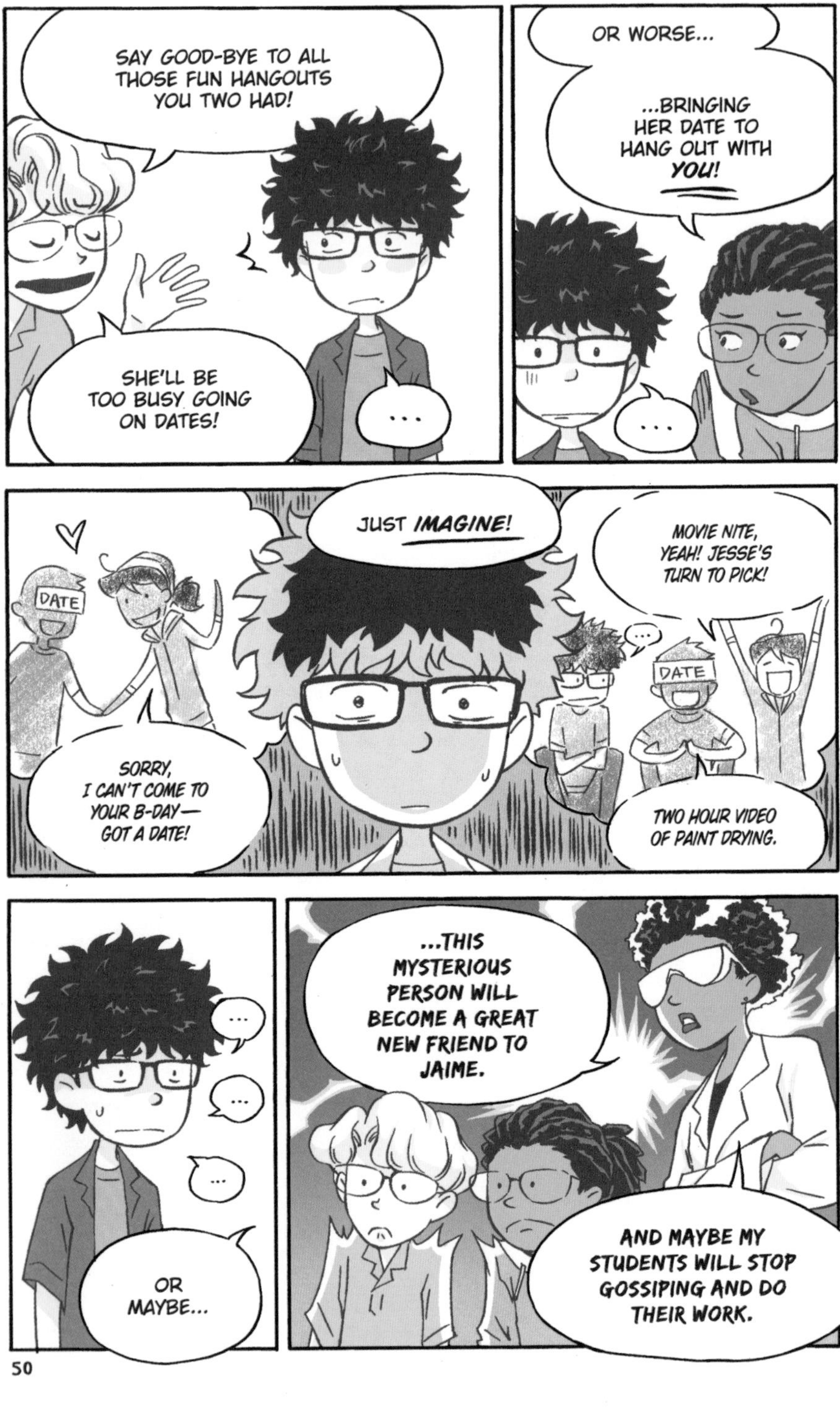
SAY GOOD-BYE TO ALL THOSE FUN HANGOUTS YOU TWO HAD!
SHE'LL BE TOO BUSY GOING ON DATES!
...
OR WORSE...
...BRINGING HER DATE TO HANG OUT WITH ***YOU!***
...
JUST ***IMAGINE!***
DATE
SORRY, I CAN'T COME TO YOUR B-DAY— GOT A DATE!
MOVIE NITE, YEAH! JESSE'S TURN TO PICK!
...
DATE
TWO HOUR VIDEO OF PAINT DRYING.
...
...
...
OR MAYBE...
...THIS MYSTERIOUS PERSON WILL BECOME A GREAT NEW FRIEND TO JAIME.
AND MAYBE MY STUDENTS WILL STOP GOSSIPING AND DO THEIR WORK.

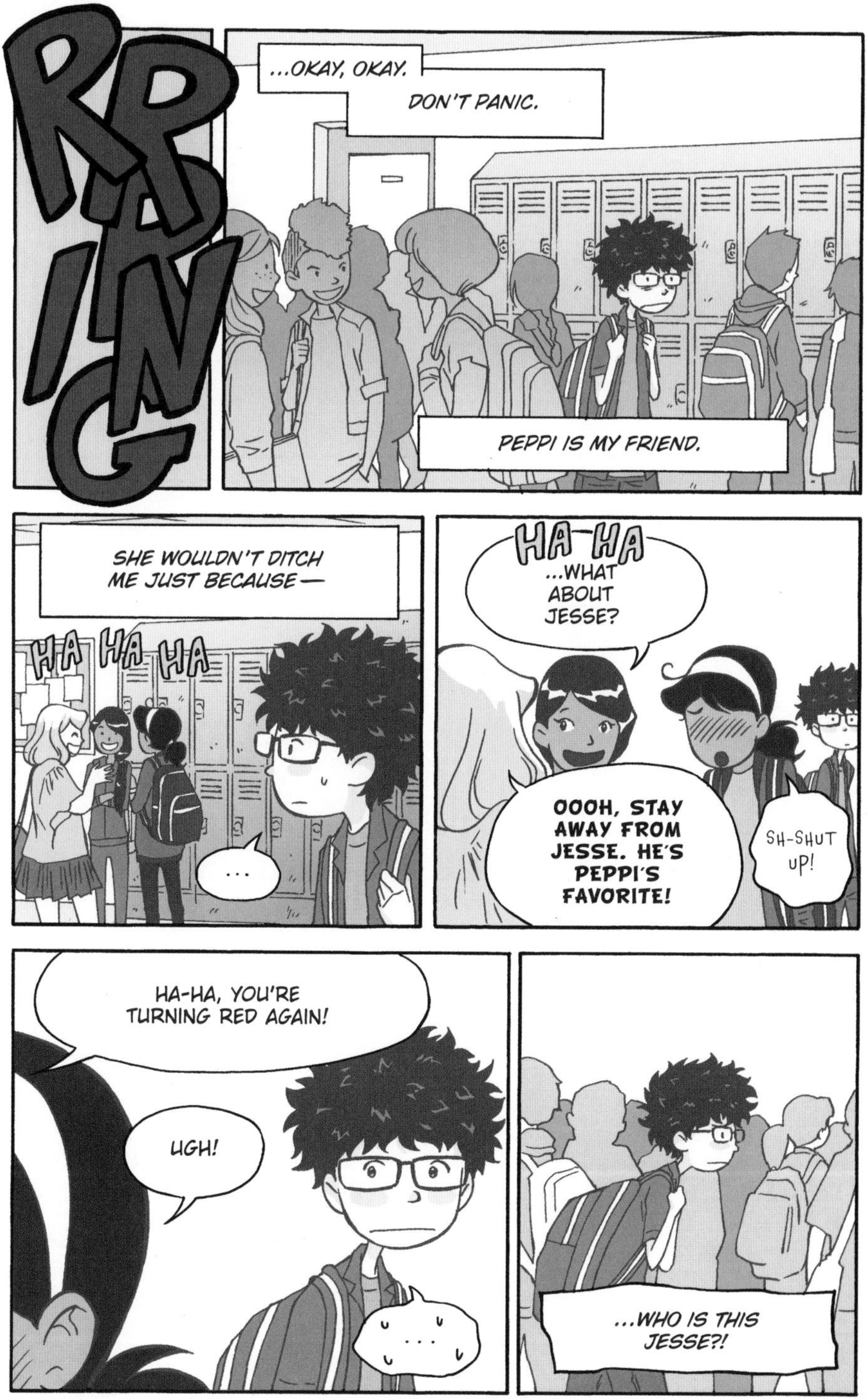
RRRIIINNNG
...OKAY, OKAY.
DON'T PANIC.
PEPPI IS MY FRIEND.
SHE WOULDN'T DITCH ME JUST BECAUSE—
HA HA HA
...
HA HA ...WHAT ABOUT JESSE?
OOOH, STAY AWAY FROM JESSE. HE'S PEPPI'S FAVORITE!
SH-SHUT UP!
HA-HA, YOU'RE TURNING RED AGAIN!
UGH!
...
...WHO IS THIS JESSE?!

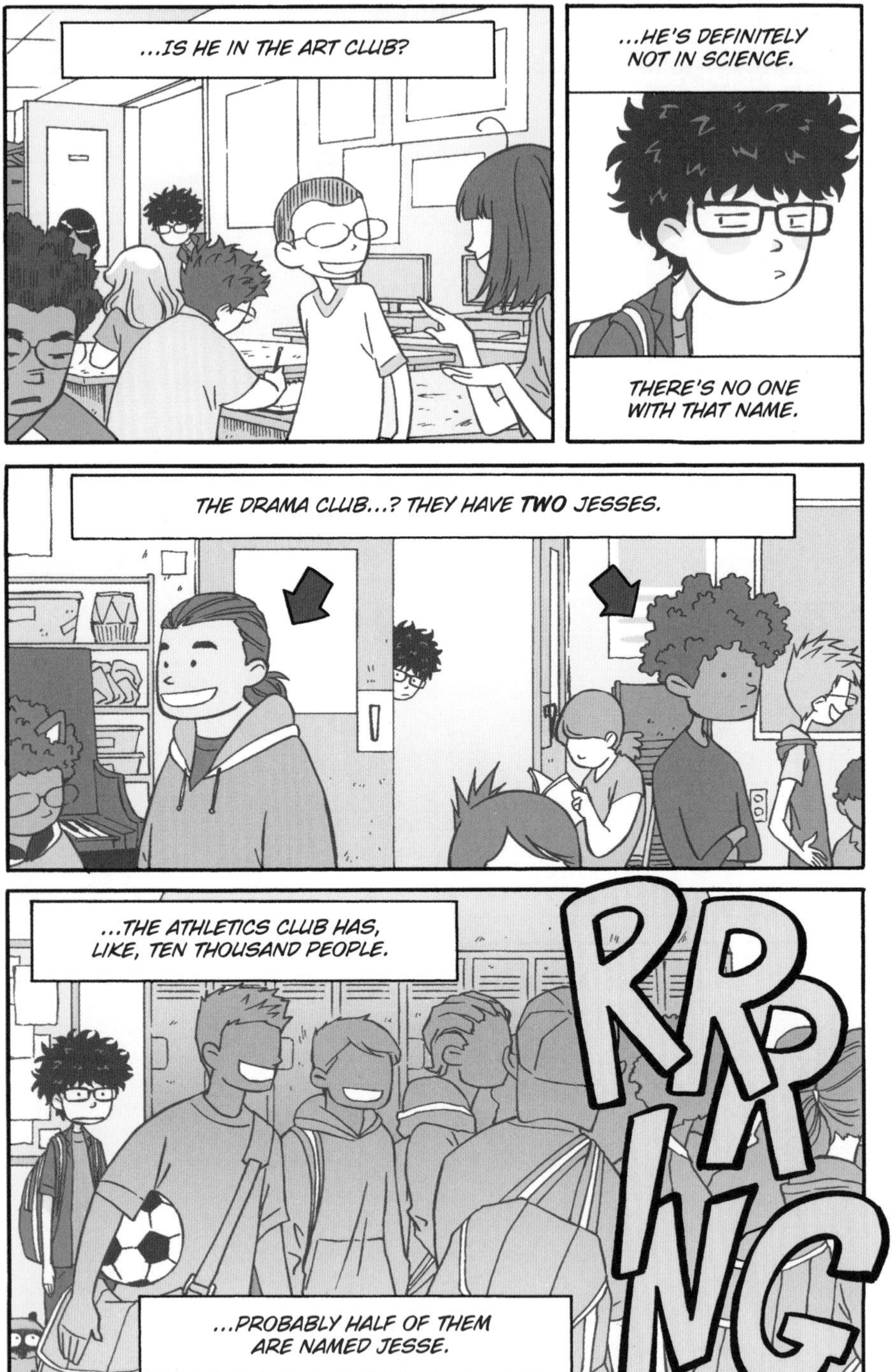
...IS HE IN THE ART CLUB?
...HE'S DEFINITELY NOT IN SCIENCE.
THERE'S NO ONE WITH THAT NAME.
THE DRAMA CLUB...? THEY HAVE **TWO** JESSES.
...THE ATHLETICS CLUB HAS, LIKE, TEN THOUSAND PEOPLE.
...PROBABLY HALF OF THEM ARE NAMED JESSE.
RRRRING

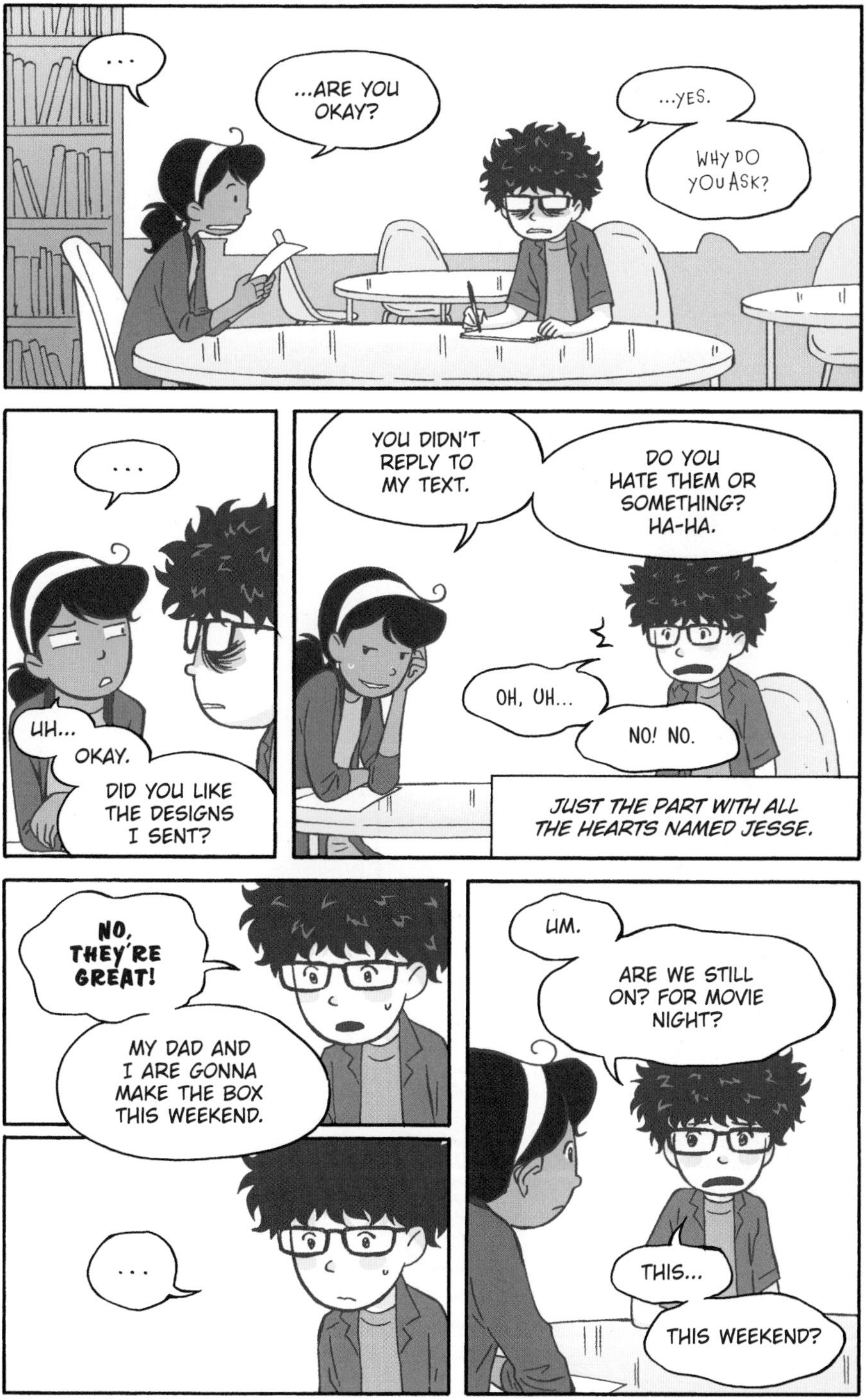
...
...ARE YOU OKAY?
...YES.
WHY DO YOU ASK?
...
UH...
OKAY.
DID YOU LIKE THE DESIGNS I SENT?
YOU DIDN'T REPLY TO MY TEXT.
DO YOU HATE THEM OR SOMETHING? HA-HA.
OH, UH...
NO! NO.
JUST THE PART WITH ALL THE HEARTS NAMED JESSE.
NO, THEY'RE GREAT!
MY DAD AND I ARE GONNA MAKE THE BOX THIS WEEKEND.
...
UM.
ARE WE STILL ON? FOR MOVIE NIGHT?
THIS...
THIS WEEKEND?

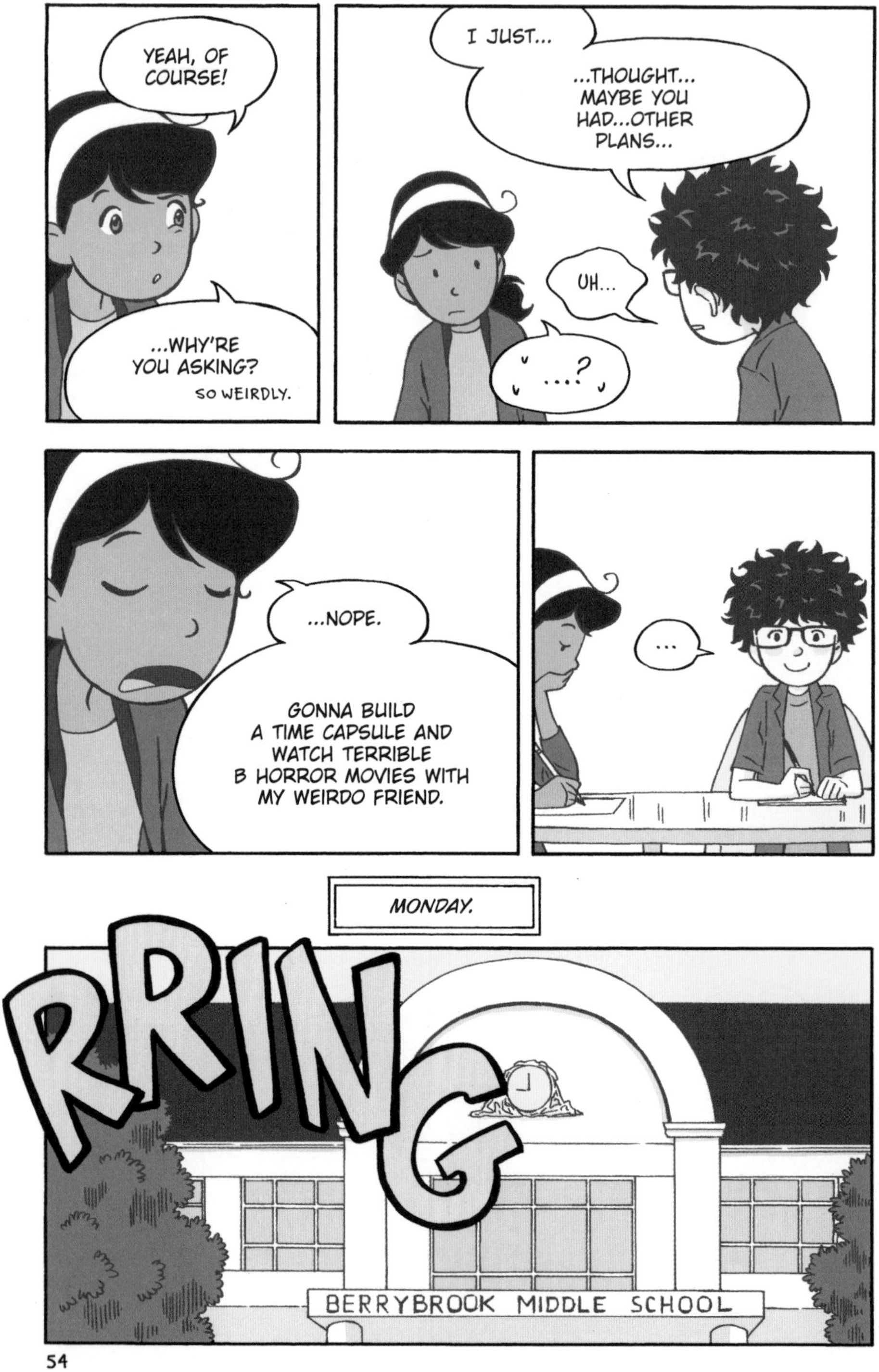

YEAH, OF COURSE!
...WHY'RE YOU ASKING?
SO WEIRDLY.
I JUST...
...THOUGHT... MAYBE YOU HAD...OTHER PLANS...
UH...
...?
...NOPE.
GONNA BUILD A TIME CAPSULE AND WATCH TERRIBLE B HORROR MOVIES WITH MY WEIRDO FRIEND.
...
MONDAY.
RRING
BERRYBROOK MIDDLE SCHOOL

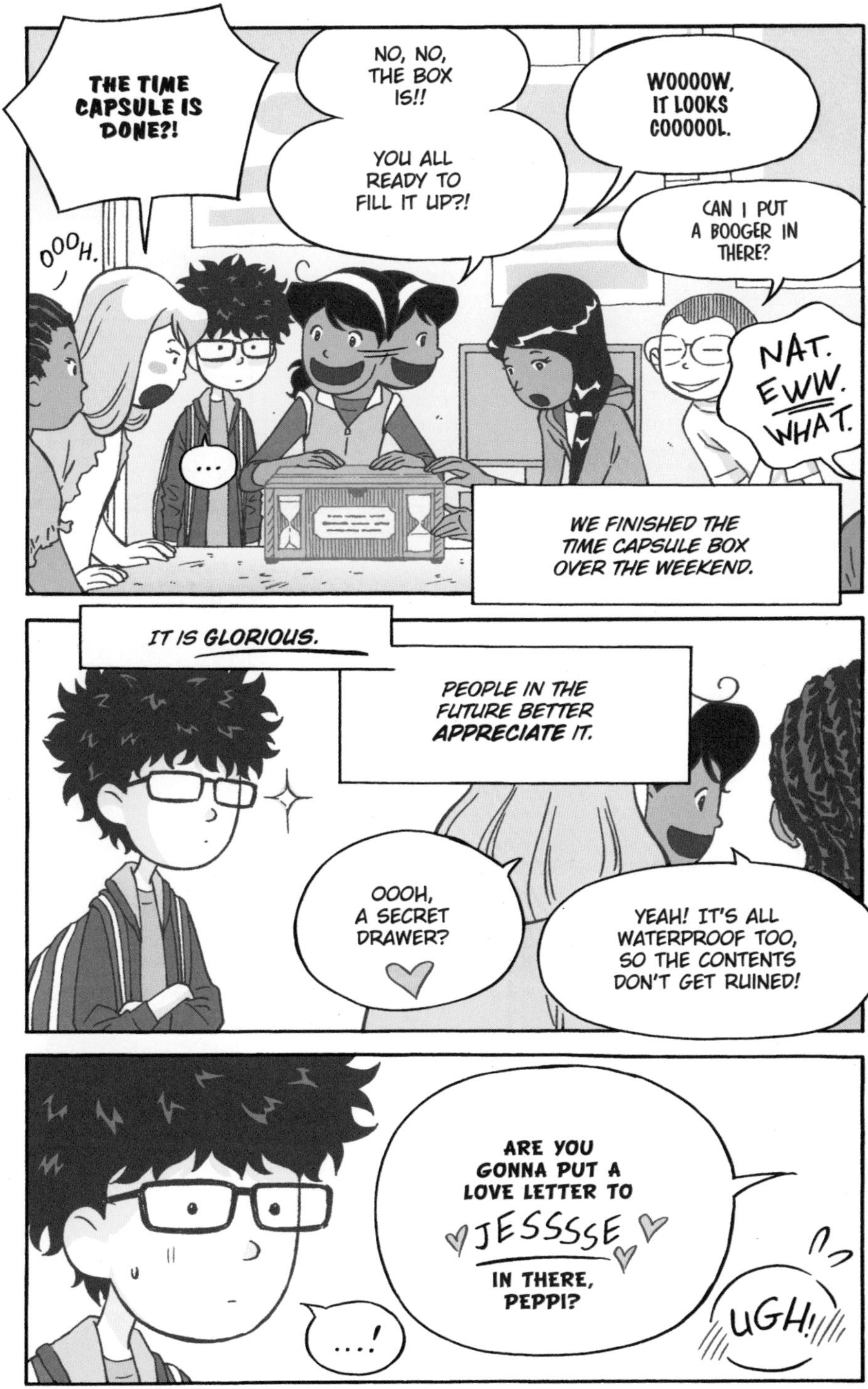
THE TIME CAPSULE IS DONE?!
NO, NO, THE BOX IS!!
YOU ALL READY TO FILL IT UP?!
WOOOOW, IT LOOKS COOOOOL.
CAN I PUT A BOOGER IN THERE?
OOOH.
NAT. EWW. WHAT.
...
WE FINISHED THE TIME CAPSULE BOX OVER THE WEEKEND.
IT IS GLORIOUS.
PEOPLE IN THE FUTURE BETTER APPRECIATE IT.
OOOH, A SECRET DRAWER?
YEAH! IT'S ALL WATERPROOF TOO, SO THE CONTENTS DON'T GET RUINED!
ARE YOU GONNA PUT A LOVE LETTER TO JESSSSE IN THERE, PEPPI?
...!
UGH!

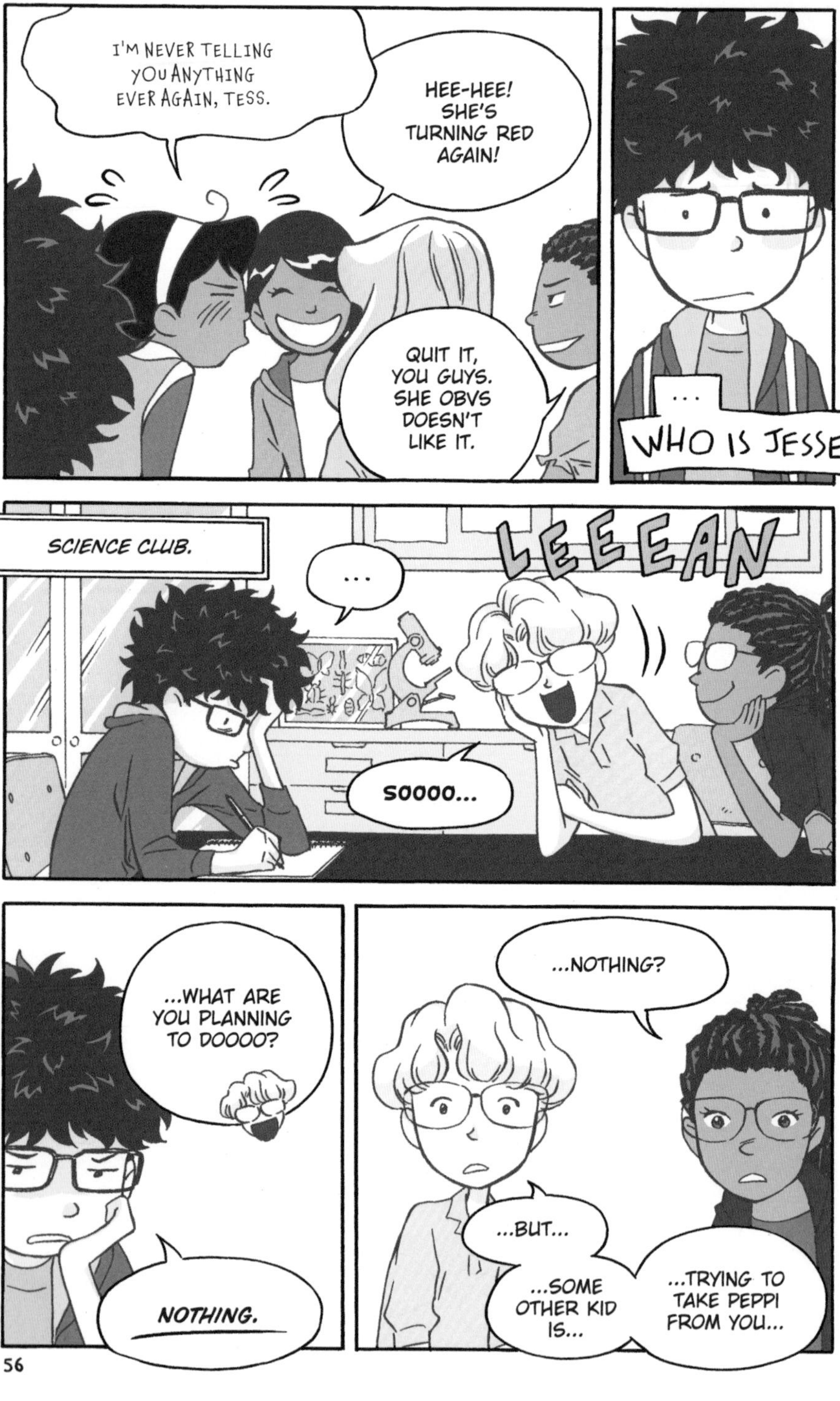

I'M NEVER TELLING YOU ANYTHING EVER AGAIN, TESS.
HEE-HEE! SHE'S TURNING RED AGAIN!
QUIT IT, YOU GUYS. SHE OBVS DOESN'T LIKE IT.
...
WHO IS JESSE
SCIENCE CLUB.
LEEEAN
...
SOOOO...
...WHAT ARE YOU PLANNING TO DOOOO?
NOTHING.
...NOTHING?
...BUT...
...SOME OTHER KID IS...
...TRYING TO TAKE PEPPI FROM YOU...

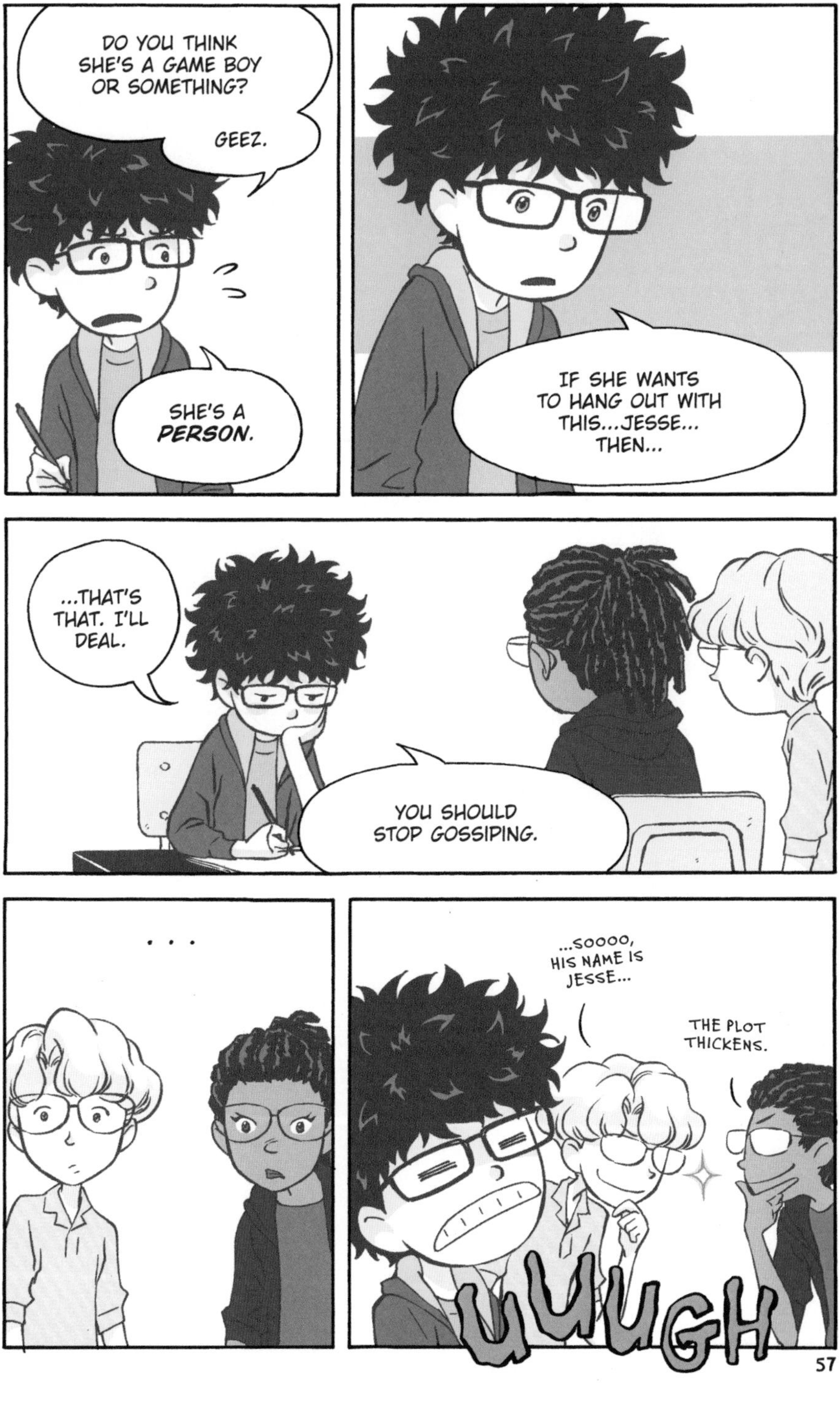
DO YOU THINK SHE'S A GAME BOY OR SOMETHING?
GEEZ.
SHE'S A *PERSON.*
IF SHE WANTS TO HANG OUT WITH THIS...JESSE... THEN...
...THAT'S THAT. I'LL DEAL.
YOU SHOULD STOP GOSSIPING.
. . .
...SOOOO, HIS NAME IS JESSE...
THE PLOT THICKENS.
UUUGH

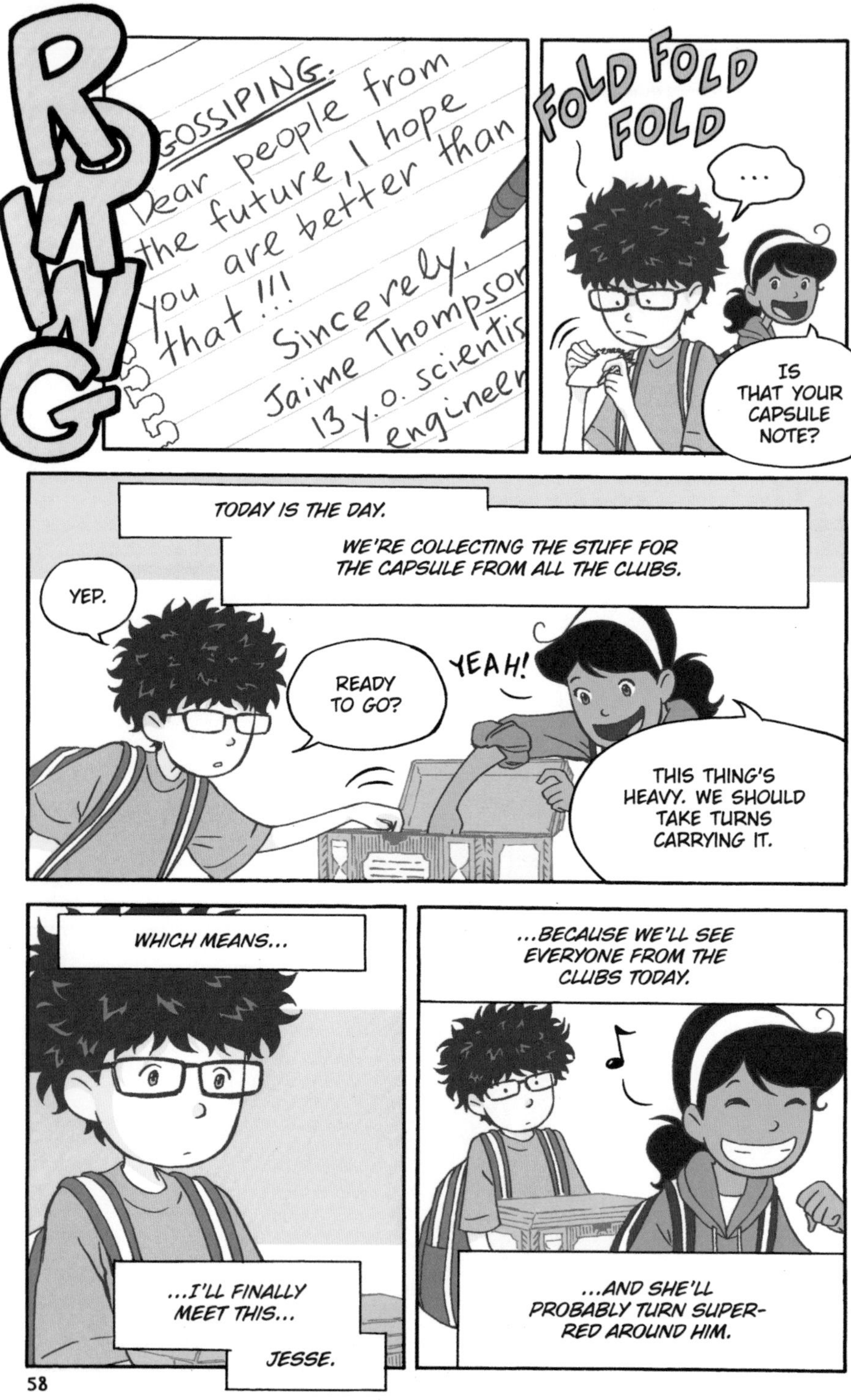
RRWG
GOSSIPING.
Dear people from the future, I hope you are better than that!!!
Sincerely, Jaime Thompson 13 y.o. scientist engineer
FOLD FOLD FOLD
...
IS THAT YOUR CAPSULE NOTE?
TODAY IS THE DAY.
WE'RE COLLECTING THE STUFF FOR THE CAPSULE FROM ALL THE CLUBS.
YEP.
READY TO GO?
YEAH!
THIS THING'S HEAVY. WE SHOULD TAKE TURNS CARRYING IT.
WHICH MEANS...
...I'LL FINALLY MEET THIS...
JESSE.
...BECAUSE WE'LL SEE EVERYONE FROM THE CLUBS TODAY.
...AND SHE'LL PROBABLY TURN SUPER-RED AROUND HIM.

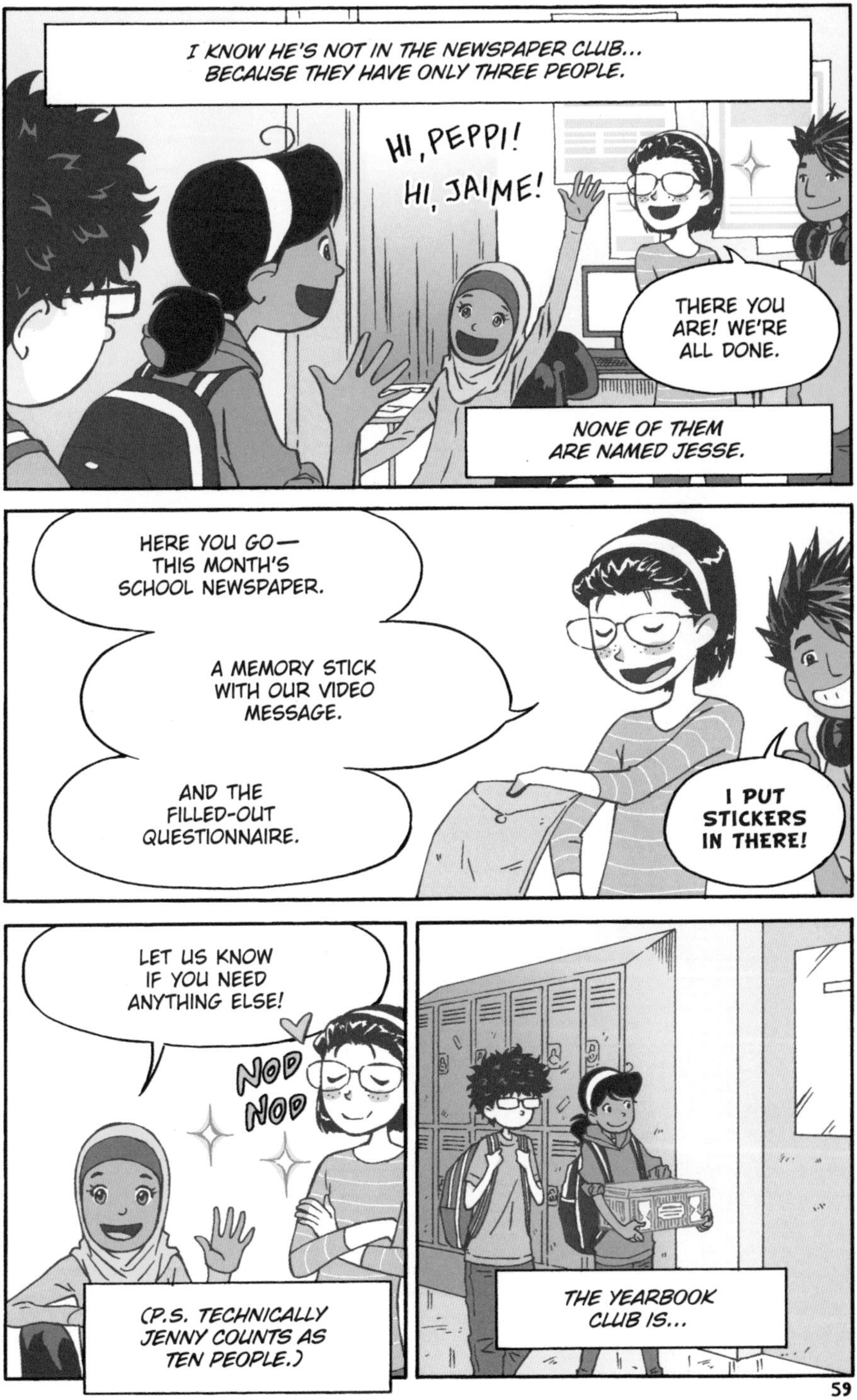
I KNOW HE'S NOT IN THE NEWSPAPER CLUB... BECAUSE THEY HAVE ONLY THREE PEOPLE.
HI, PEPPI!
HI, JAIME!
THERE YOU ARE! WE'RE ALL DONE.
NONE OF THEM ARE NAMED JESSE.
HERE YOU GO— THIS MONTH'S SCHOOL NEWSPAPER.
A MEMORY STICK WITH OUR VIDEO MESSAGE.
AND THE FILLED-OUT QUESTIONNAIRE.
I PUT STICKERS IN THERE!
LET US KNOW IF YOU NEED ANYTHING ELSE!
NOD NOD
(P.S. TECHNICALLY JENNY COUNTS AS TEN PEOPLE.)
THE YEARBOOK CLUB IS...

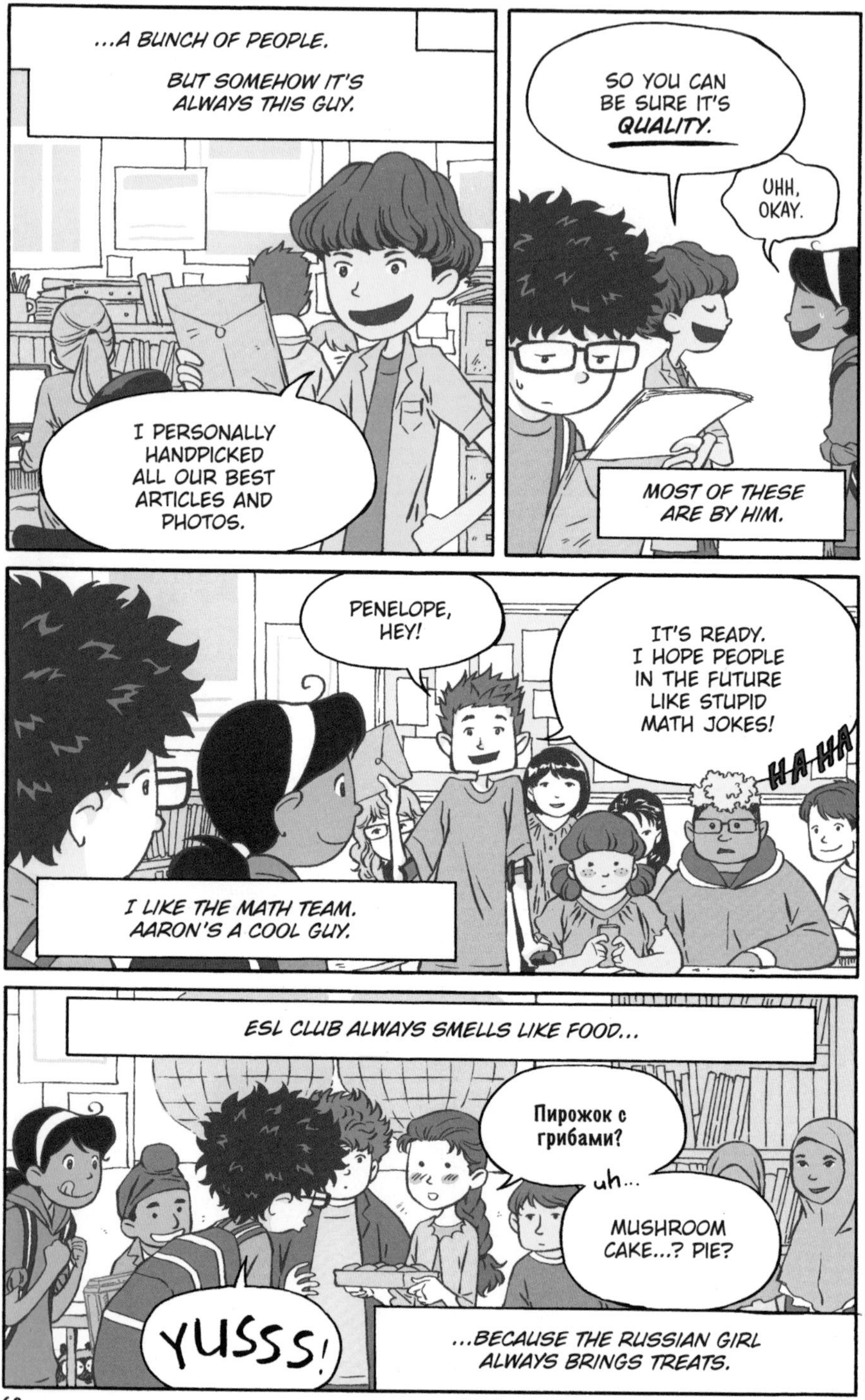
...A BUNCH OF PEOPLE.
BUT SOMEHOW IT'S ALWAYS THIS GUY.
I PERSONALLY HANDPICKED ALL OUR BEST ARTICLES AND PHOTOS.
SO YOU CAN BE SURE IT'S QUALITY.
UHH, OKAY.
MOST OF THESE ARE BY HIM.
PENELOPE, HEY!
IT'S READY. I HOPE PEOPLE IN THE FUTURE LIKE STUPID MATH JOKES!
HA HA
I LIKE THE MATH TEAM. AARON'S A COOL GUY.
ESL CLUB ALWAYS SMELLS LIKE FOOD...
Пирожок с грибами?
uh...
MUSHROOM CAKE...? PIE?
YUSSS!
...BECAUSE THE RUSSIAN GIRL ALWAYS BRINGS TREATS.

*ESL: ENGLISH AS A SECOND LANGUAGE

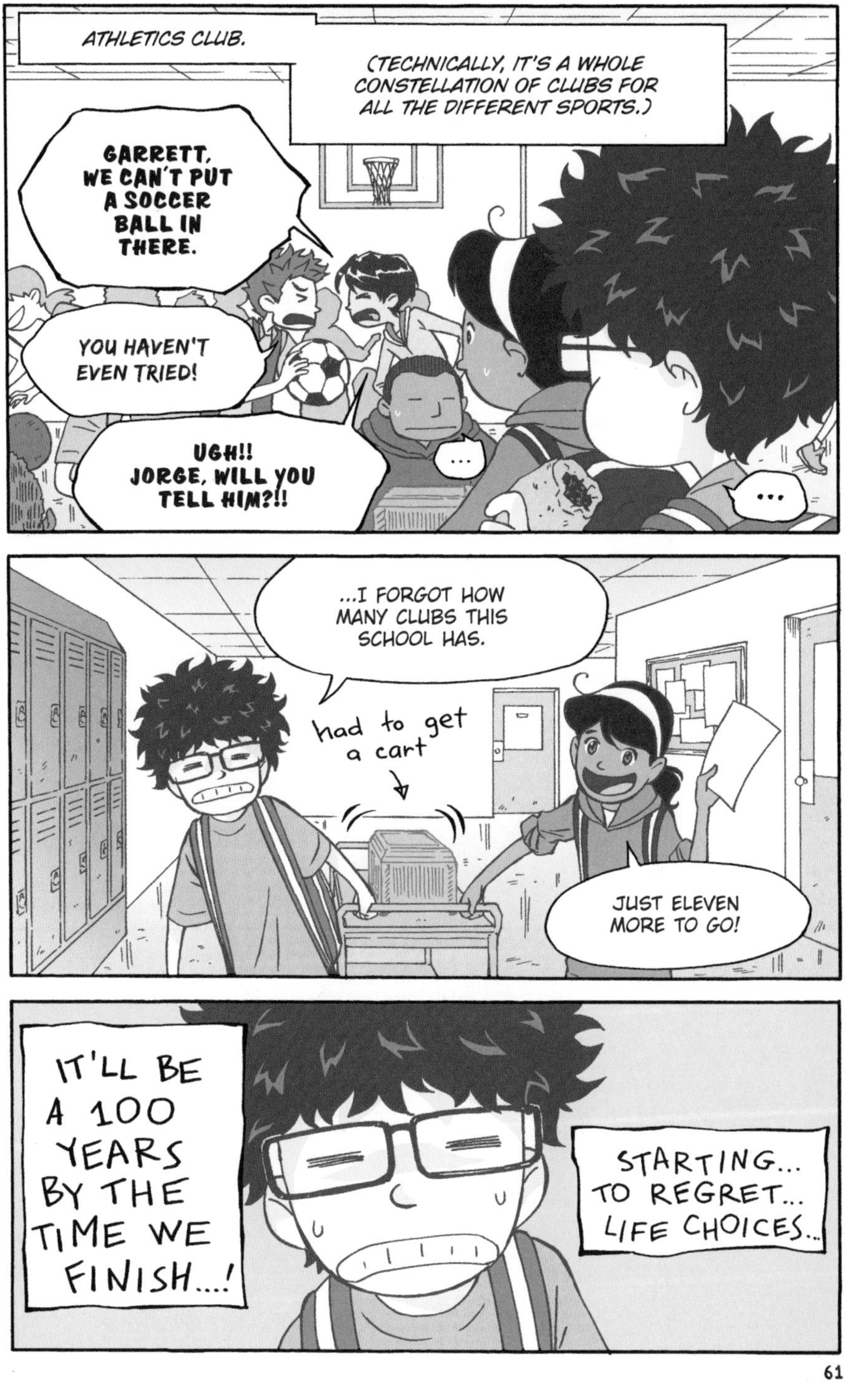

ATHLETICS CLUB.
(TECHNICALLY, IT'S A WHOLE CONSTELLATION OF CLUBS FOR ALL THE DIFFERENT SPORTS.)
GARRETT, WE CAN'T PUT A SOCCER BALL IN THERE.
YOU HAVEN'T EVEN TRIED!
UGH!! JORGE, WILL YOU TELL HIM?!!
...
...
...I FORGOT HOW MANY CLUBS THIS SCHOOL HAS.
had to get a cart
JUST ELEVEN MORE TO GO!
IT'LL BE A 100 YEARS BY THE TIME WE FINISH...!
STARTING... TO REGRET... LIFE CHOICES...

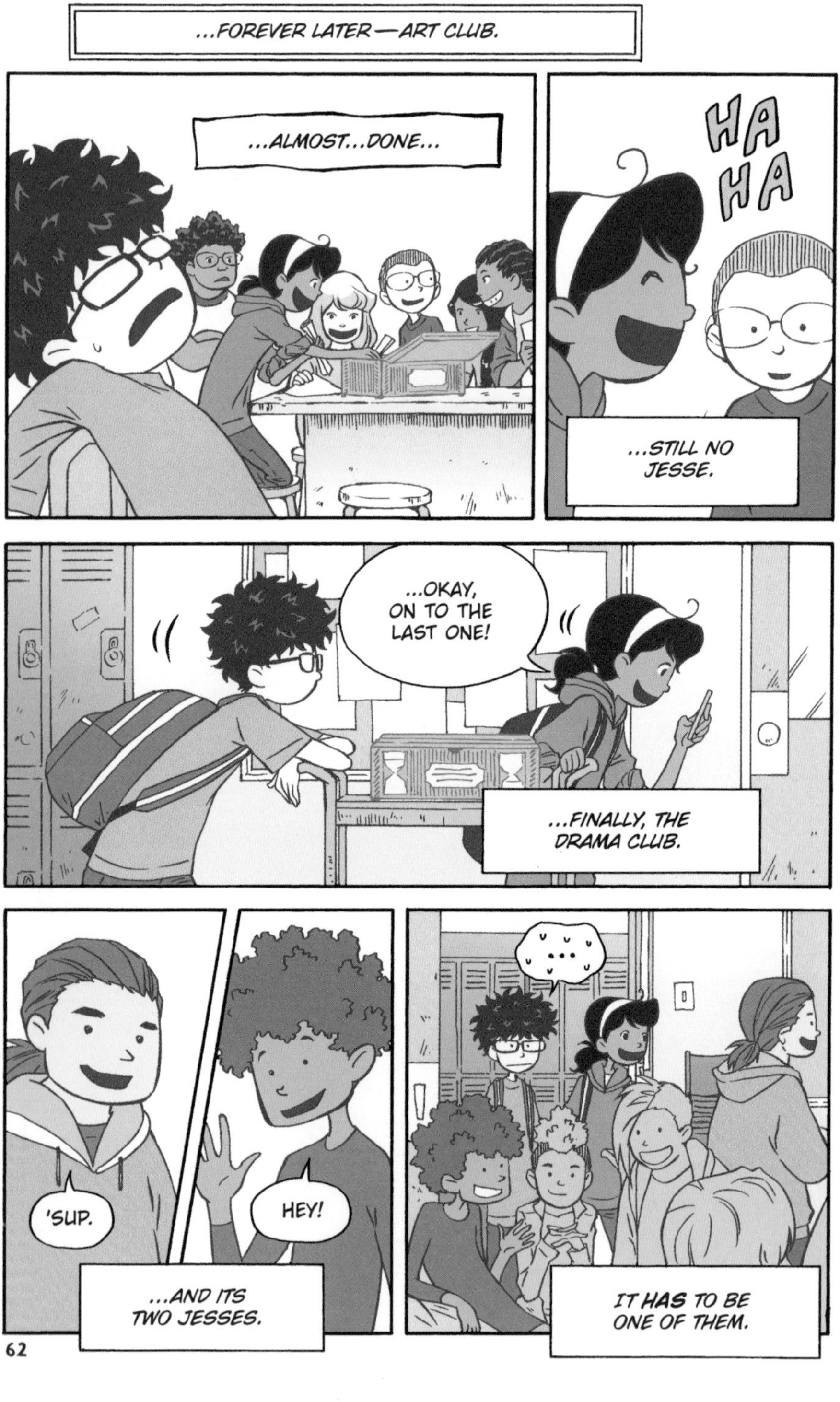
...FOREVER LATER—ART CLUB.
...ALMOST...DONE...
HA HA
...STILL NO JESSE.
...OKAY, ON TO THE LAST ONE!
...FINALLY, THE DRAMA CLUB.
'SUP.
HEY!
...AND ITS TWO JESSES.
...
IT HAS TO BE ONE OF THEM.

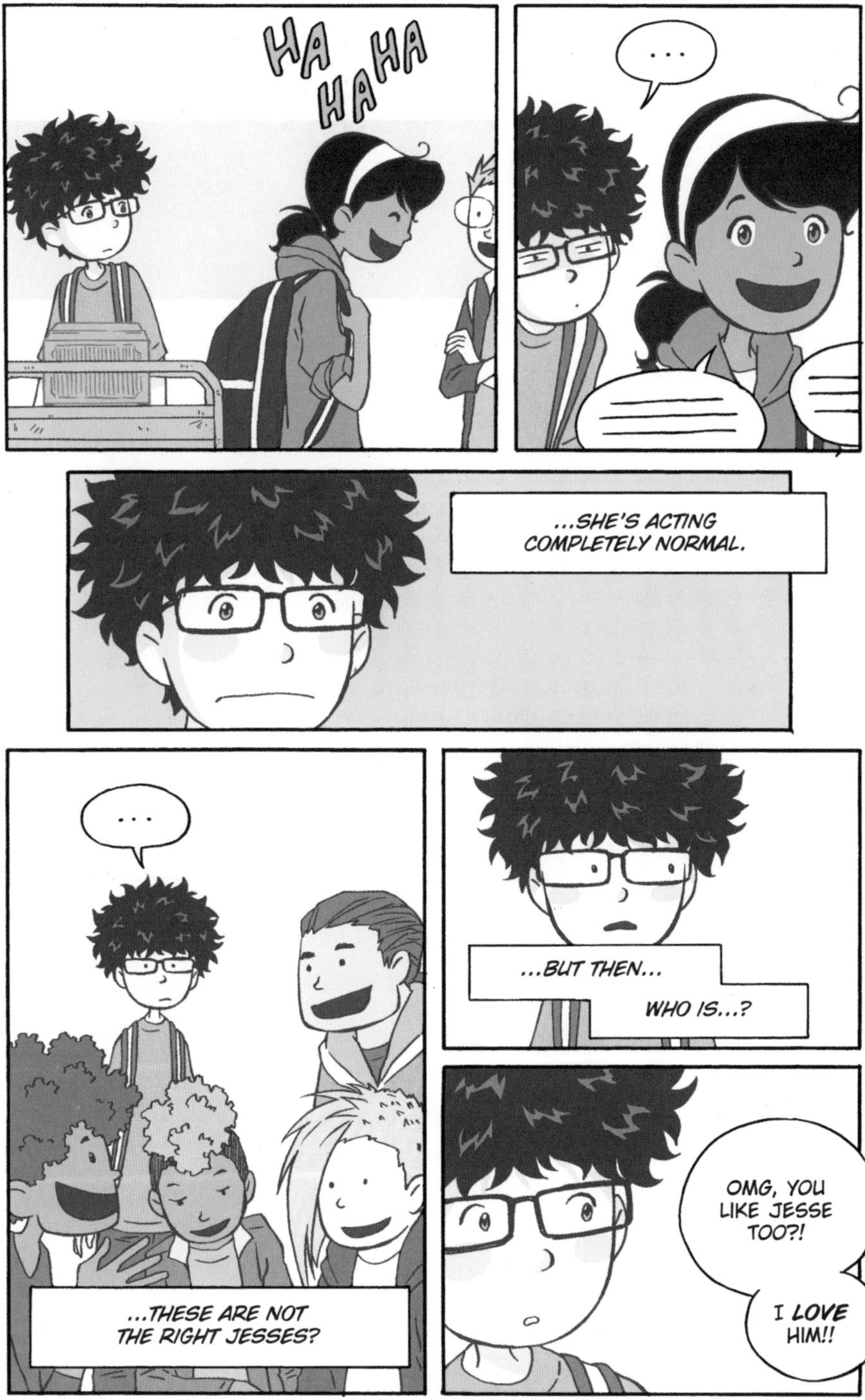
HA HA HA HA
...
...SHE'S ACTING COMPLETELY NORMAL.
...
...THESE ARE NOT THE RIGHT JESSES?
...BUT THEN...
WHO IS...?
OMG, YOU LIKE JESSE TOO?!
I LOVE HIM!!

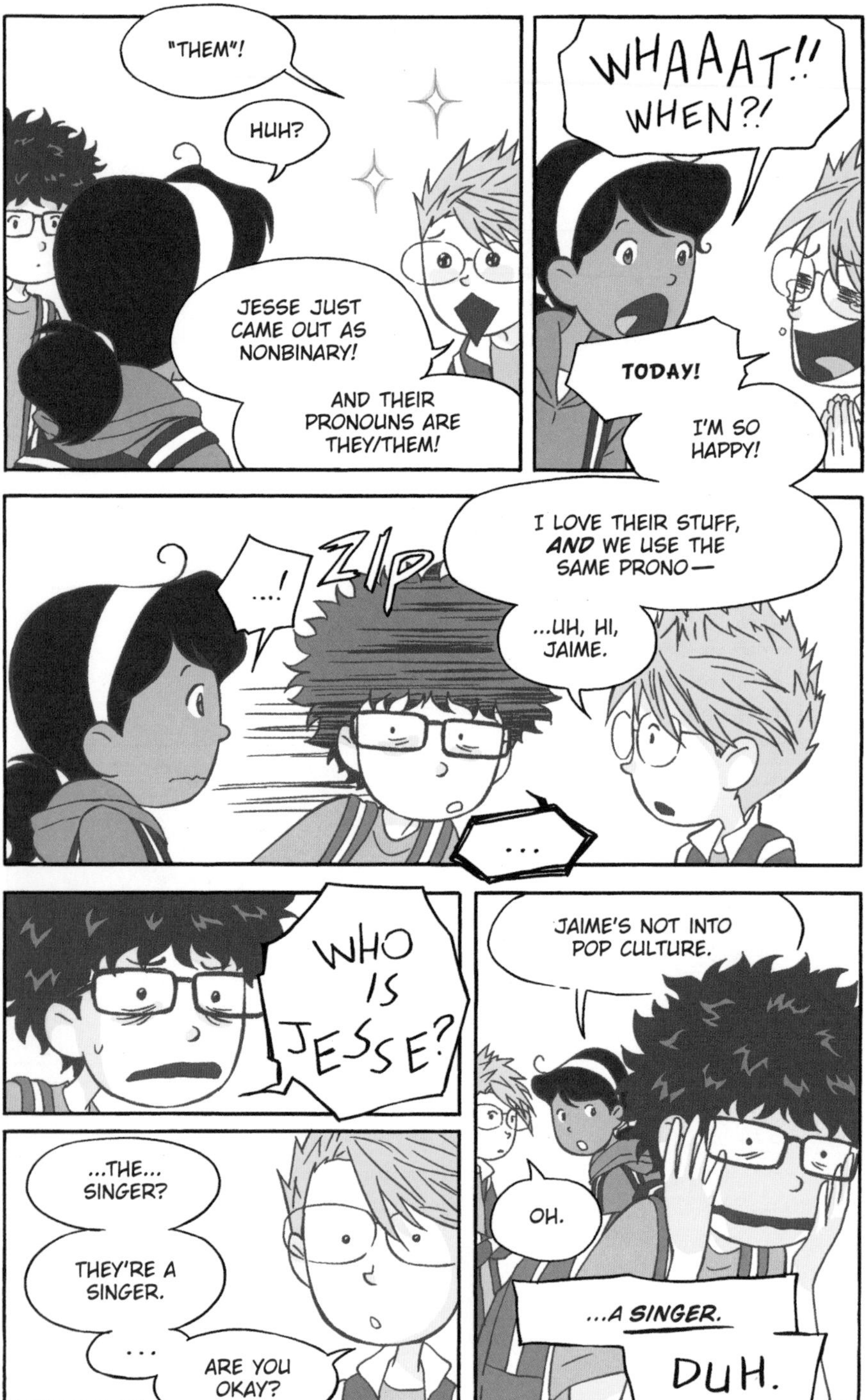
"THEM"!
HUH?
JESSE JUST CAME OUT AS NONBINARY!
AND THEIR PRONOUNS ARE THEY/THEM!
WHAAAT!! WHEN?!
TODAY!
I'M SO HAPPY!
I LOVE THEIR STUFF, AND WE USE THE SAME PRONO—
...!
ZIP
...UH, HI, JAIME.
...
WHO IS JESSE?
JAIME'S NOT INTO POP CULTURE.
...THE... SINGER?
THEY'RE A SINGER.
...
ARE YOU OKAY?
OH.
...A SINGER.
DUH.

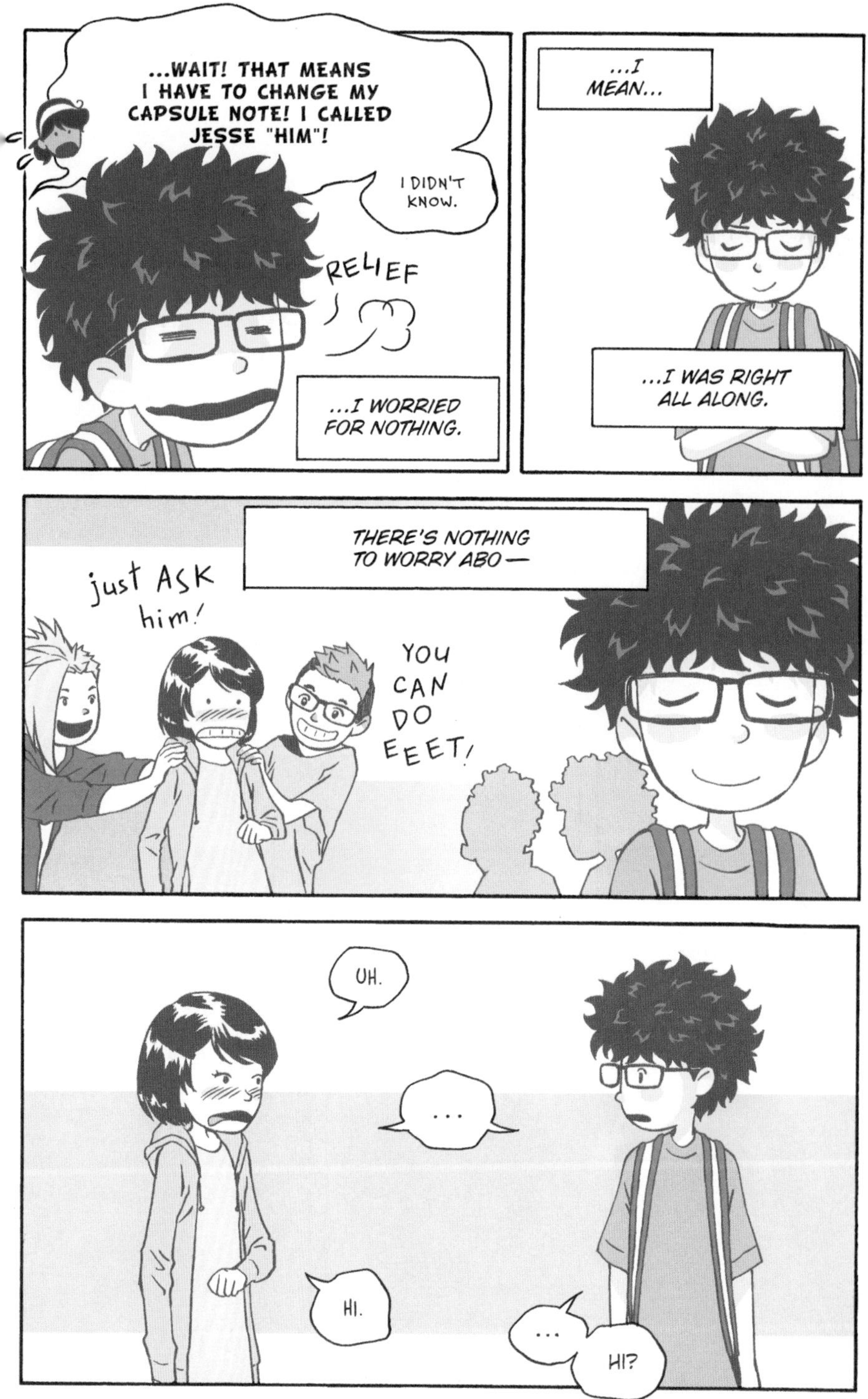
...WAIT! THAT MEANS I HAVE TO CHANGE MY CAPSULE NOTE! I CALLED JESSE "HIM"!
I DIDN'T KNOW.
RELIEF
...I WORRIED FOR NOTHING.
...I MEAN...
...I WAS RIGHT ALL ALONG.
THERE'S NOTHING TO WORRY ABO—
just ASK him!
YOU CAN DO EEEET!
UH.
...
HI.
...
HI?

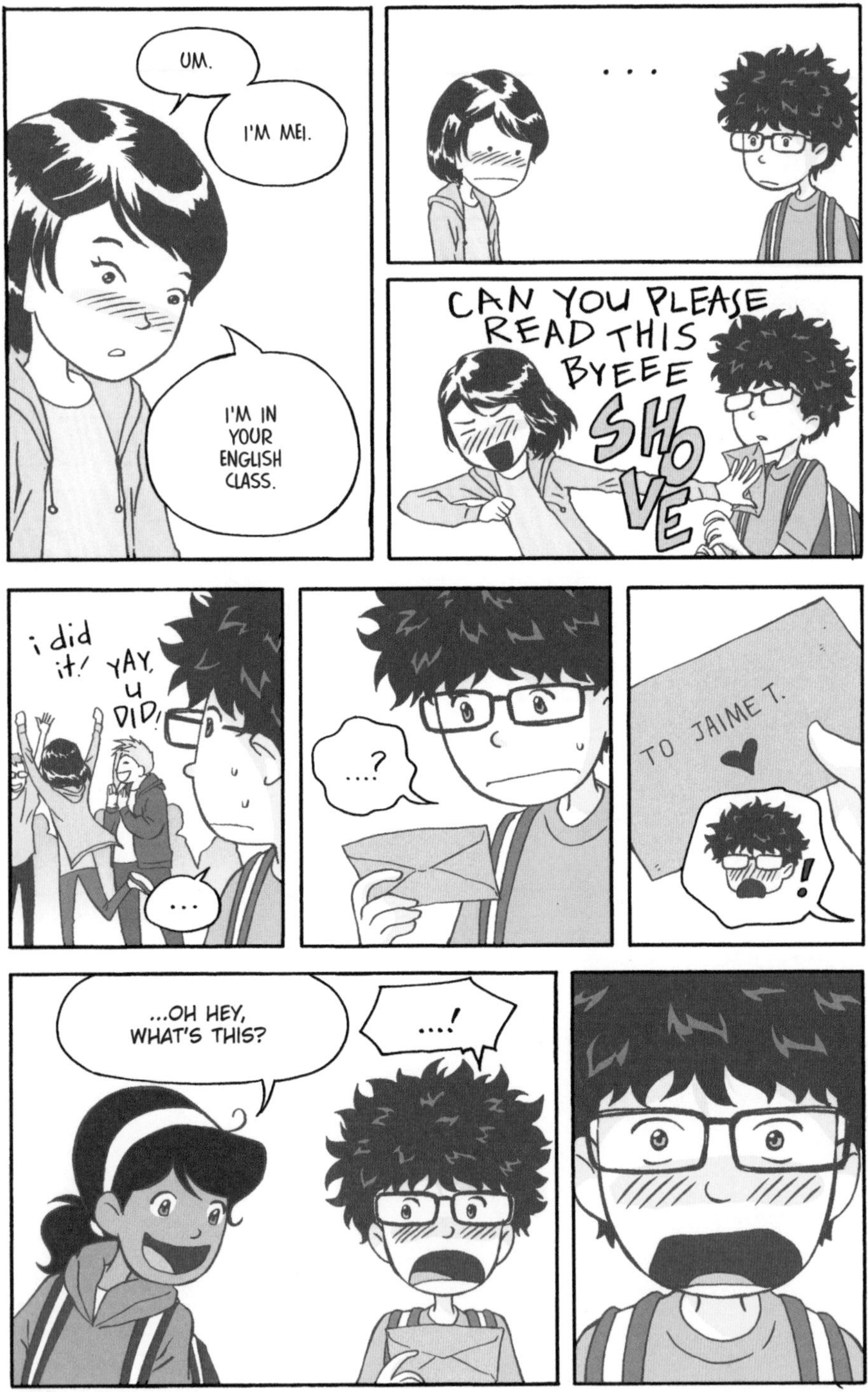
UM.
I'M MEI.
I'M IN YOUR ENGLISH CLASS.
. . .
CAN YOU PLEASE READ THIS BYEEE
SHOVE
i did it!
YAY, u DID!
...
...?
TO JAIME T.
!
...OH HEY, WHAT'S THIS?
...!

TIME CAPSULE: THE END

Time Capsule

If you could put something in a time capsule, what would it be?

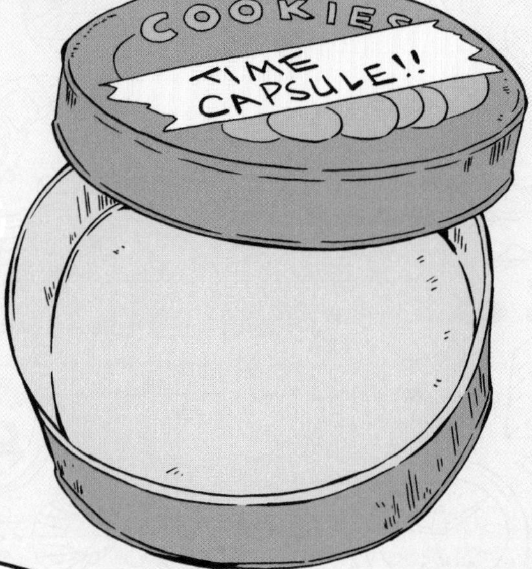
COOKIES
TIME CAPSULE!!

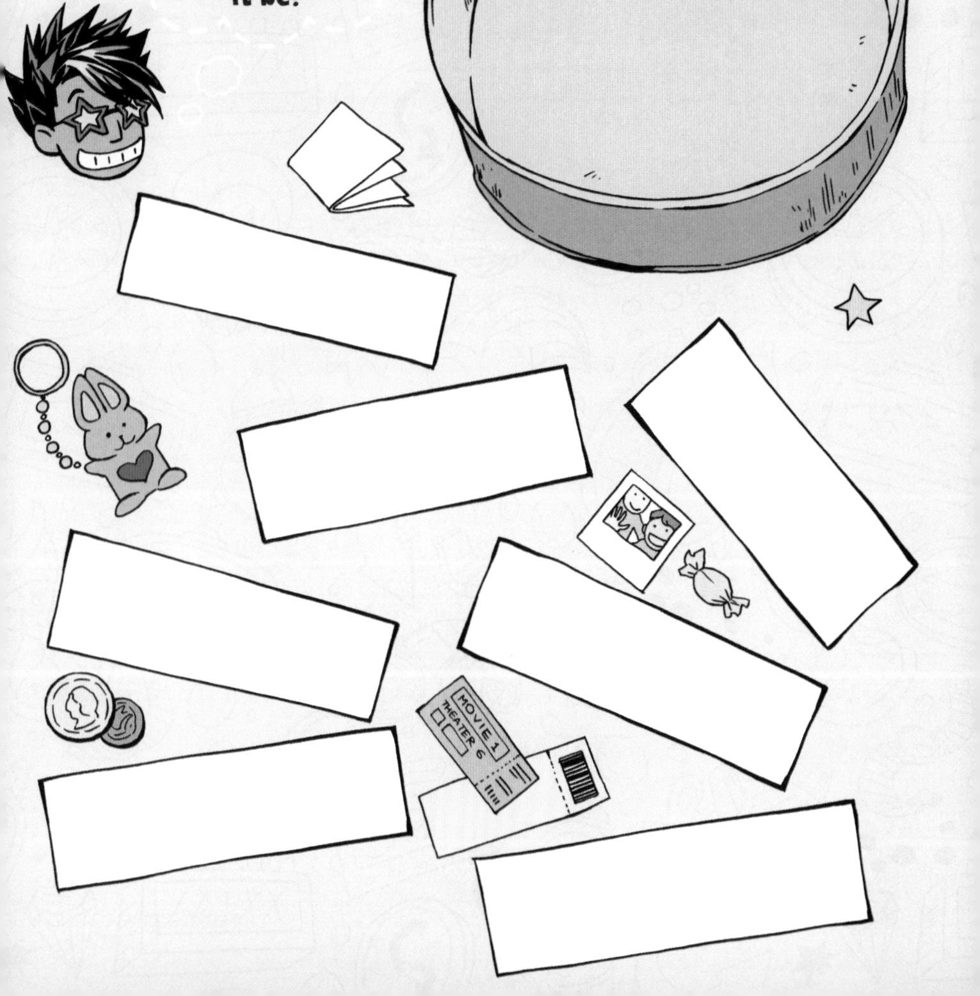
MOVIE 1
THEATER 6

Drawing Is Awesome
~PRACTICE IS KEY!

- Start with underdrawing (basic shapes/forms).
- Add details last!

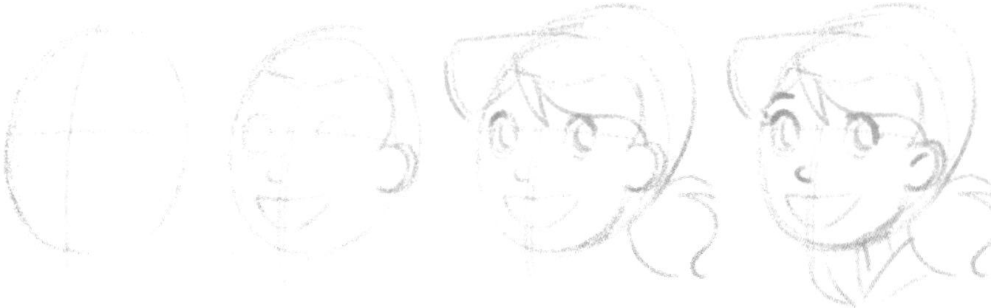

- Eyes are tricky. Draw them a lot!

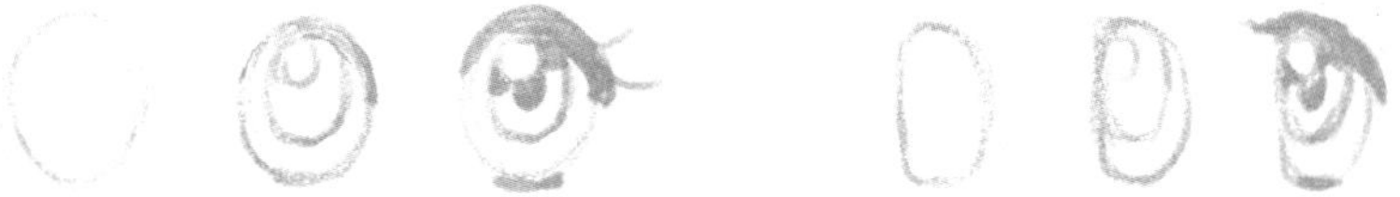

- Poses are hard to draw. Get references!!

(You can ask a friend to pose or pause movies and practice poses from that. This trick is great for fighting poses!)

Start with a rough gesture.

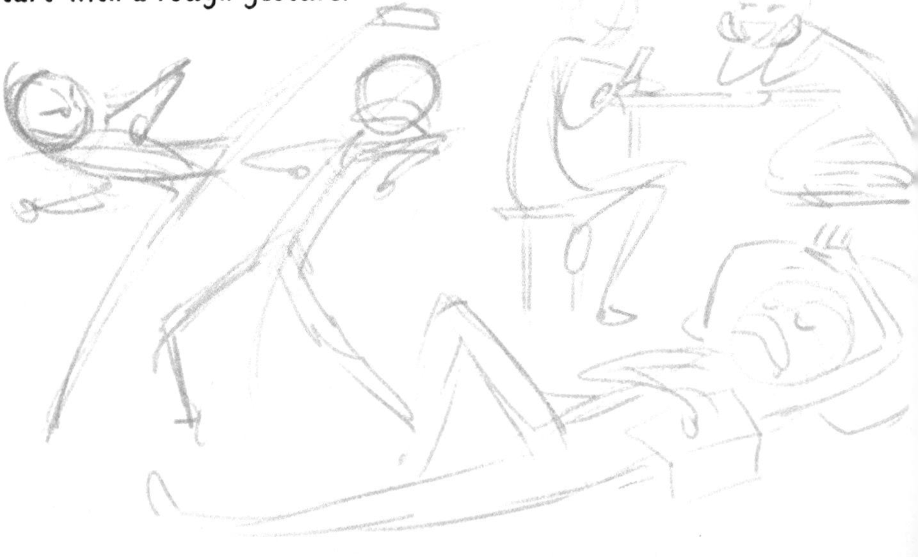

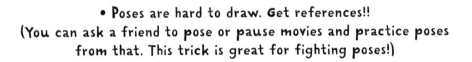

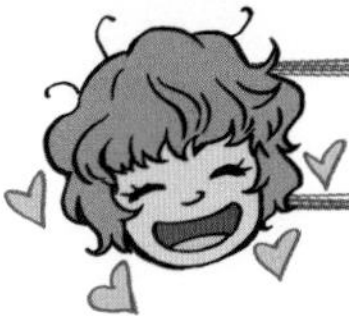

Show us how you draw, Svet!

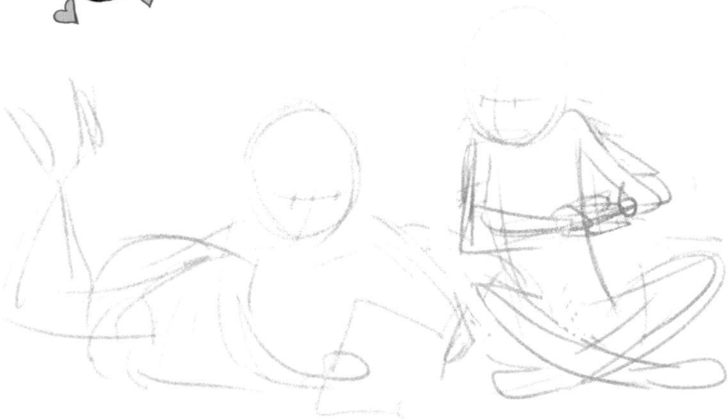

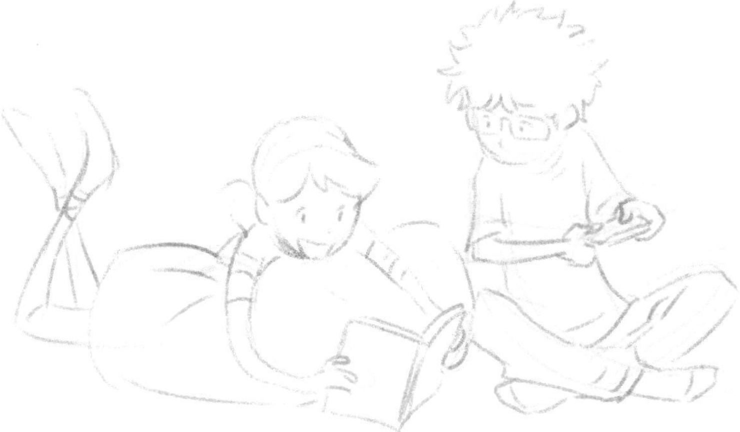

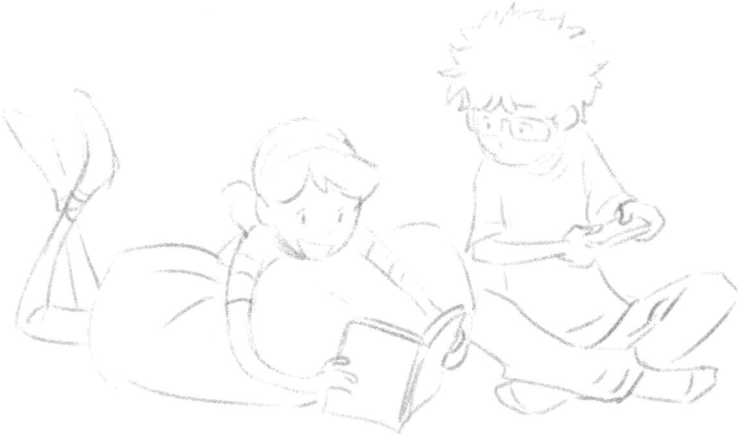

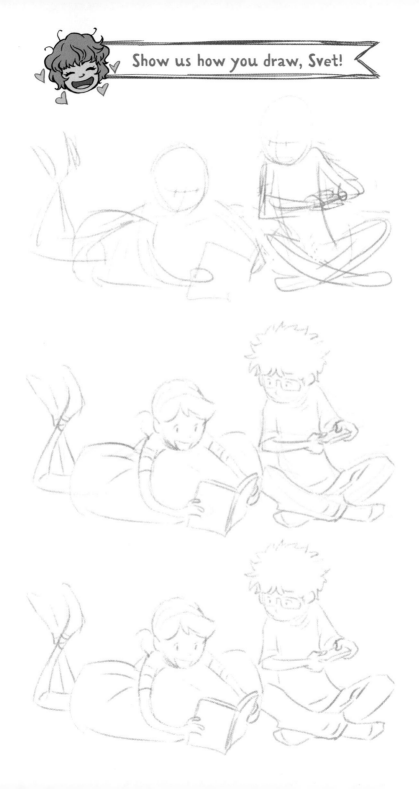

ONE SKETCH A DAY

DATE: ____________

DATE: ____________

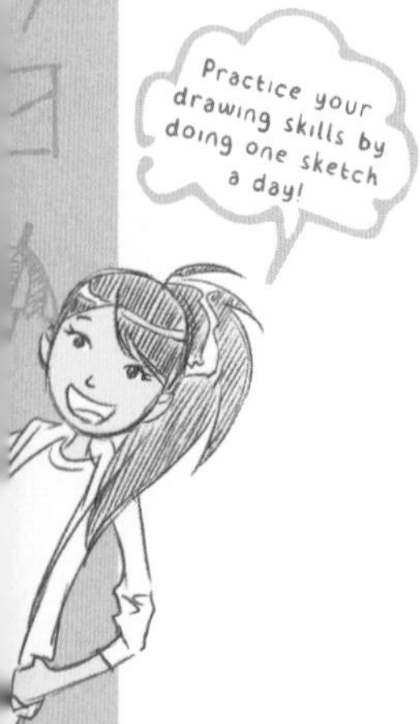
Practice your drawing skills by doing one sketch a day!

DATE: _____

Draw a dinosaur with a Mohawk having a party!

DATE: _____

DATE: _____

DATE: _____

Draw a
rain puddle with
a reflection.

DATE: _____

DATE: _____

DATE: _____

DATE: _____

Draw a
mermaid
eating a
birthday
cake!

DATE: _____

_____

DATE: _____

DATE: _____

_____

DATE: _____

DATE: _____

DATE: _____

Draw
Mr. Raccoon
eating a
cookie on
top of a
mountain
of
biscuits!

DATE: _____

DATE: _____

DATE: _____

Draw the floorplan for your dream room!

DATE: _____

Draw your favorite outfit and shoes!

ONE SKETCH A DAY

DATE: _____

DATE: _____

DATE: _____

DATE: _____

DATE: _____

_____

DATE: _____

Draw a
squirrel with its
cheeks stuffed
with too
many nuts!

DATE: _____

DATE: _____

DATE: _____

DATE: _____

DATE: _____

Draw
Peppi
like the
Mona Lisa
painting!

DATE: _____

DATE: _____

Draw six different kinds of insects and name them!

DATE: _____

DATE: _____

DATE: _____

DATE: _____

DATE: _____

Draw a realistic eye and a cartoon eye.

DATE: _____

DATE: _____

DATE: _____

DATE: _____

DATE: _____

DATE: _____

Draw a snail wearing a
raincoat in the rain.

DATE: _____

DATE: _____

Draw
your favorite
foods with
faces.

DATE: _____

DATE: _____

ONE SKETCH A DAY

DATE: _____

DATE: _____

DATE: _____

DATE: _____

Draw
like your
favorite
artist.

DATE: _____

Draw an
elf riding
a dragon.

DATE: _____

DATE: _____

DATE: _____

DATE: _____

_____

DATE: _____

DATE: _____

Draw what's on your desk.

DATE: _____

DATE: _____

Draw your
favorite heroine
from a story.

DATE: _____

DATE: _____

_____

DATE: _____

DATE: _____

_____

DATE: _____

Draw you
and your
friends
on a
camping
trip.

DATE: _____

DATE: _____

• **Cartooning doesn't have to be fancy and complicated. You can draw a story using just stick figures! They are VERY customizable for all your story needs. Look:**

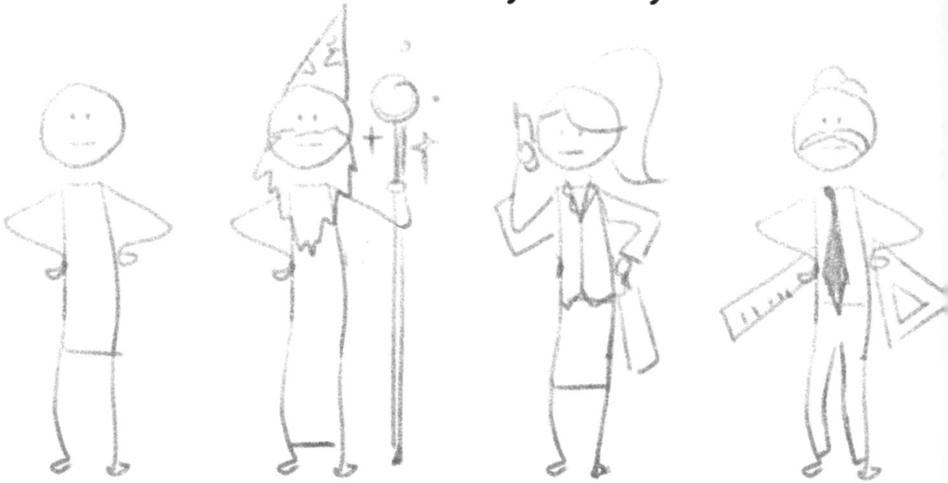

Person Wizard Business lady Geometry Teacher

• **Maybe you need children and animals in your story? Stick figures will help!**

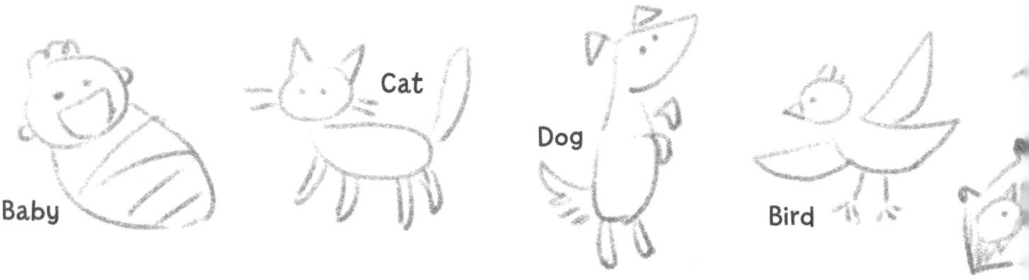
Baby
Cat
Dog
Bird

• **EXPRESSIONS! Endless variations of eyes, brows, and mouths are here for youuu!**

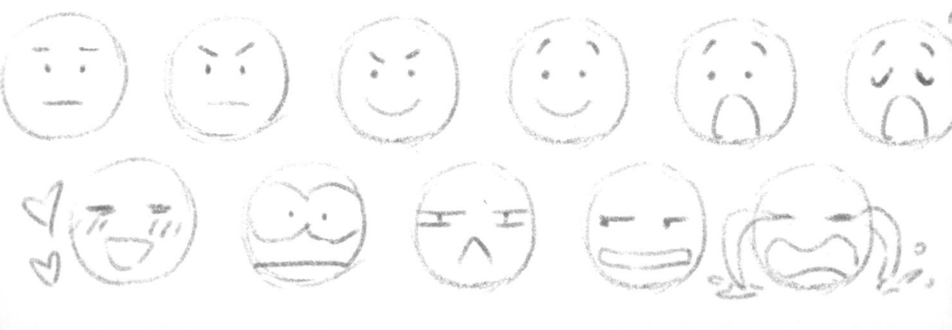

- **Locations also don't have to be complicated!**

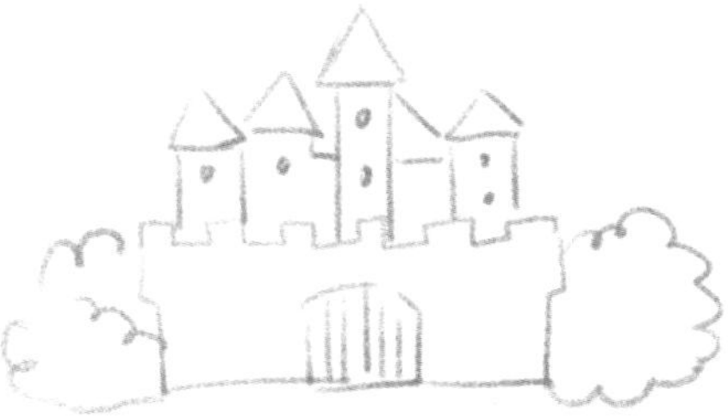

Castle

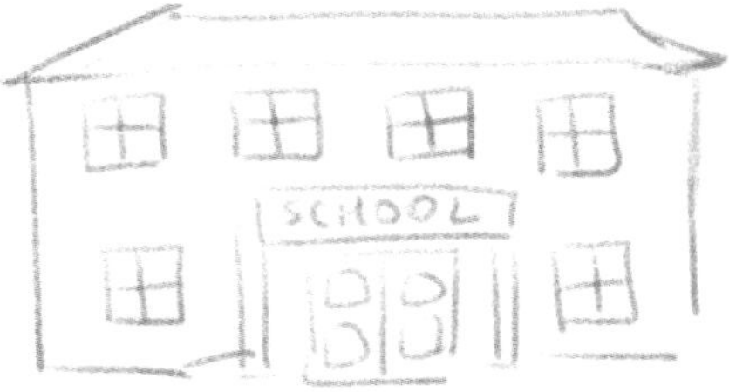
SCHOOL

School

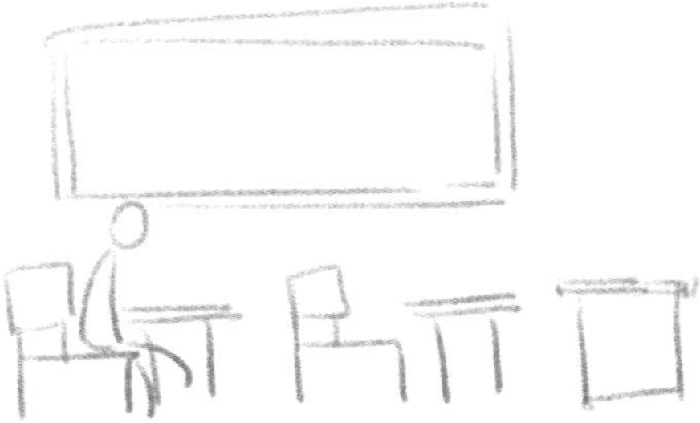

Classroom

Space Station

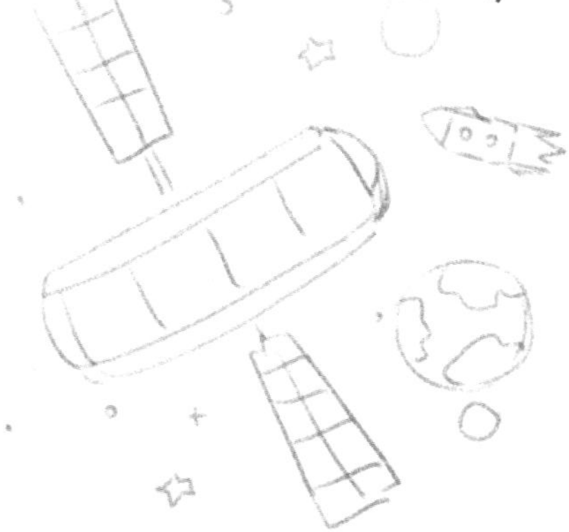

With cartooning, you can let your imagination fly!

The next few pages have Jensen's cartoon diary of his imaginary adventures.

What adventures will YOU have?

Turn to the next page to read:

The Captain's Log

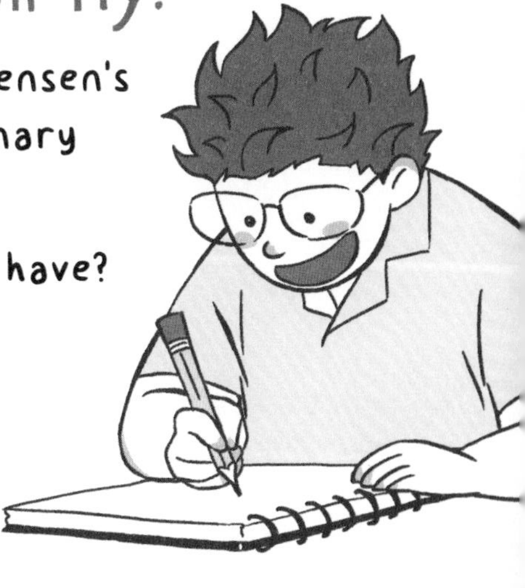

MISSION LOG: Day 1

0900 hours — landed on surface of Alpha Zeta Prime in search of intelligent life

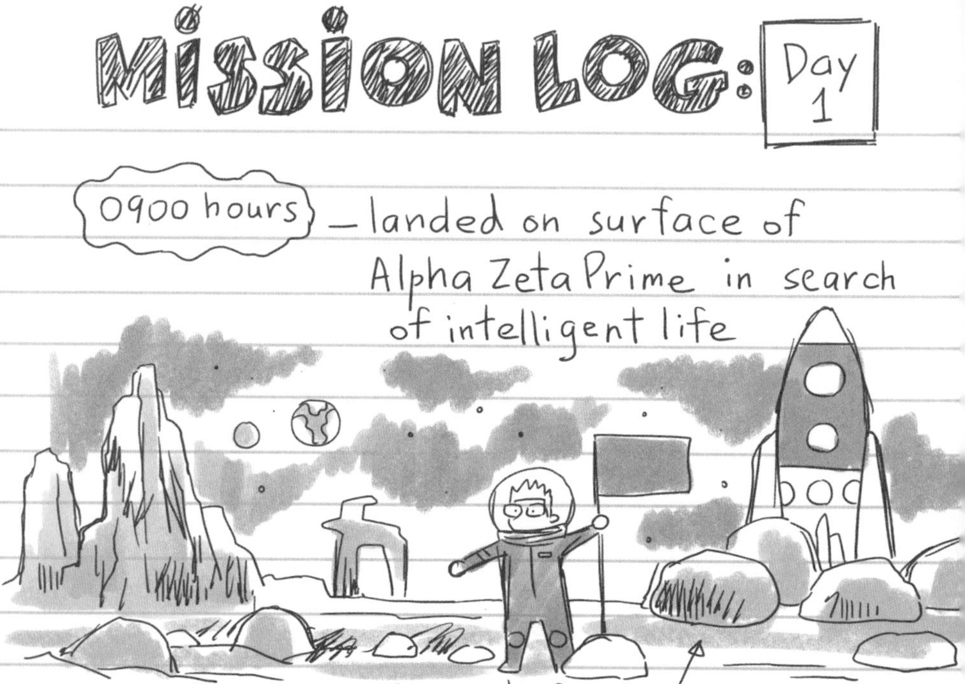

(so far only found a bunch of rocks)

Crew is setting up the station and snack area.

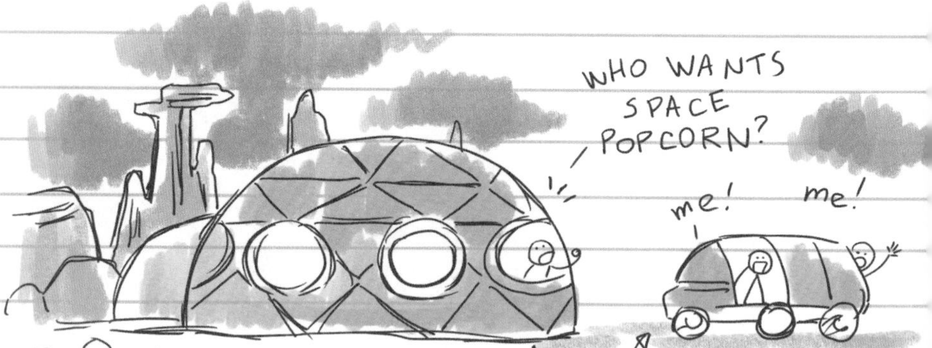
WHO WANTS SPACE POPCORN?
me!
me!

(bio-dome station)

(space ATV)

1200 hours – My chief security officer and co-captain return from their scout mission

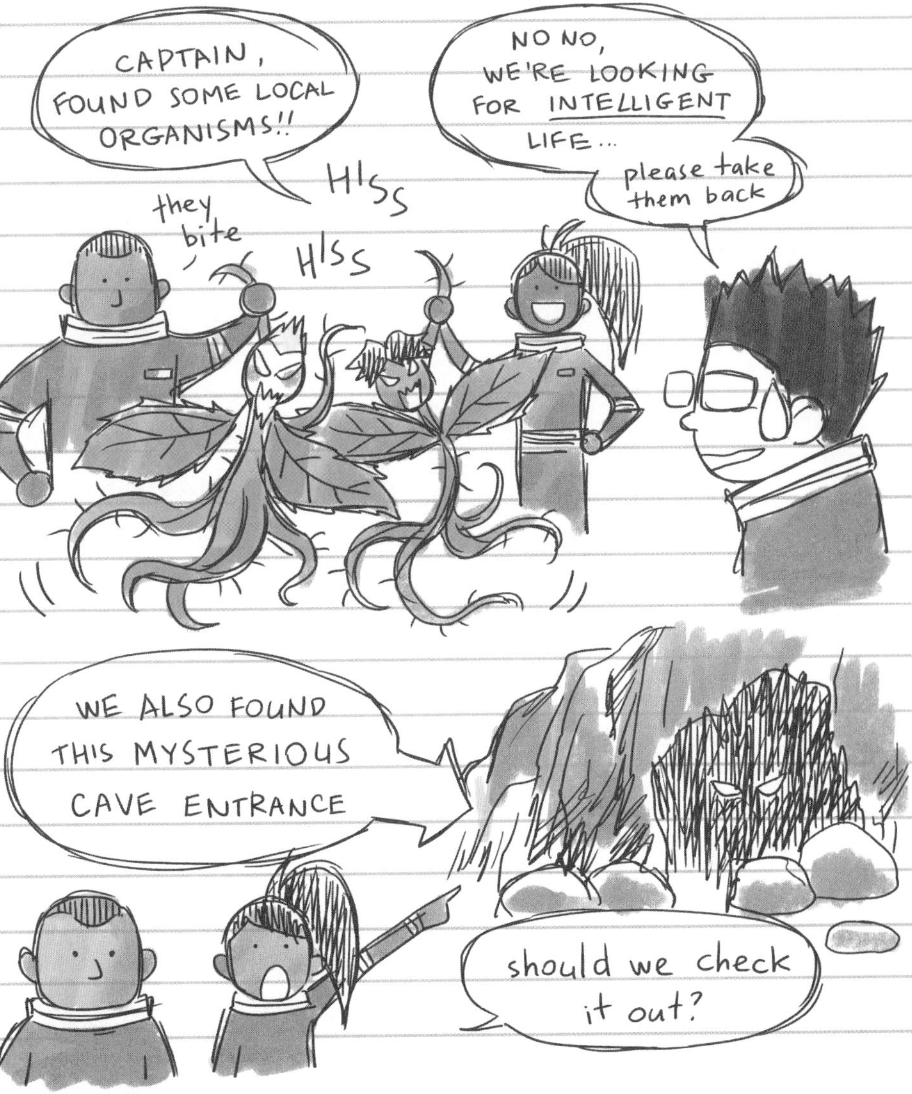
CAPTAIN, FOUND SOME LOCAL ORGANISMS!!
HISS
they bite
HISS
NO NO, WE'RE LOOKING FOR INTELLIGENT LIFE...
please take them back
WE ALSO FOUND THIS MYSTERIOUS CAVE ENTRANCE
should we check it out?

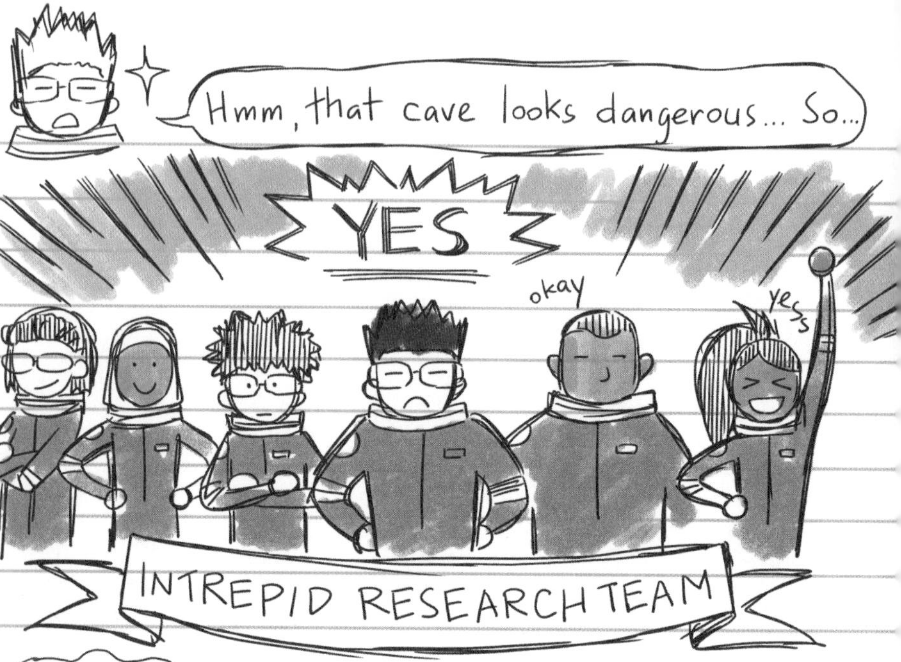
Hmm, that cave looks dangerous... So...
YES
okay
yesss
INTREPID RESEARCH TEAM

1300 hours We break for lunch first, because lunch is **space hot dogs** and **space tacos** and no one wants to miss that.

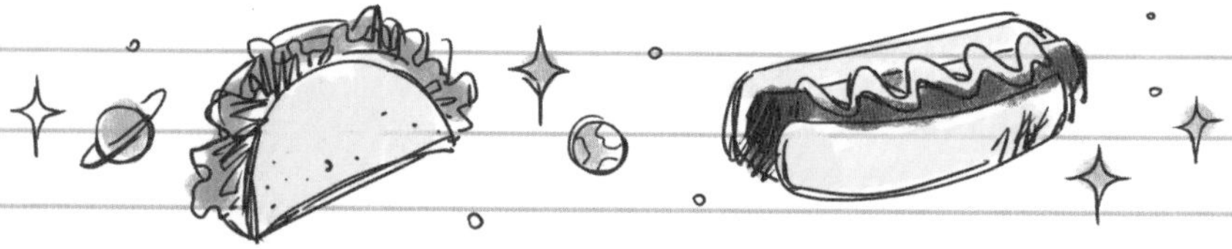

1500 hours We are ready!

Our intrepid research team sets out to explore the MYSTERIOUS CAVE.

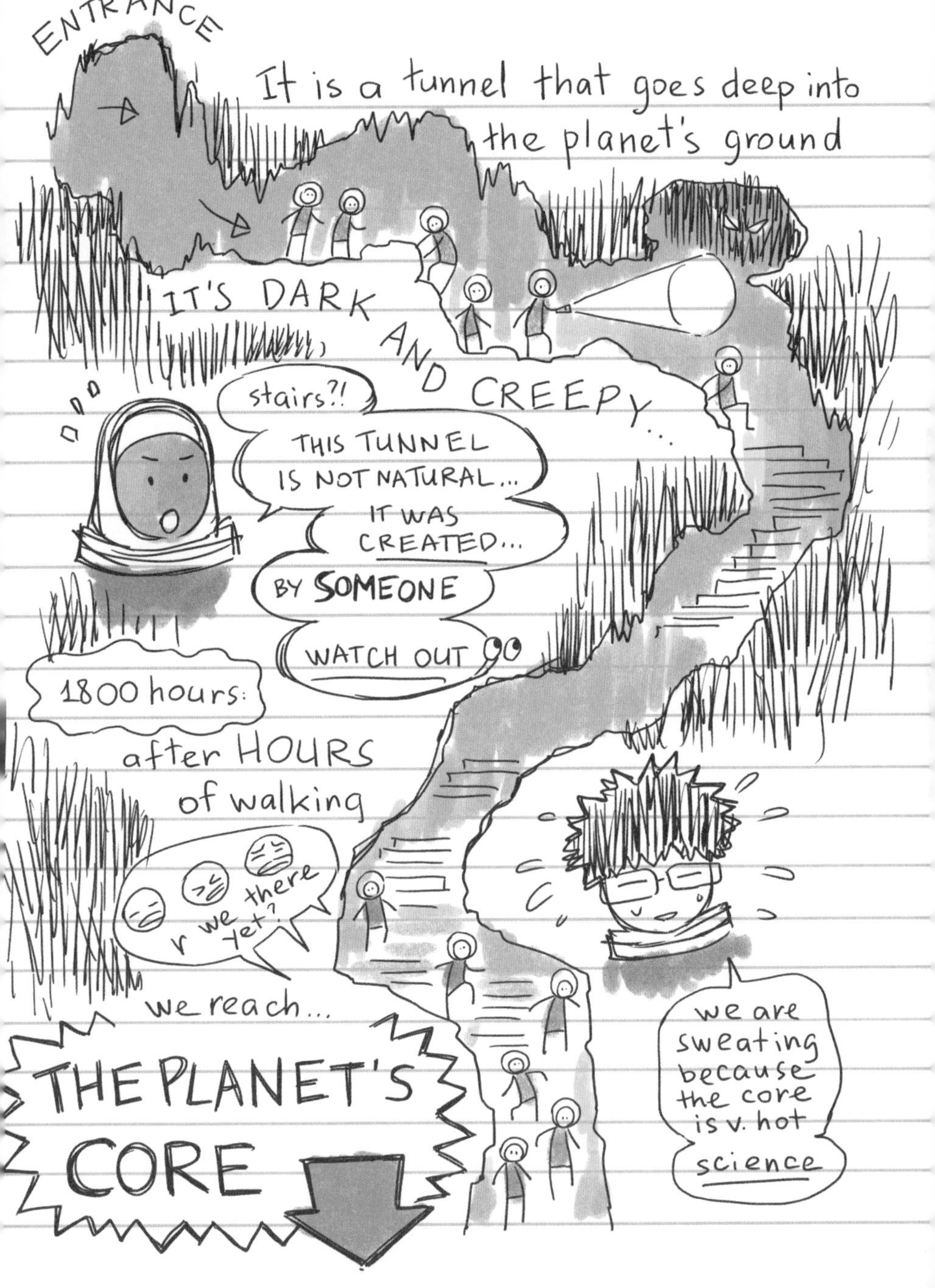
ENTRANCE
It is a tunnel that goes deep into the planet's ground
IT'S DARK AND CREEPY...
stairs?!
THIS TUNNEL IS NOT NATURAL...
IT WAS CREATED...
BY SOMEONE
WATCH OUT
1800 hours:
after HOURS of walking
r we there yet?
we reach...
THE PLANET'S CORE
we are sweating because the core is v. hot
science

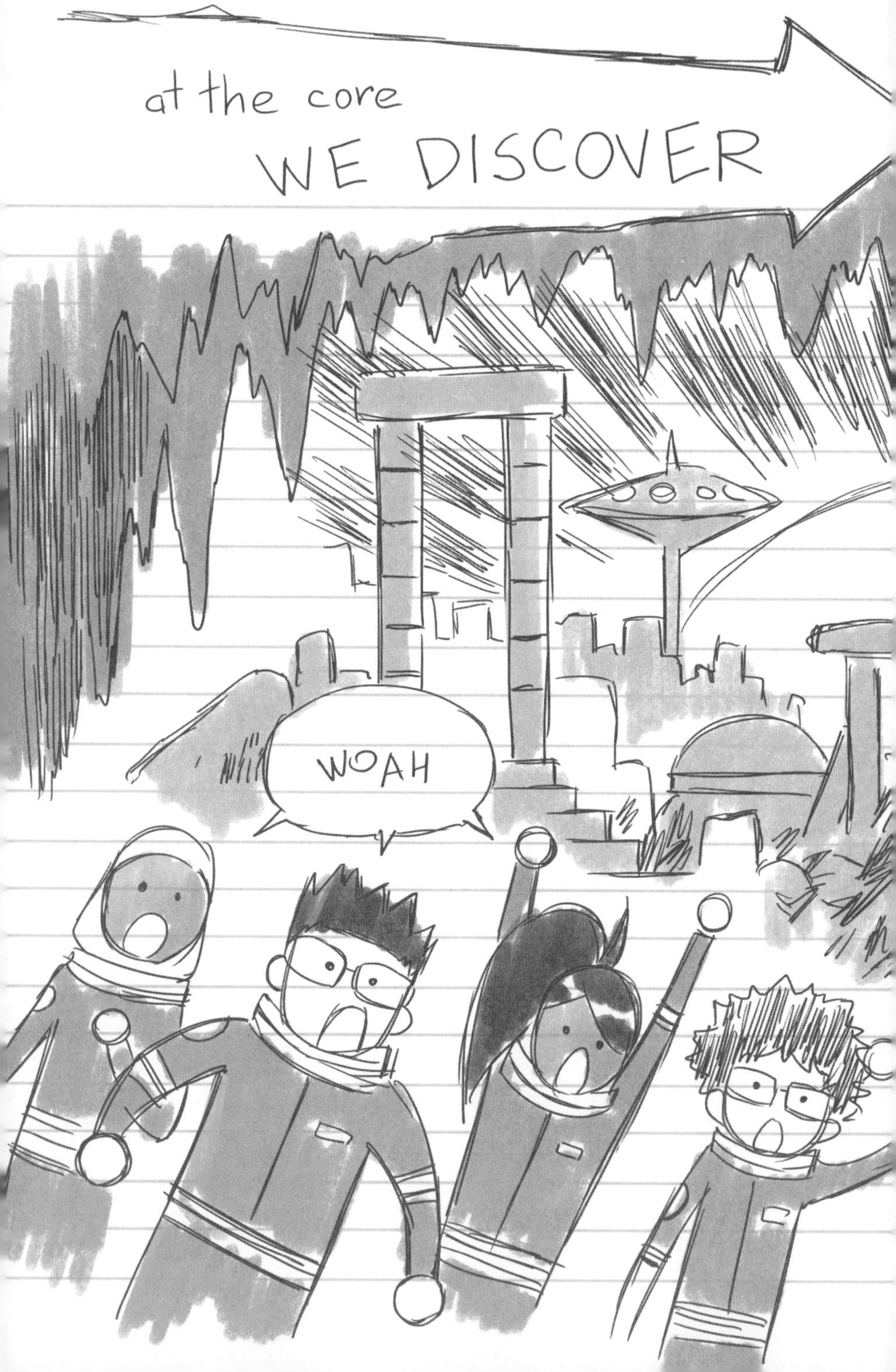
at the core
WE DISCOVER
WOAH

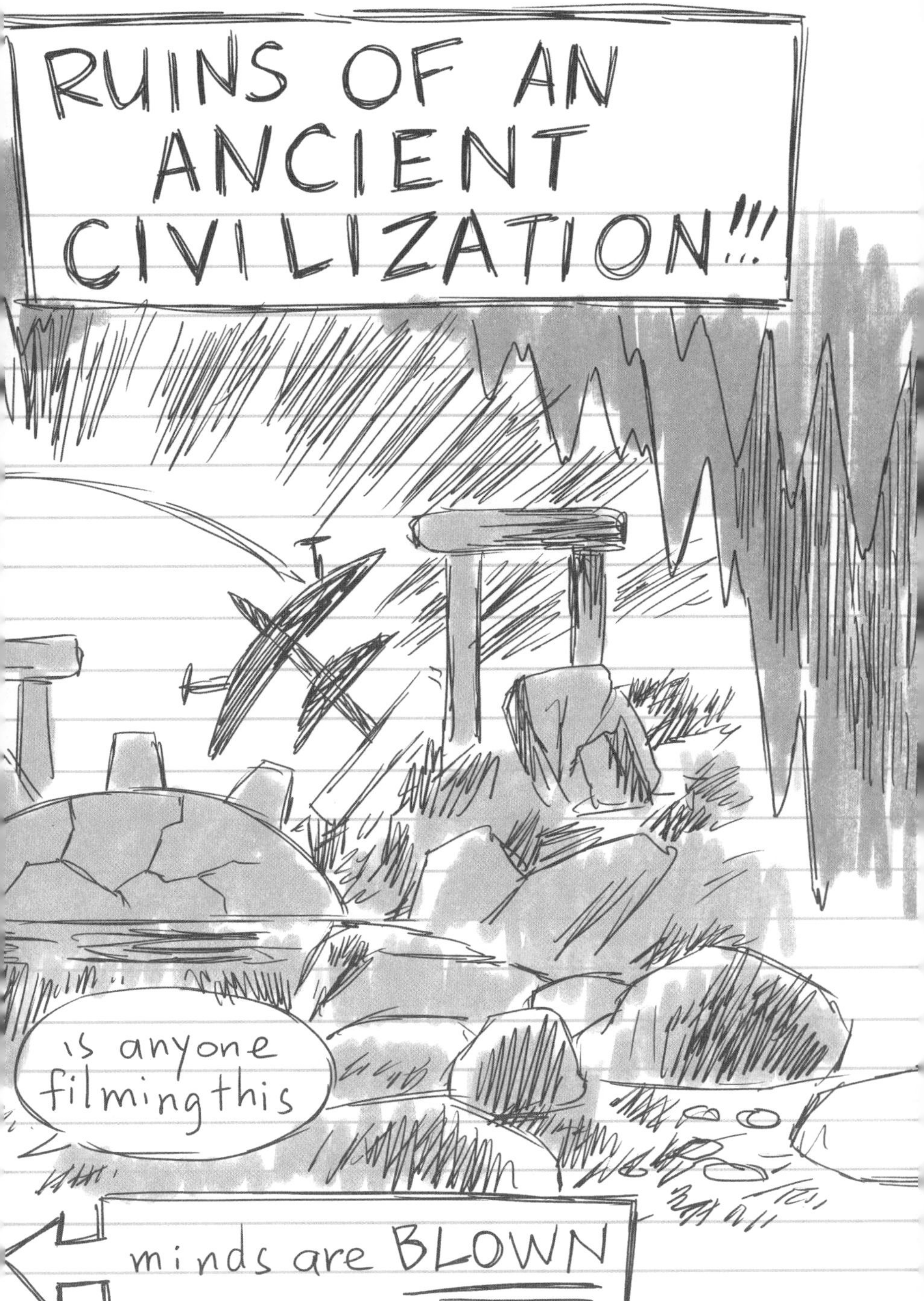
RUINS OF AN ANCIENT CIVILIZATION!!!
is anyone filming this
minds are BLOWN

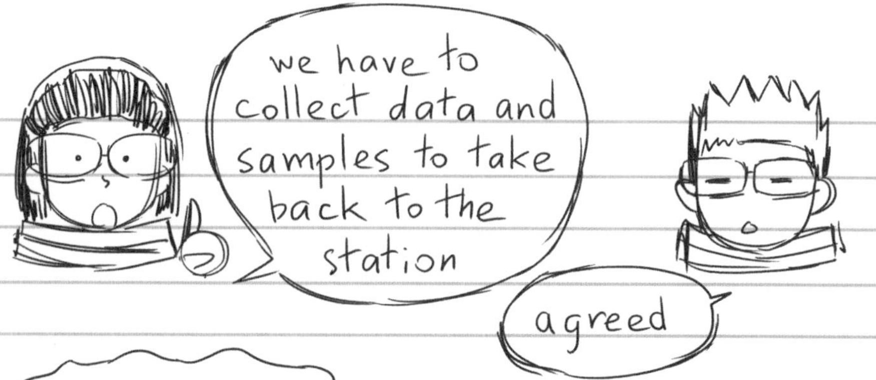
we have to collect data and samples to take back to the station
agreed

2000 hours: we do what Jenny said.

...WHEN SUDDENLY...!!

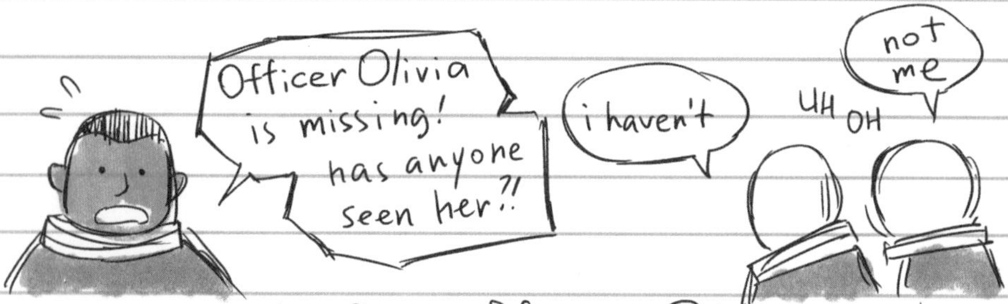
Officer Olivia is missing! has anyone seen her?!
i haven't
UH OH
not me

We look for officer Olivia and find her hiding behind a rock. She seems... Strange.

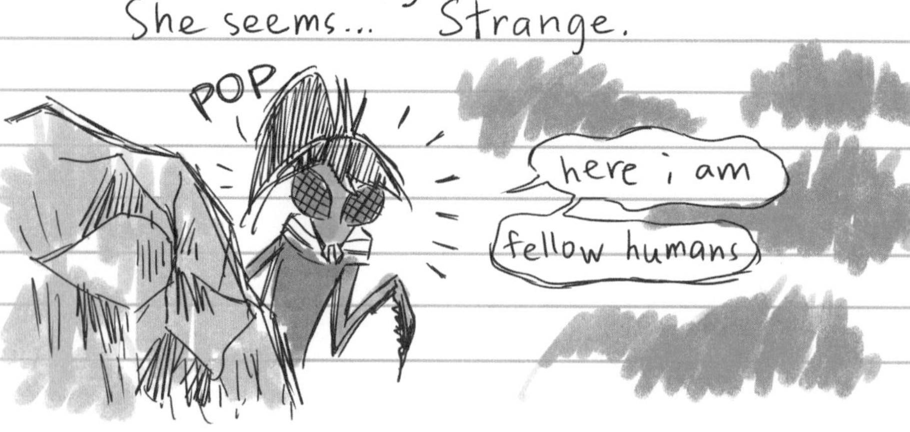
POP
here i am
fellow humans

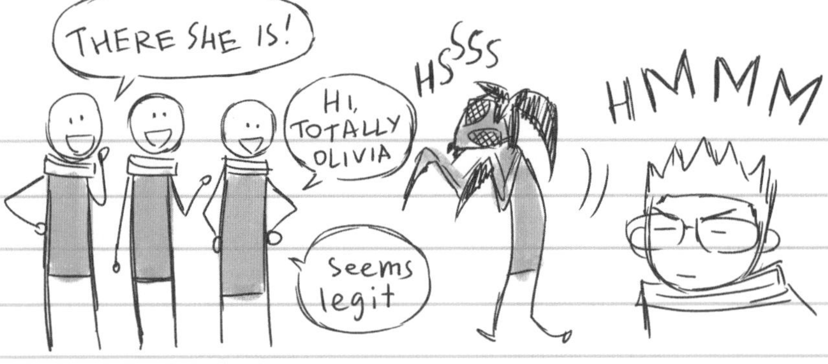
THERE SHE IS!
HI, TOTALLY OLIVIA
Seems legit
HSSSS
HMMM

2100 hours: It's space bedtime soon, so we head back to the station.

I suspect there is something wrong with officer Olivia...

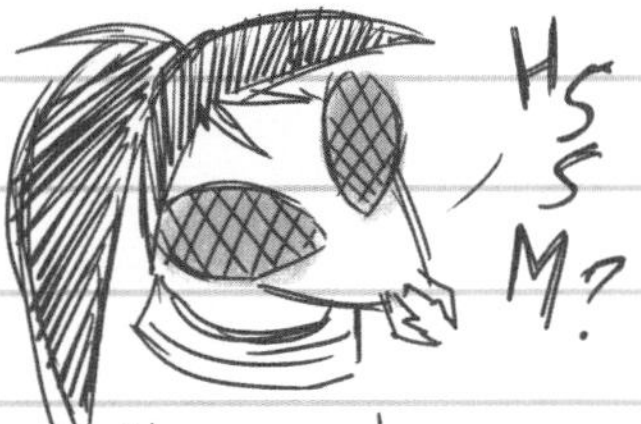
HSSM?

But I seem to be the only one.

MISSION LOG: Day 2

0800 hours: Breakfast is ✧space eggs✧ and ✧space waffles with syrup✧

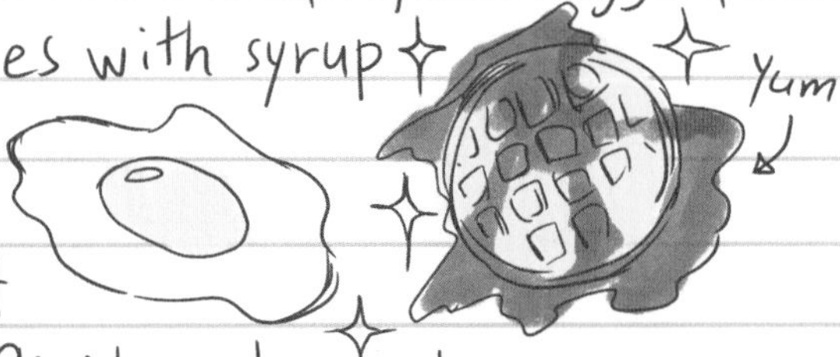
Yum

Everyone is excited about that and the Ancient Civilization discovery.

0830 hours: So many questions, so few answers... And so many waffles

Officer Olivia still seems weird. No one else notices.

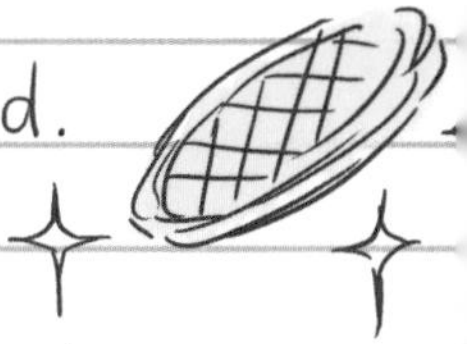

Am I just imagining it?

...WHEN SUDDENLY...!!

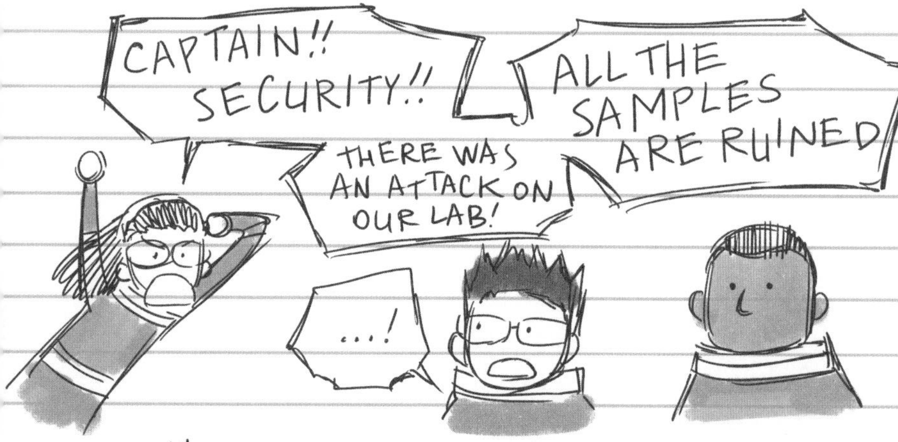
CAPTAIN!! SECURITY!!
THERE WAS AN ATTACK ON OUR LAB!
ALL THE SAMPLES ARE RUINED
...!

...WAS IT OFFICER OLIVIA?!!!

we RUN to the lab!!!

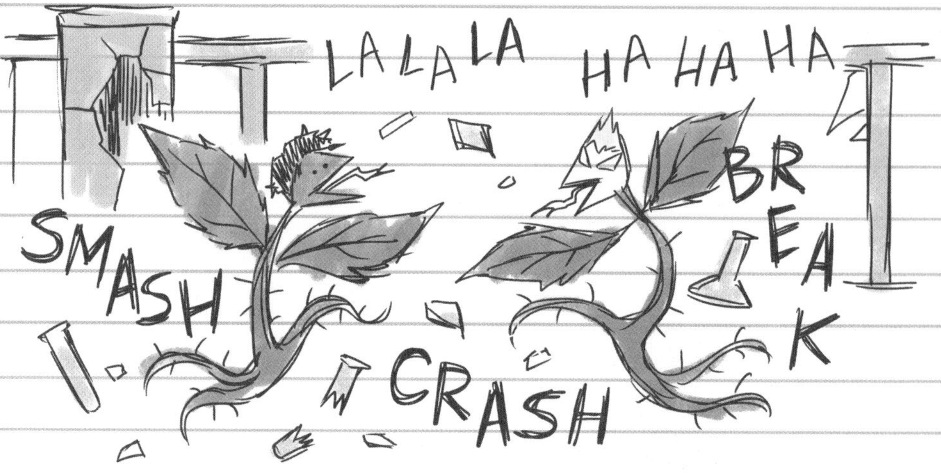
LALALA
HA HA HA HA
SMASH
BREAK
CRASH

...but it wasn't officer Olivia!

it was the local organisms!

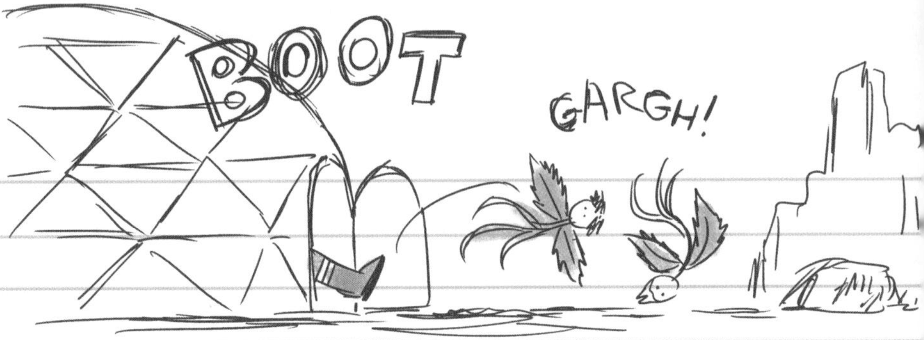
BOOT
GARGH!

Chief of security gives them the boot and everyone is relieved.

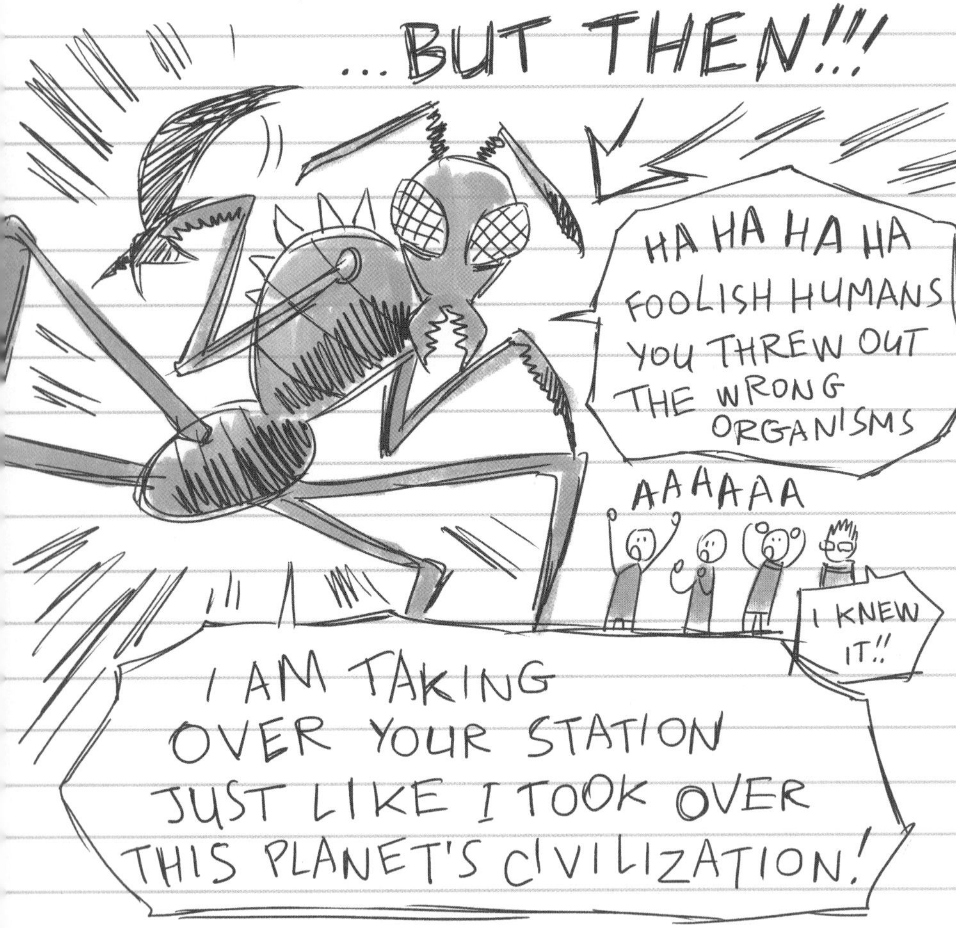
...BUT THEN!!!
HA HA HA HA
FOOLISH HUMANS
YOU THREW OUT
THE WRONG
ORGANISMS
AAAAAA
I KNEW IT!!
I AM TAKING
OVER YOUR STATION
JUST LIKE I TOOK OVER
THIS PLANET'S CIVILIZATION!

WITH MY ARMY OF SPACE BUGS!!
MWAH HA HA HA HA
NOT ON MY WATCH!! RUN, EVERYONE! GET TO THE SHIP! I WILL HOLD THEM OFF!!
But... There are too many bugs...
at least...
i saved...
the crew...
good-by—

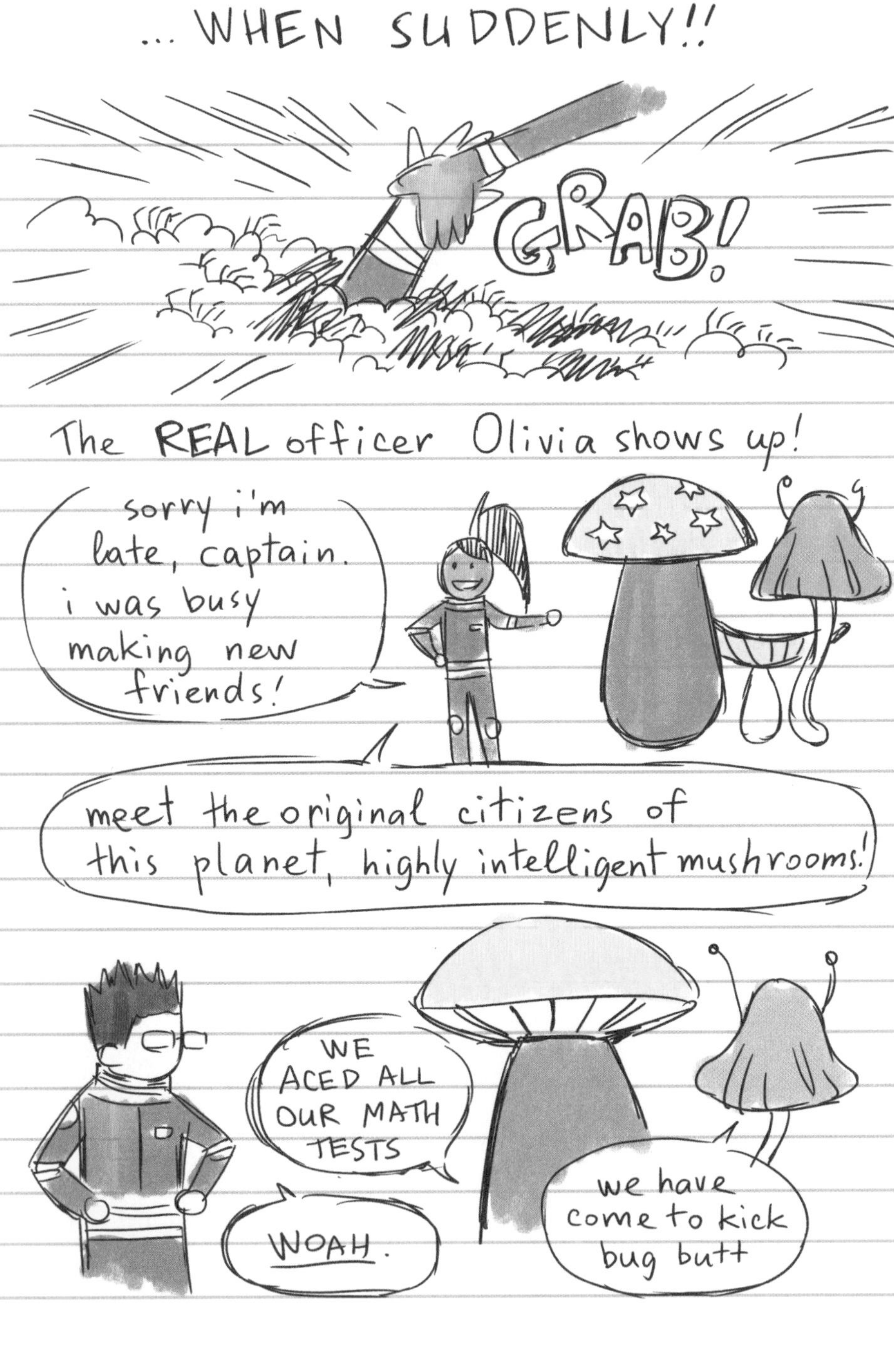

... WHEN SUDDENLY!!
GRAB!
The REAL officer Olivia shows up!
sorry i'm late, captain. i was busy making new friends!
meet the original citizens of this planet, highly intelligent mushrooms!
WE ACED ALL OUR MATH TESTS
we have come to kick bug butt
WOAH.

AND SO WE DID

(and totally won)

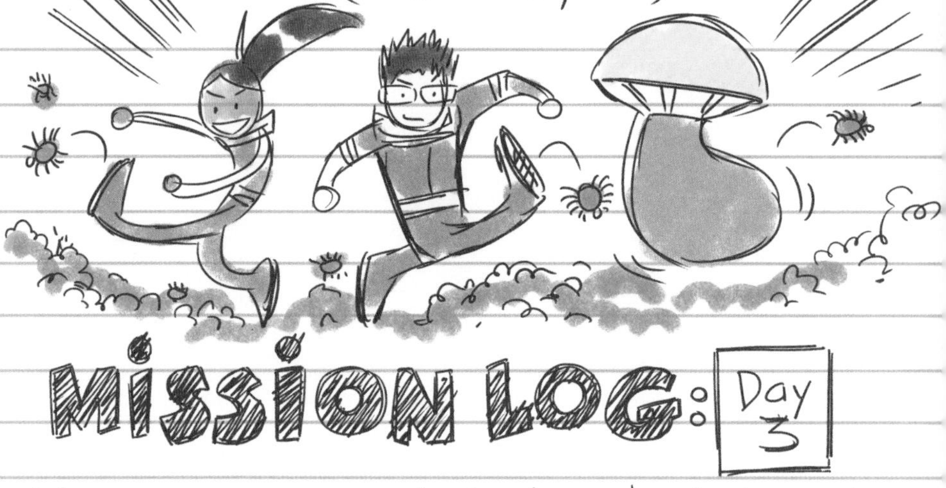

MISSION LOG: Day 3

Mission is accomplished and intelligent life found! Mushroniums are SUPER nice

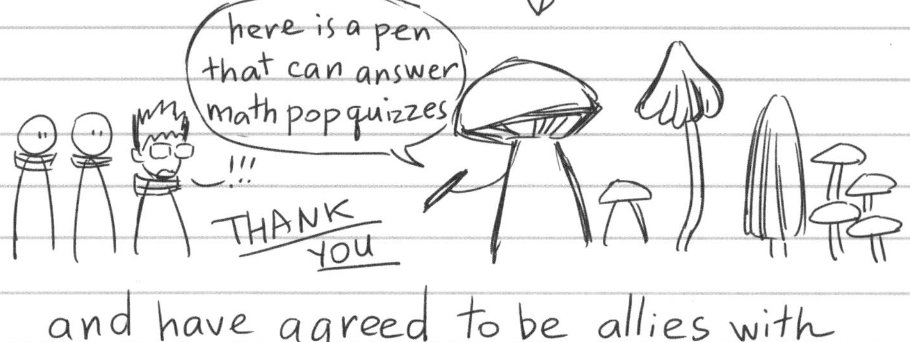

here is a pen that can answer math pop quizzes
!!!
THANK YOU

and have agreed to be allies with the Planet Federation.

The ancient ruins turned out to be a big insectarium for the Space Bugs (oops, we weren't supposed to go in there...)

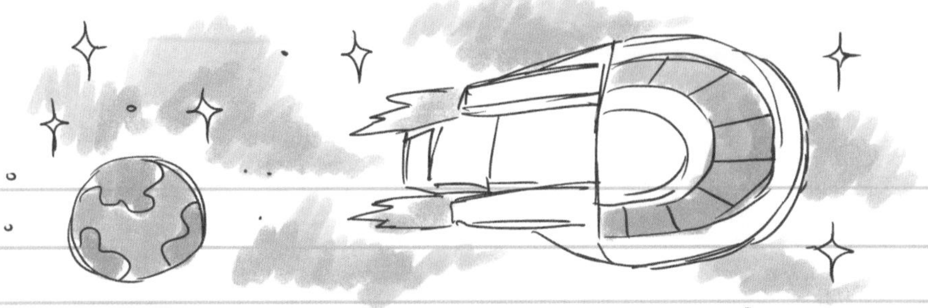

We are off the planet's surface
and ready for our next mission!
What is it?

UNKNOWN.
(i haven't opened Mission Control's
e-mail yet.)

But whatever it is, we will
accomplish that, too.

Captain Jensen, over and out.

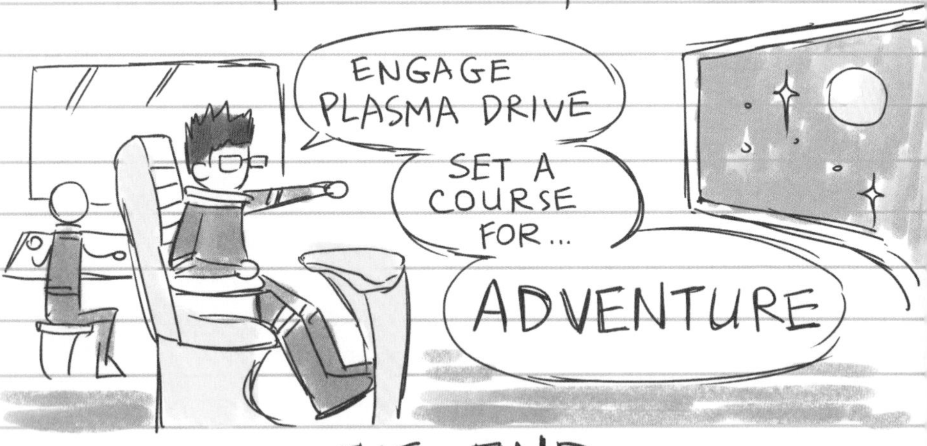
ENGAGE PLASMA DRIVE
SET A COURSE FOR...
ADVENTURE

THE END

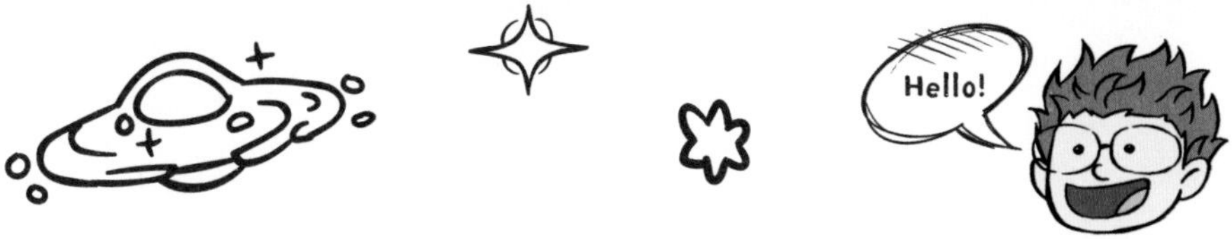
Hello!

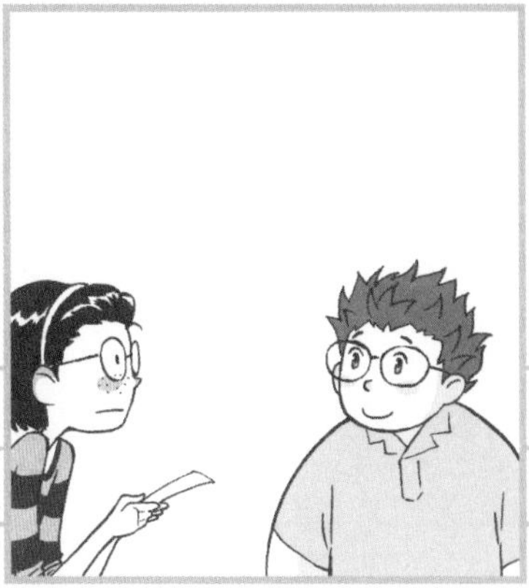

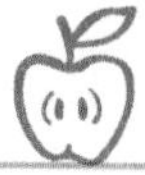

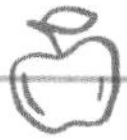

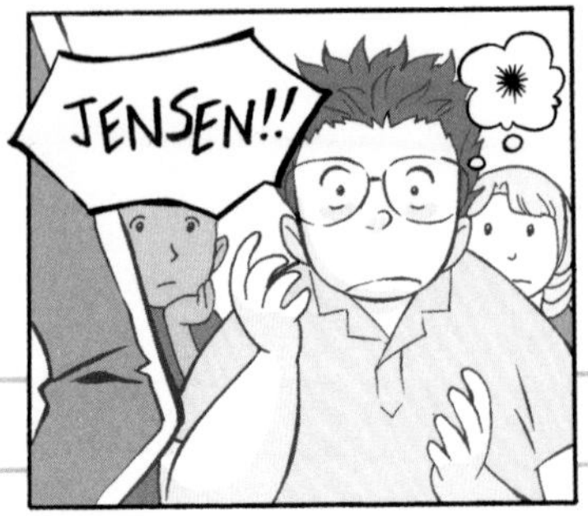
JENSEN!!

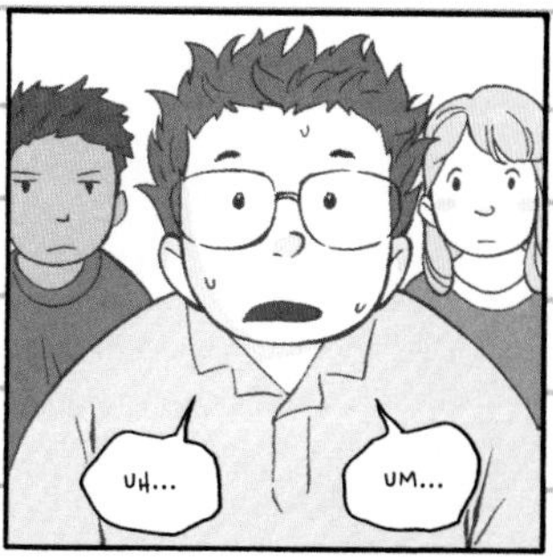
UH...
UM...

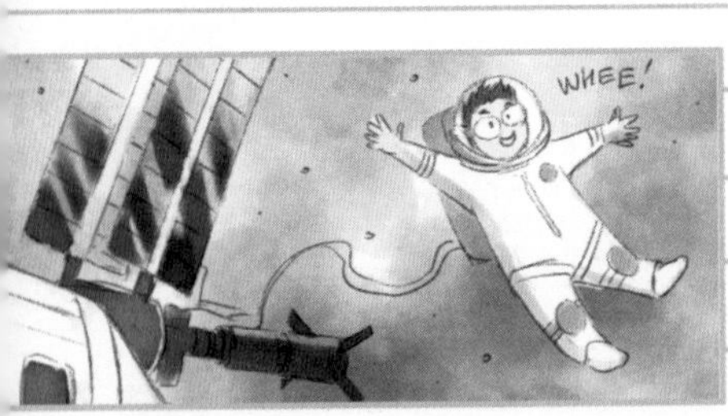
WHEE!

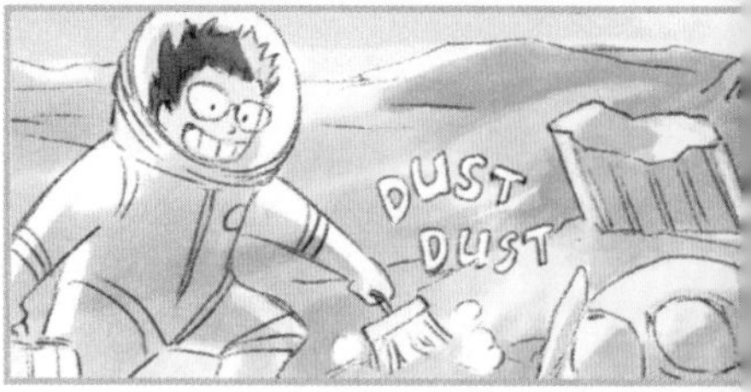
DUST
DUST

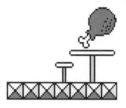

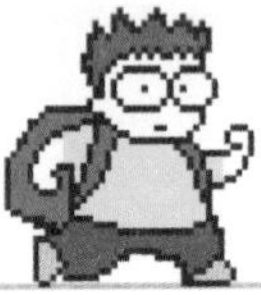

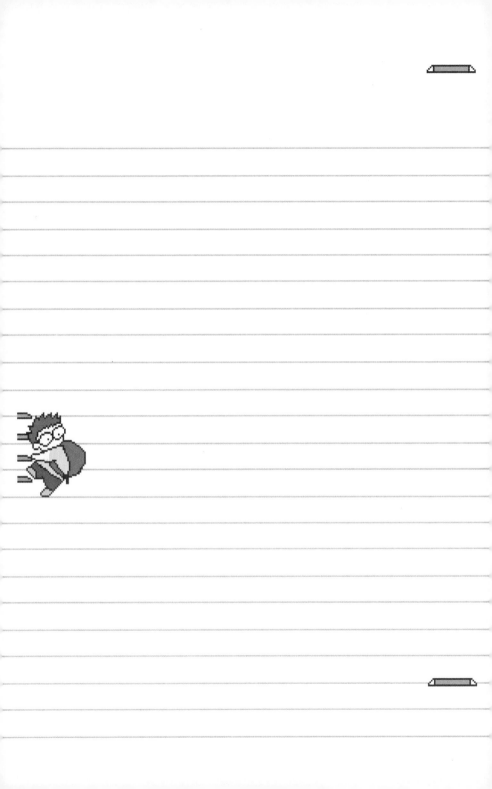

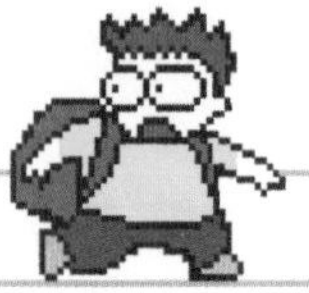

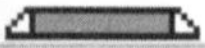

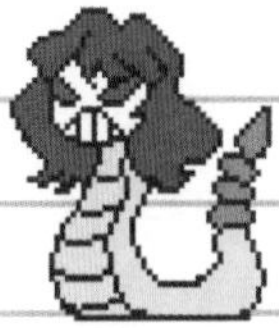

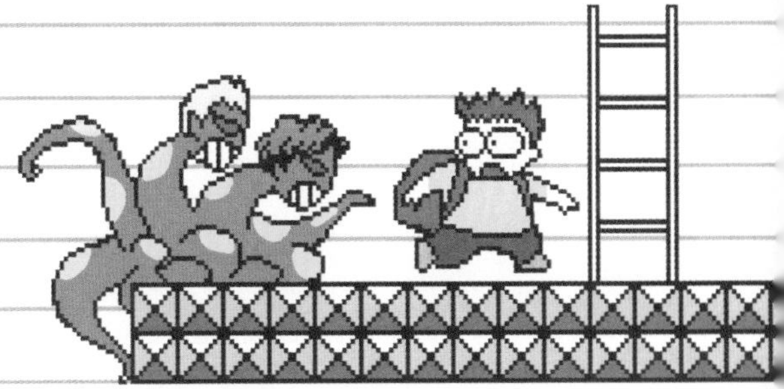

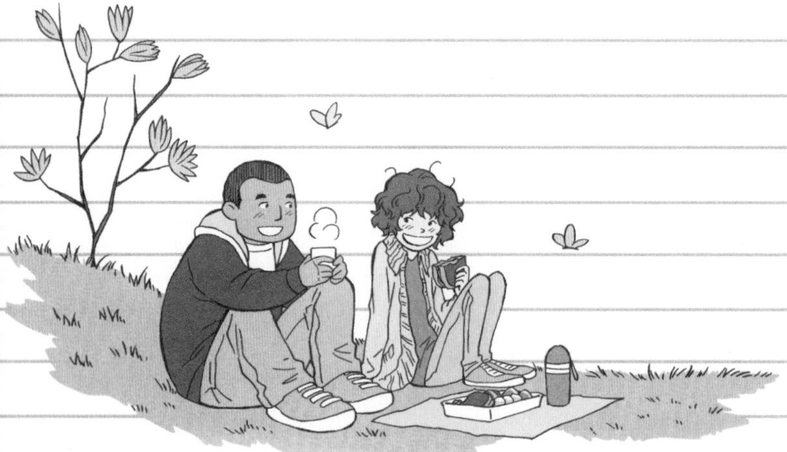

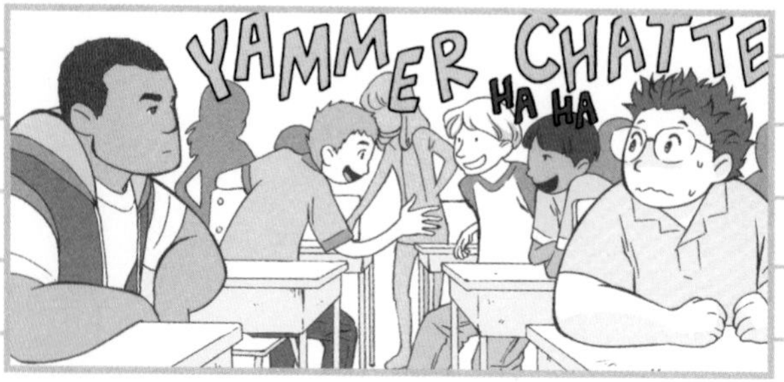

YAMMER
HA HA
CHATTE

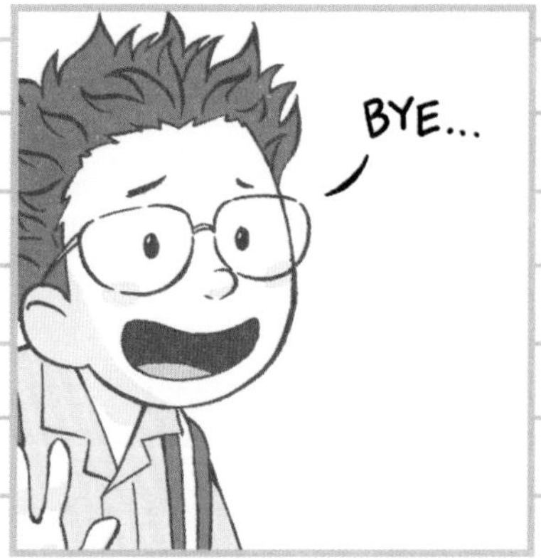
BYE...

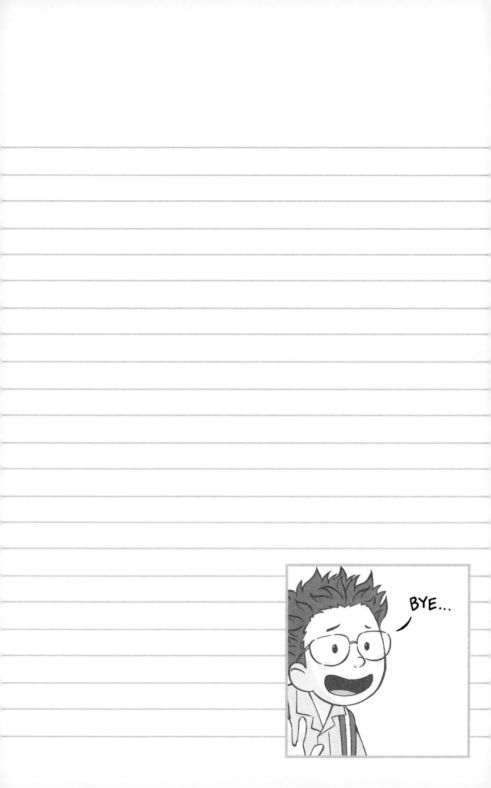

New Girl

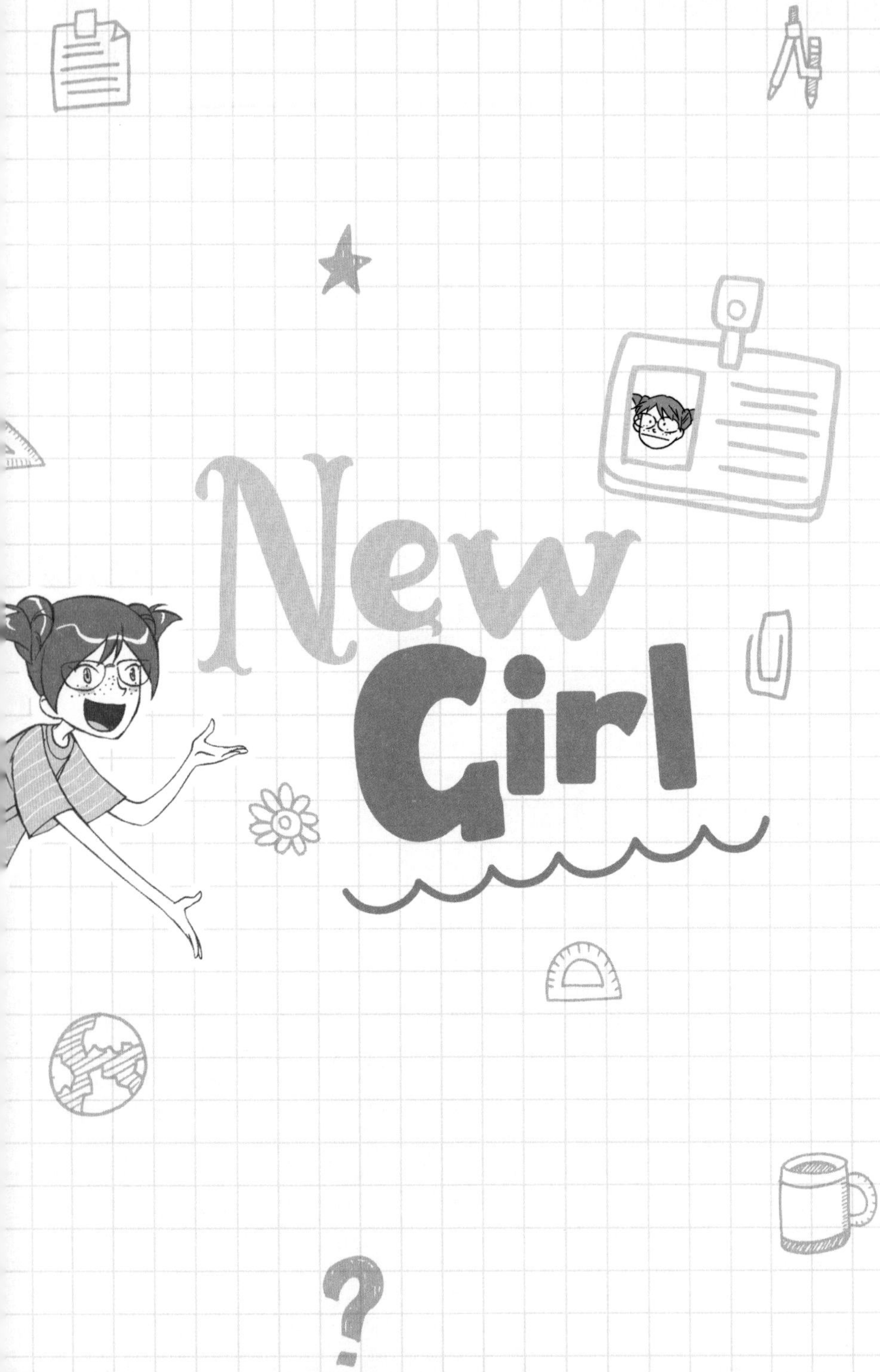

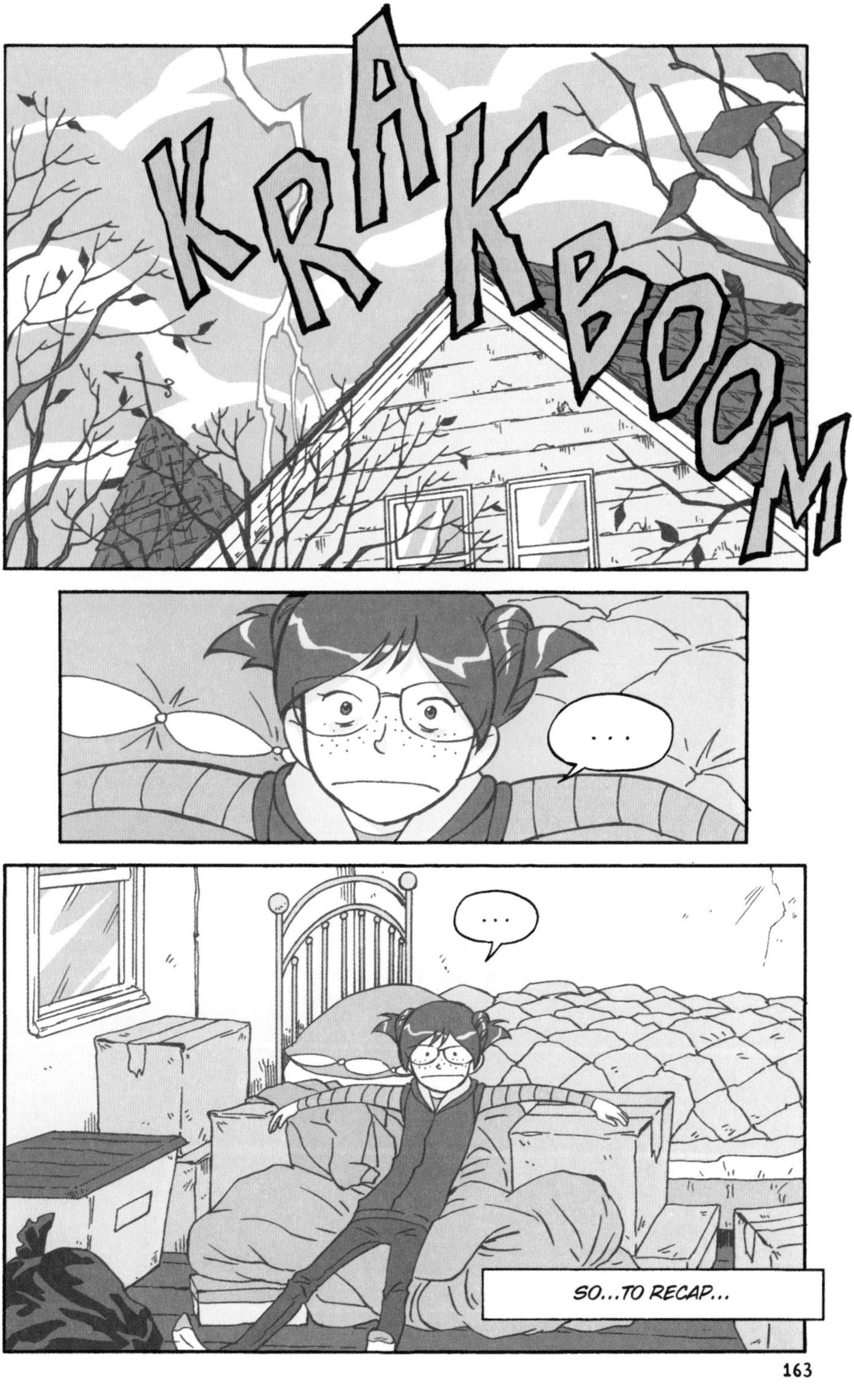
KRAKBOOM
. . .
. . .
SO...TO RECAP...

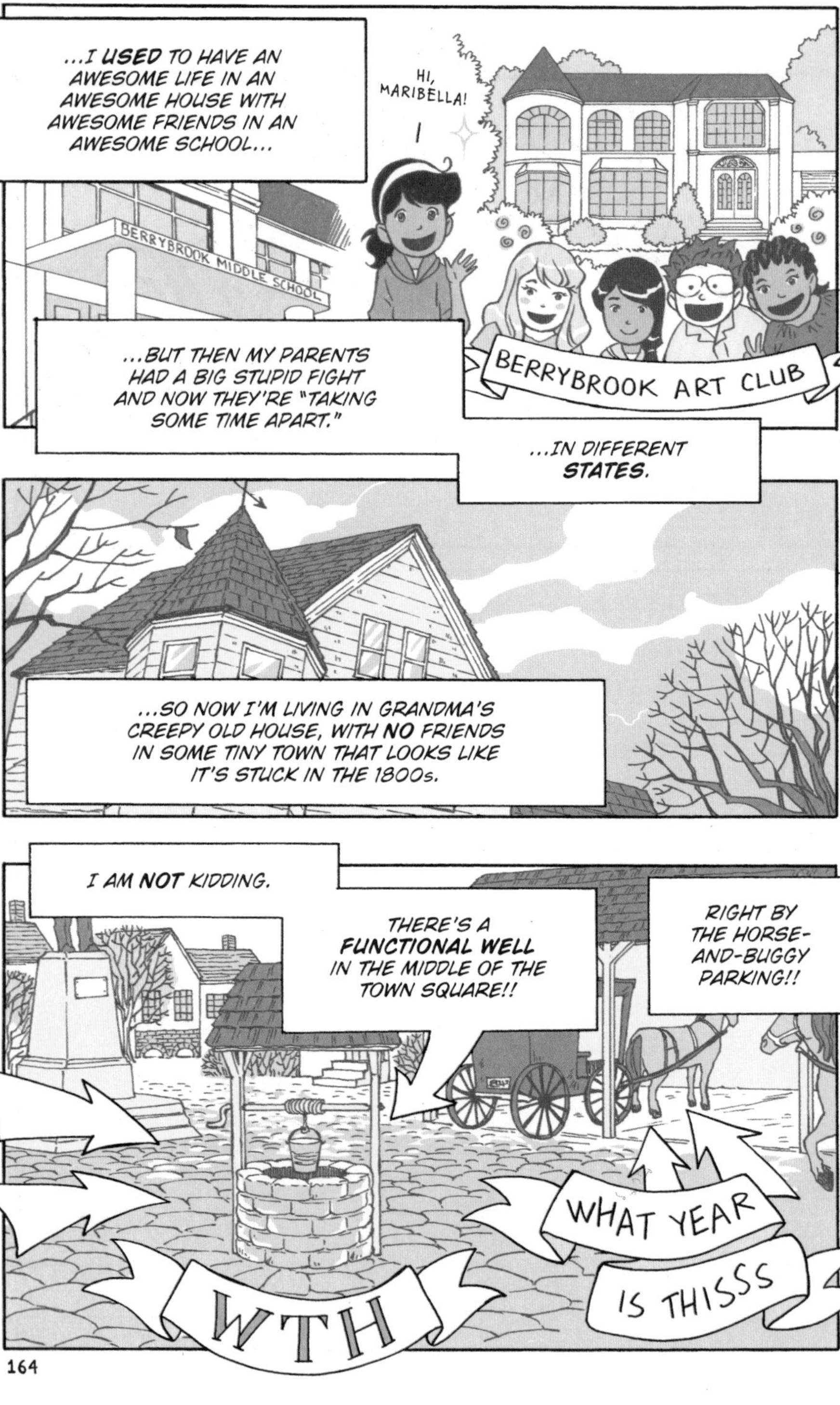
...I USED TO HAVE AN AWESOME LIFE IN AN AWESOME HOUSE WITH AWESOME FRIENDS IN AN AWESOME SCHOOL...
HI, MARIBELLA!
BERRYBROOK MIDDLE SCHOOL
BERRYBROOK ART CLUB
...BUT THEN MY PARENTS HAD A BIG STUPID FIGHT AND NOW THEY'RE "TAKING SOME TIME APART."
...IN DIFFERENT STATES.
...SO NOW I'M LIVING IN GRANDMA'S CREEPY OLD HOUSE, WITH NO FRIENDS IN SOME TINY TOWN THAT LOOKS LIKE IT'S STUCK IN THE 1800s.
I AM NOT KIDDING.
THERE'S A FUNCTIONAL WELL IN THE MIDDLE OF THE TOWN SQUARE!!
RIGHT BY THE HORSE-AND-BUGGY PARKING!!
WTH
WHAT YEAR IS THISSS

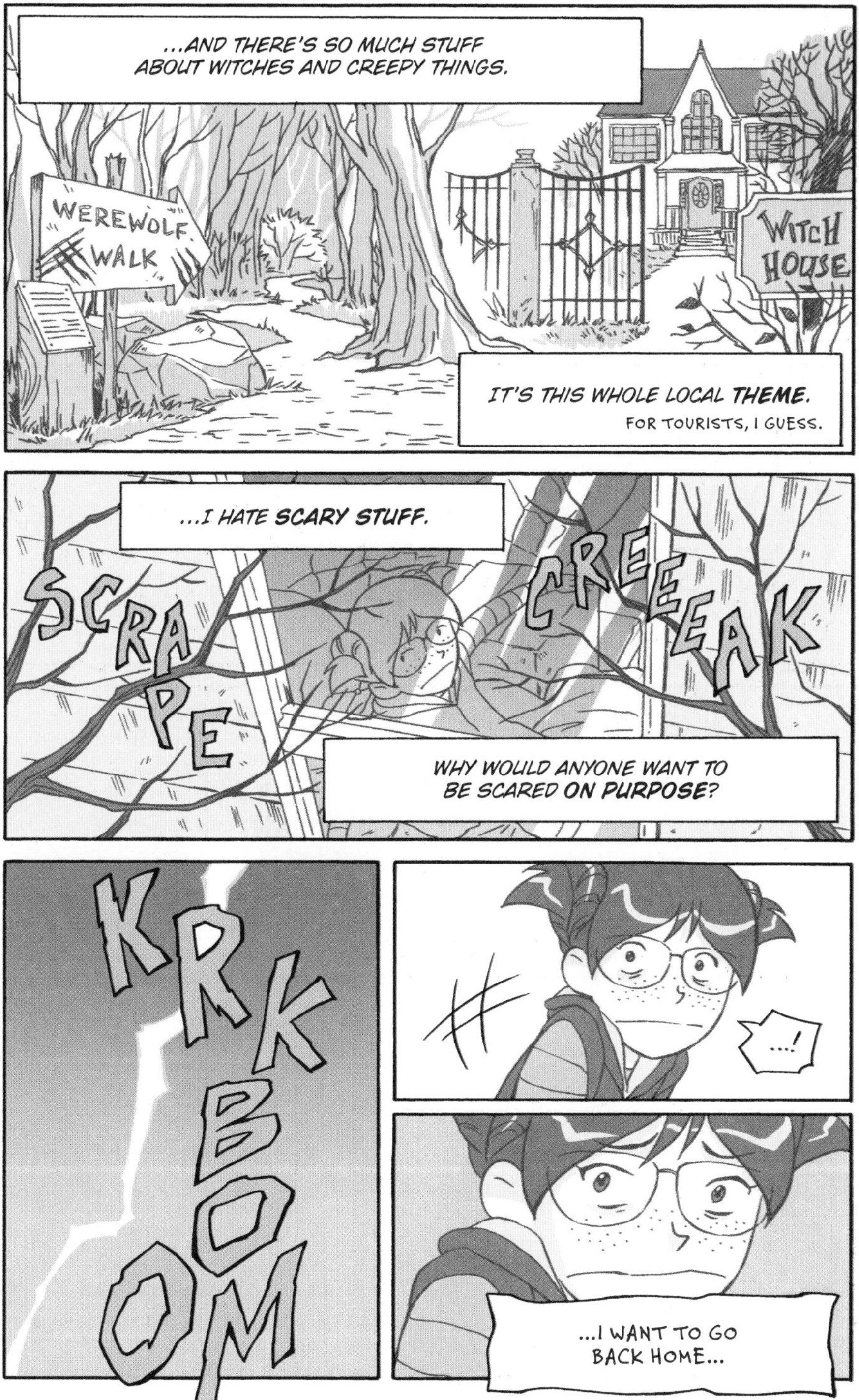
...AND THERE'S SO MUCH STUFF ABOUT WITCHES AND CREEPY THINGS.
WEREWOLF WALK
WITCH HOUSE
IT'S THIS WHOLE LOCAL **THEME.** FOR TOURISTS, I GUESS.
...I HATE **SCARY STUFF.**
SCRAPE
CREEEAK
WHY WOULD ANYONE WANT TO BE SCARED **ON PURPOSE**?
KRKBOOM
...!
...I WANT TO GO BACK HOME...

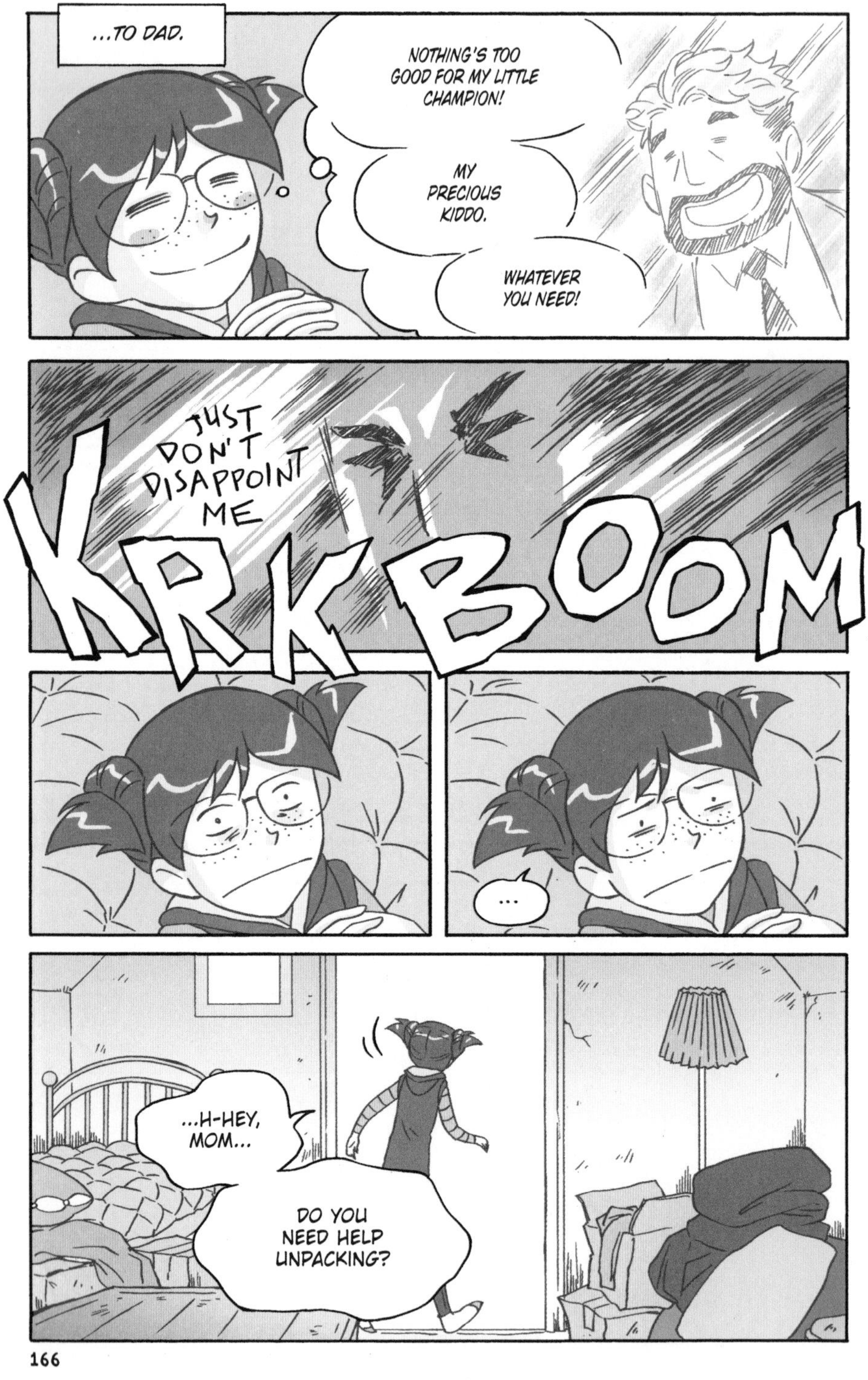

...TO DAD.
NOTHING'S TOO GOOD FOR MY LITTLE CHAMPION!
MY PRECIOUS KIDDO.
WHATEVER YOU NEED!
JUST DON'T DISAPPOINT ME
KRKBOOM
...
...H-HEY, MOM...
DO YOU NEED HELP UNPACKING?

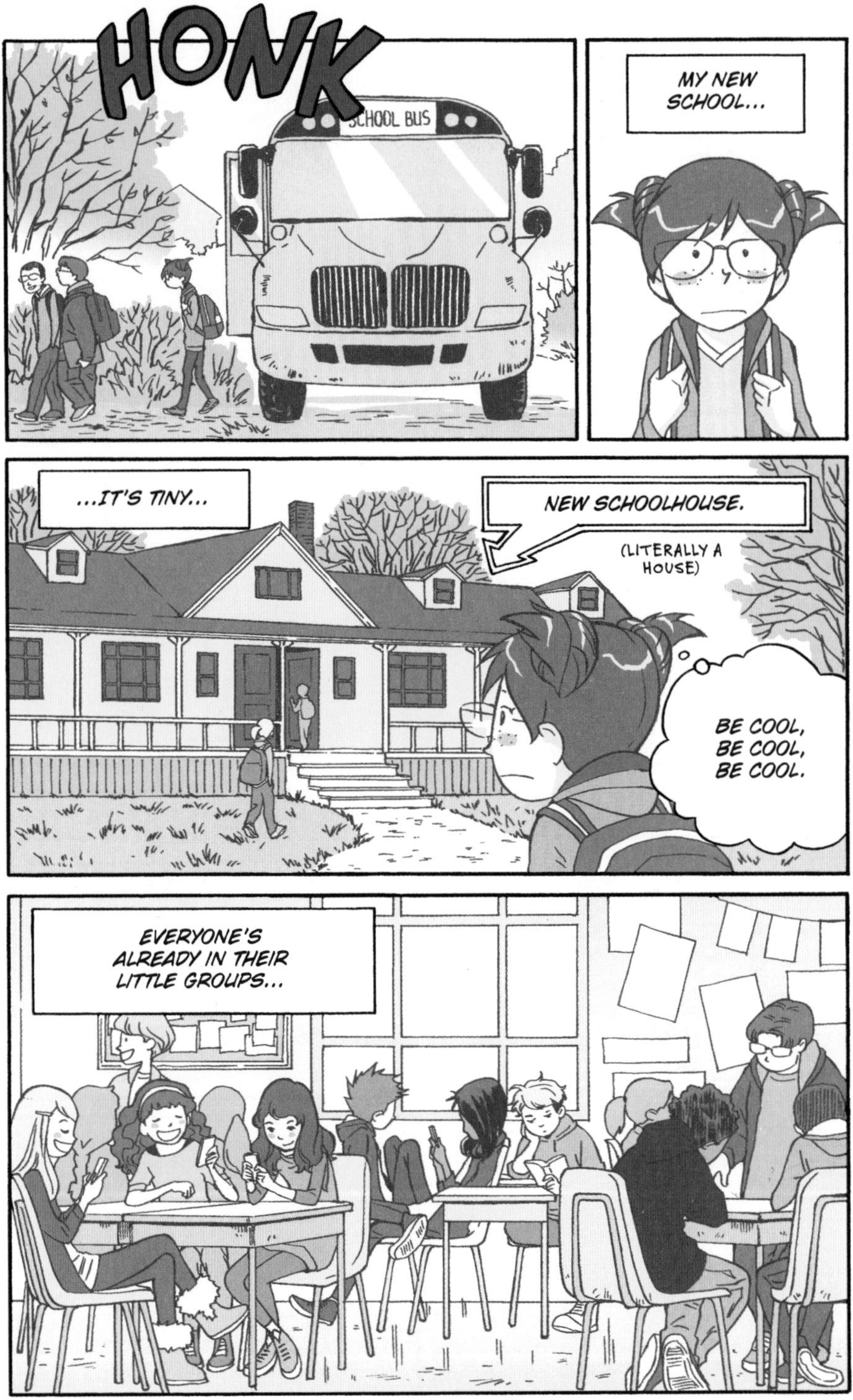
HONK
SCHOOL BUS
MY NEW SCHOOL...
...IT'S TINY...
NEW SCHOOLHOUSE.
(LITERALLY A HOUSE)
BE COOL, BE COOL, BE COOL.
EVERYONE'S ALREADY IN THEIR LITTLE GROUPS...

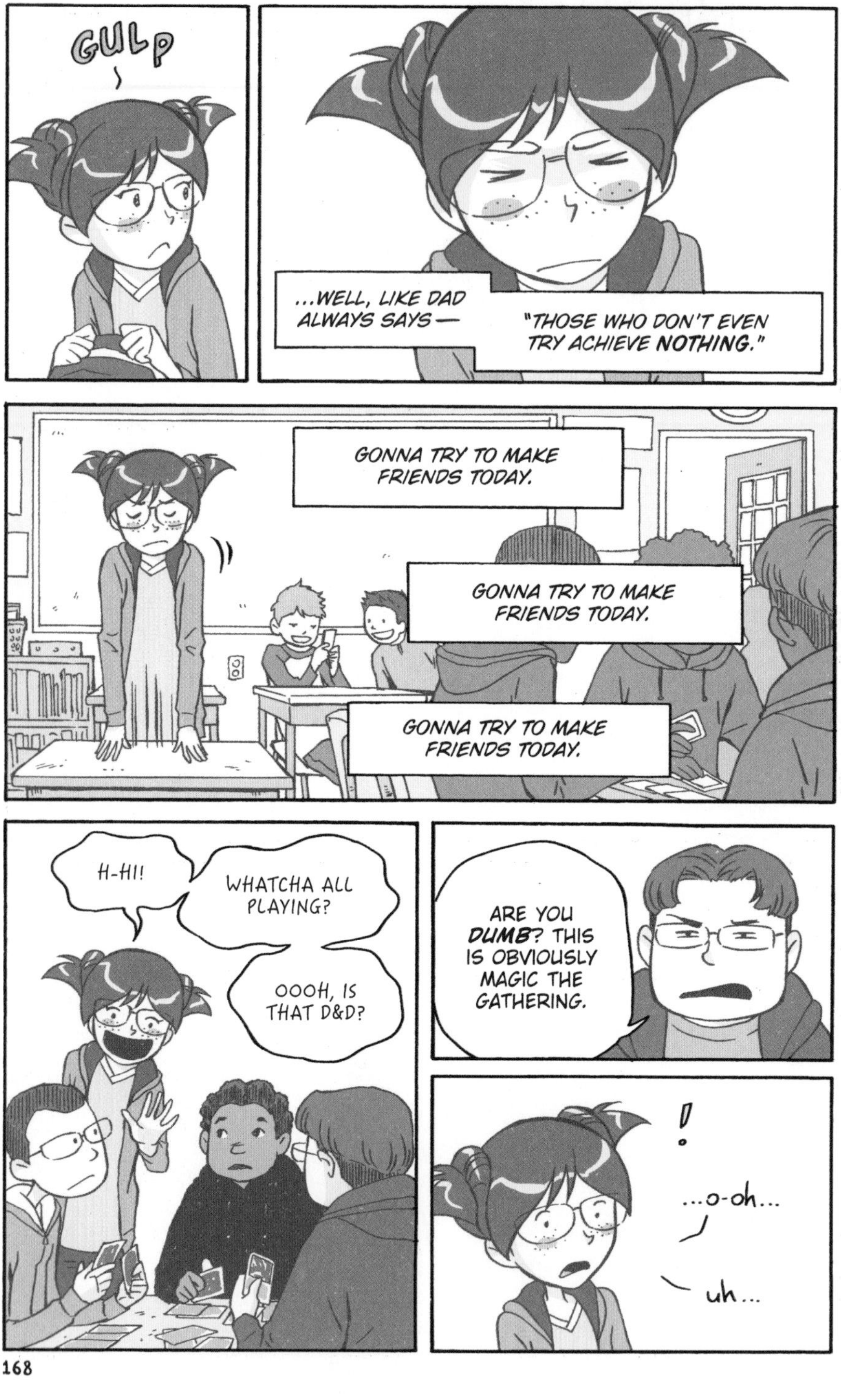
GULP
...WELL, LIKE DAD ALWAYS SAYS—
"THOSE WHO DON'T EVEN TRY ACHIEVE **NOTHING.**"
GONNA TRY TO MAKE FRIENDS TODAY.
GONNA TRY TO MAKE FRIENDS TODAY.
GONNA TRY TO MAKE FRIENDS TODAY.
H-HI!
WHATCHA ALL PLAYING?
OOOH, IS THAT D&D?
ARE YOU **DUMB**? THIS IS OBVIOUSLY MAGIC THE GATHERING.
!
...o-oh...
uh...

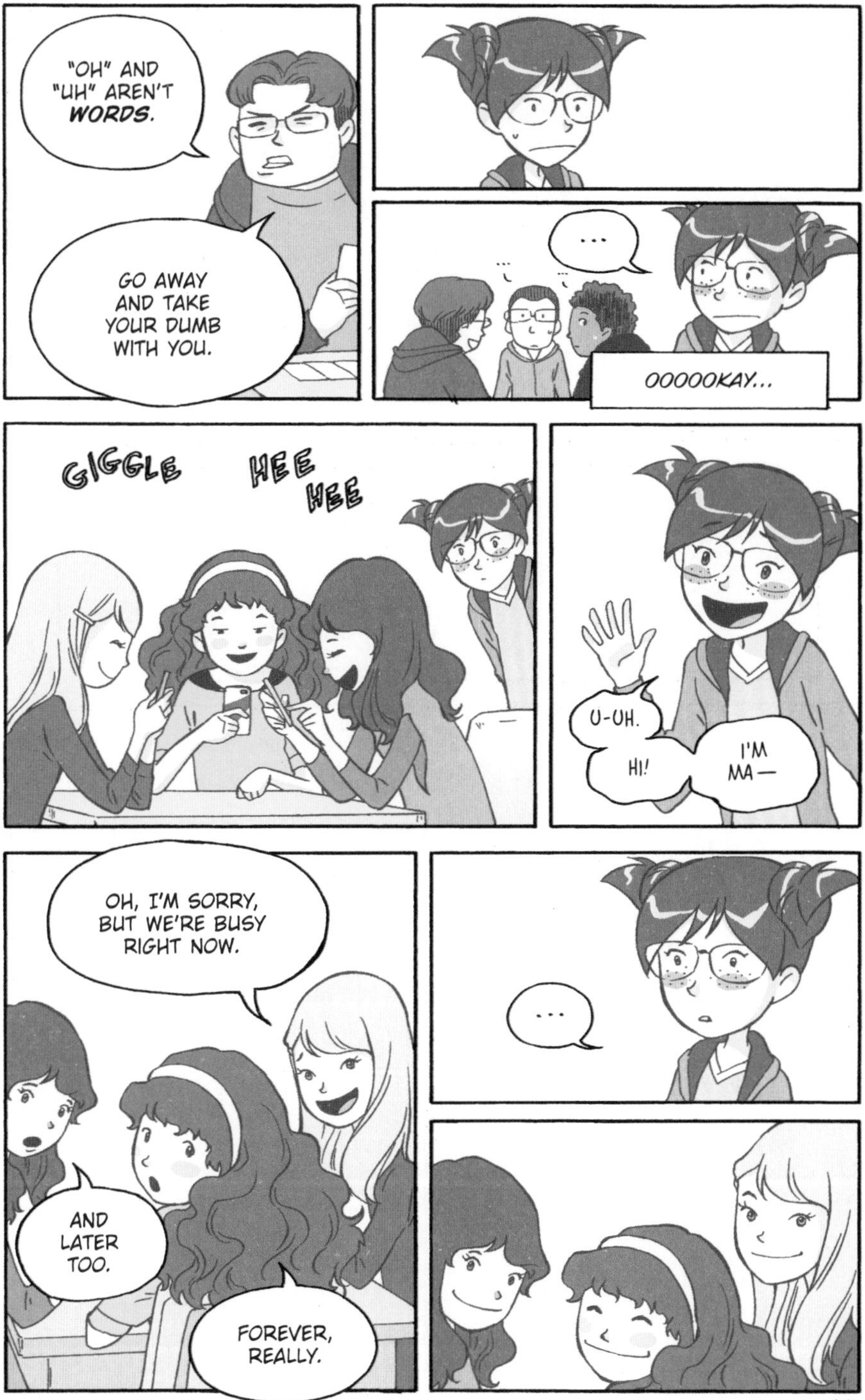
"OH" AND "UH" AREN'T WORDS.
GO AWAY AND TAKE YOUR DUMB WITH YOU.
...
OOOOOKAY...
GIGGLE
HEE HEE
U-UH.
HI!
I'M MA—
OH, I'M SORRY, BUT WE'RE BUSY RIGHT NOW.
AND LATER TOO.
FOREVER, REALLY.
...

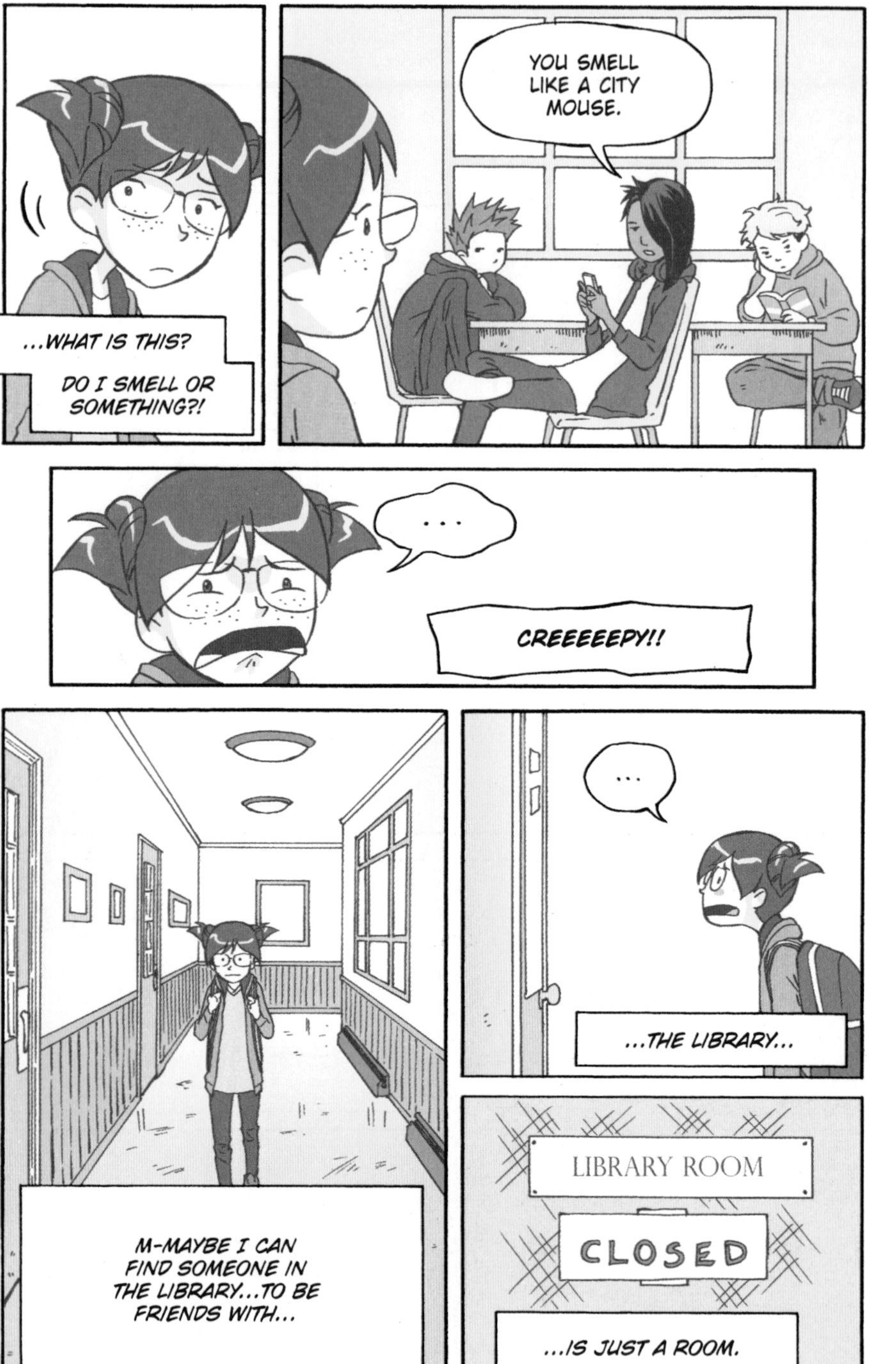
...WHAT IS THIS?
DO I SMELL OR SOMETHING?!
YOU SMELL LIKE A CITY MOUSE.
...
CREEEEEPY!!
M-MAYBE I CAN FIND SOMEONE IN THE LIBRARY...TO BE FRIENDS WITH...
...
...THE LIBRARY...
LIBRARY ROOM
CLOSED
...IS JUST A ROOM.
THAT'S CLOSED.

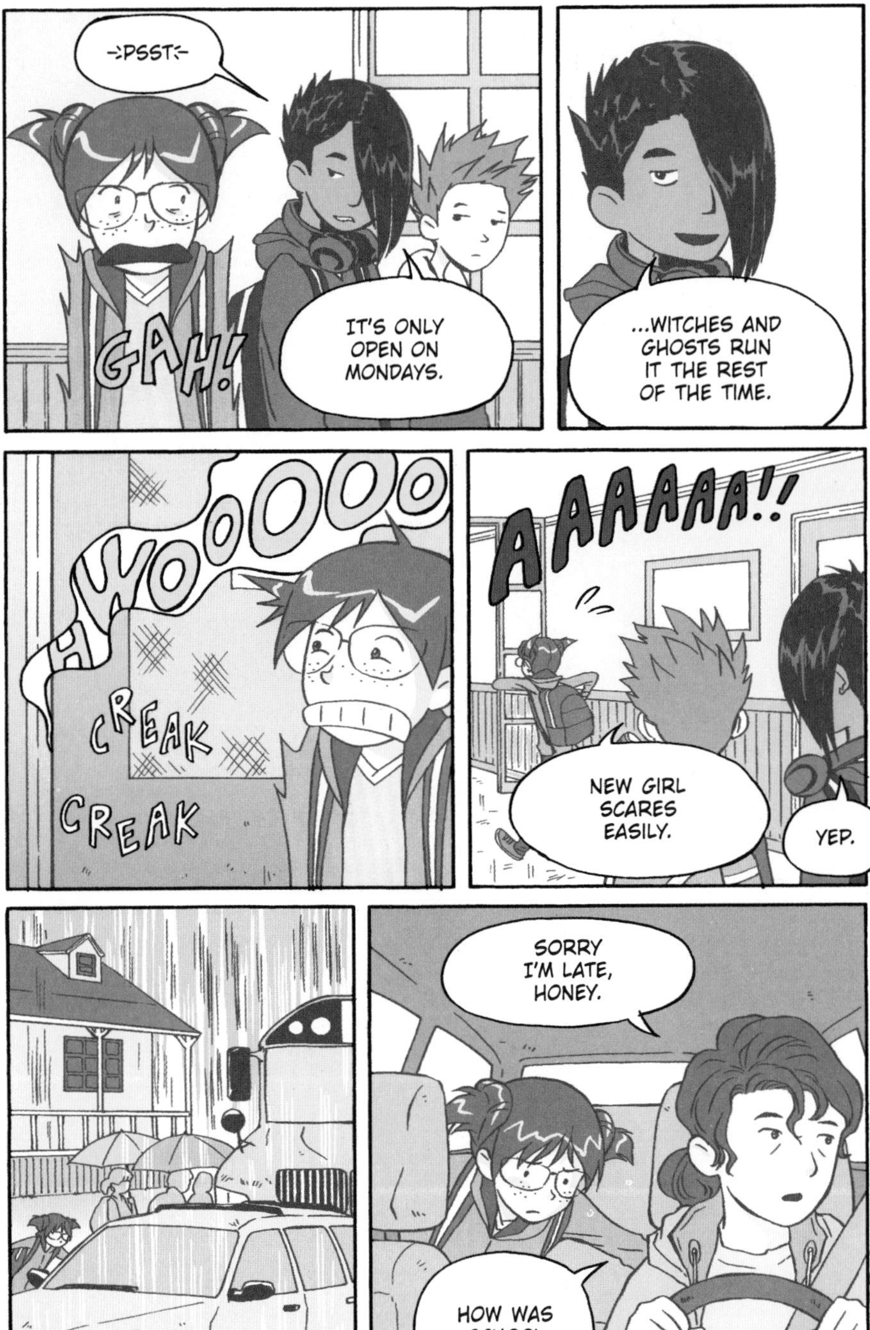
-:PSST:-
GAH!
IT'S ONLY OPEN ON MONDAYS.
...WITCHES AND GHOSTS RUN IT THE REST OF THE TIME.
HWOOOOOO
CREAK
CREAK
AAAAAA!!
NEW GIRL SCARES EASILY.
YEP.
SORRY I'M LATE, HONEY.
HOW WAS SCHOOL TODAY?

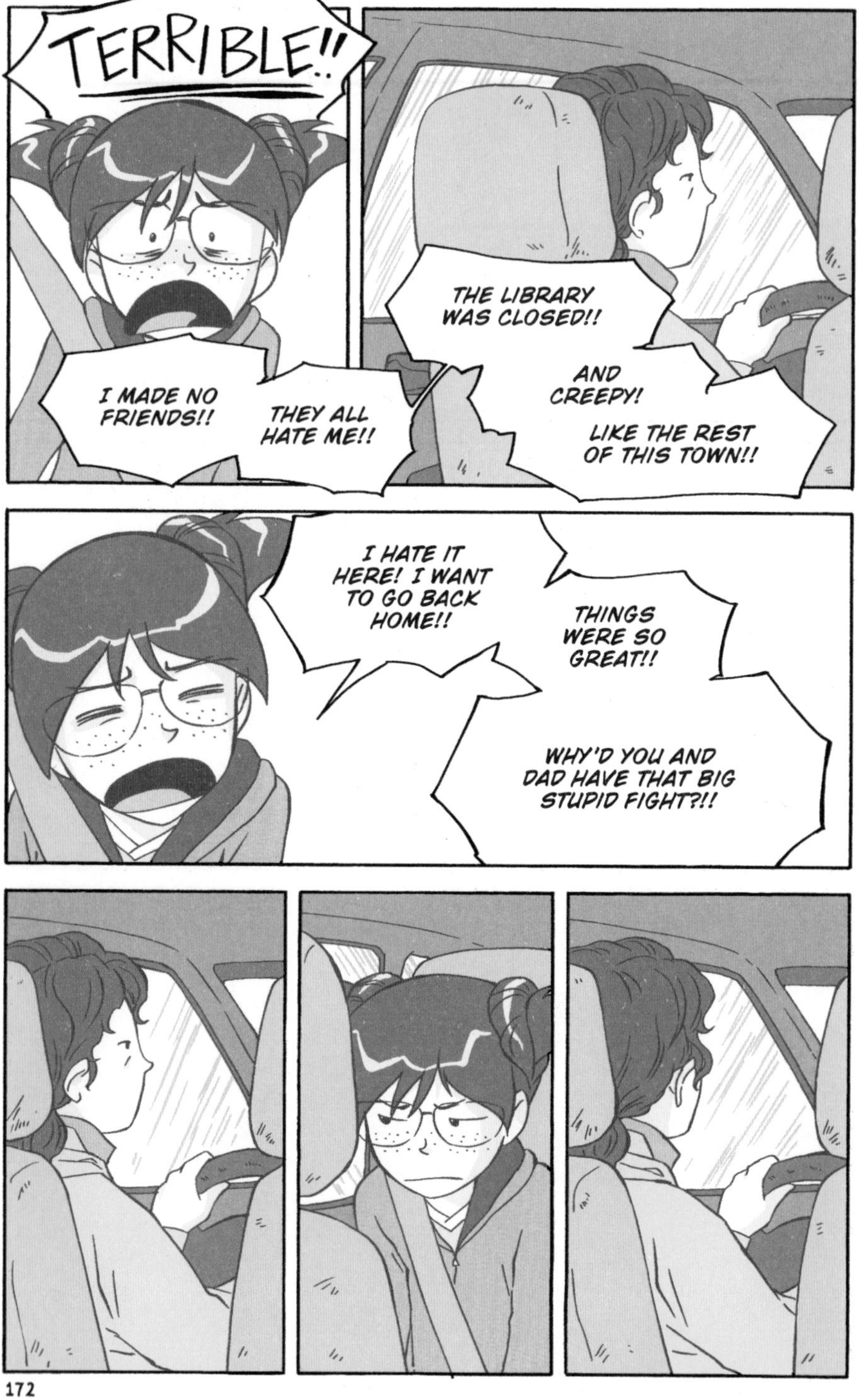
TERRIBLE!!
I MADE NO FRIENDS!!
THEY ALL HATE ME!!
THE LIBRARY WAS CLOSED!!
AND CREEPY!
LIKE THE REST OF THIS TOWN!!
I HATE IT HERE! I WANT TO GO BACK HOME!!
THINGS WERE SO GREAT!!
WHY'D YOU AND DAD HAVE THAT BIG STUPID FIGHT?!!

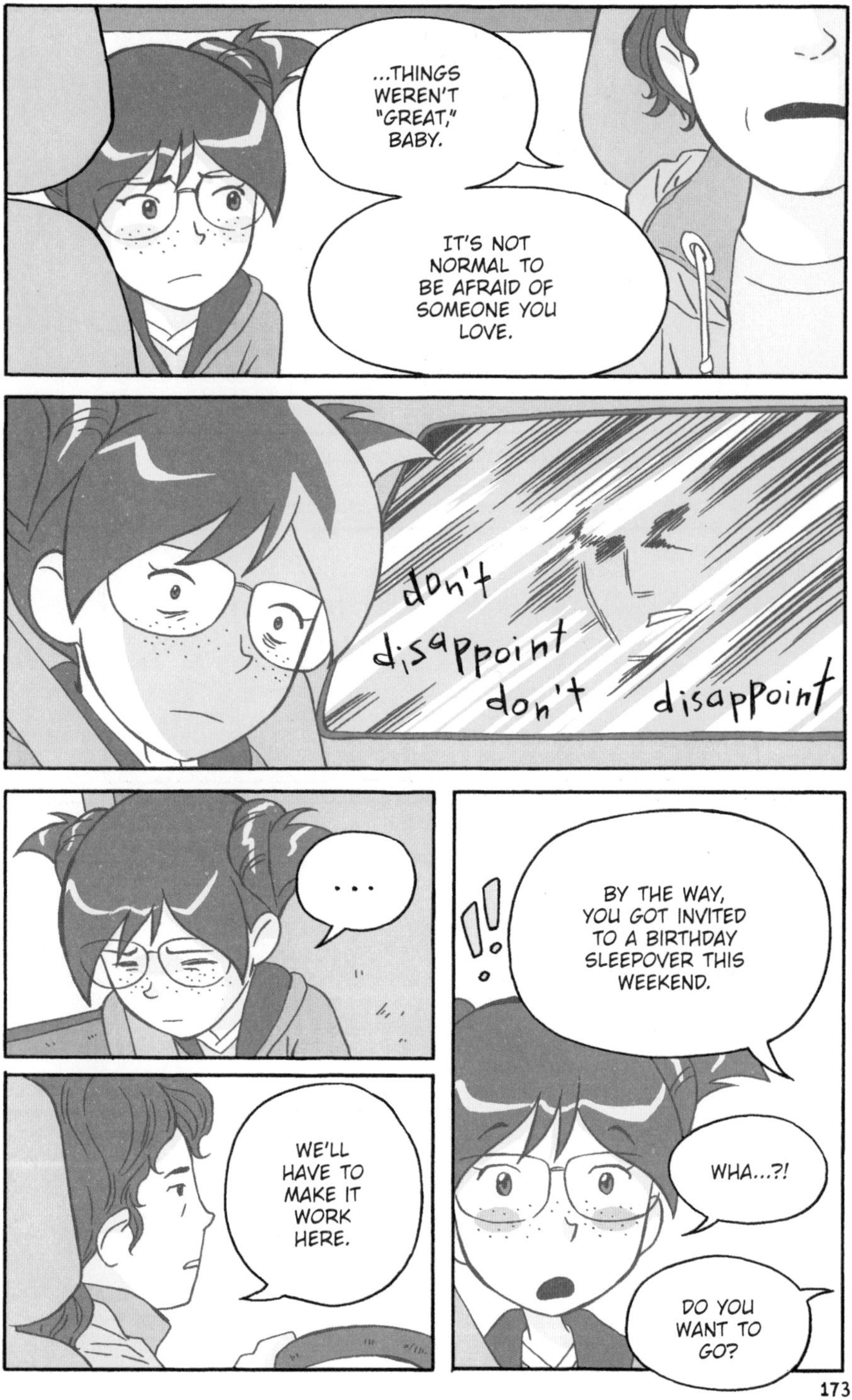
...THINGS WEREN'T "GREAT," BABY.
IT'S NOT NORMAL TO BE AFRAID OF SOMEONE YOU LOVE.
don't disappoint don't disappoint
...
!!
BY THE WAY, YOU GOT INVITED TO A BIRTHDAY SLEEPOVER THIS WEEKEND.
WE'LL HAVE TO MAKE IT WORK HERE.
WHA...?!
DO YOU WANT TO GO?

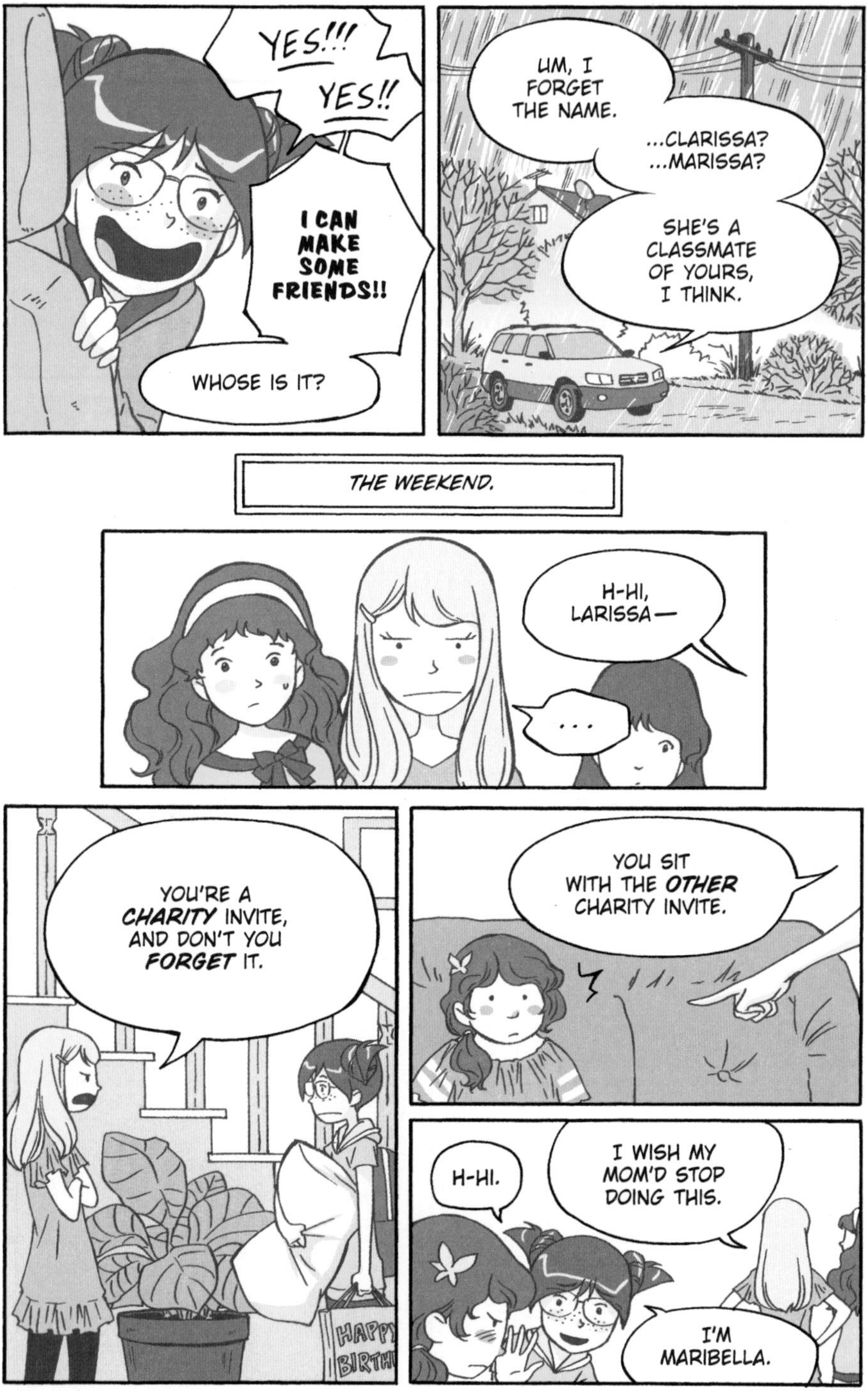
YES!!!
YES!!
I CAN MAKE SOME FRIENDS!!
WHOSE IS IT?
UM, I FORGET THE NAME.
...CLARISSA? ...MARISSA?
SHE'S A CLASSMATE OF YOURS, I THINK.
THE WEEKEND.
H-HI, LARISSA—
...
YOU'RE A CHARITY INVITE, AND DON'T YOU FORGET IT.
HAPPY BIRTH
YOU SIT WITH THE OTHER CHARITY INVITE.
H-HI.
I WISH MY MOM'D STOP DOING THIS.
I'M MARIBELLA.

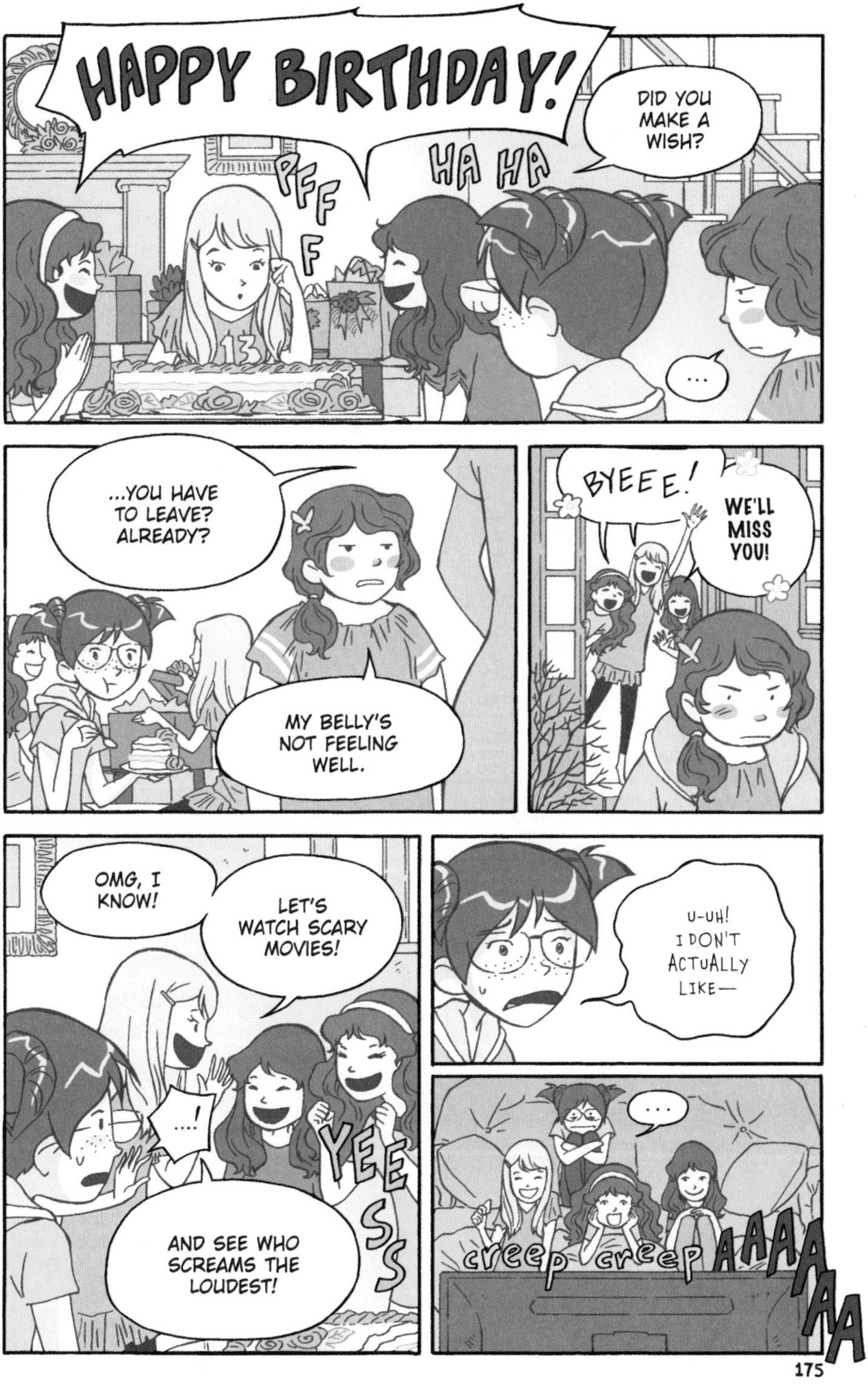
HAPPY BIRTHDAY!
PFFF
HA HA
DID YOU MAKE A WISH?
...
...YOU HAVE TO LEAVE? ALREADY?
MY BELLY'S NOT FEELING WELL.
BYEEEE!
WE'LL MISS YOU!
OMG, I KNOW!
LET'S WATCH SCARY MOVIES!
...!
AND SEE WHO SCREAMS THE LOUDEST!
YEESSS
U-UH! I DON'T ACTUALLY LIKE—
...
creep creep
AAAAAAA

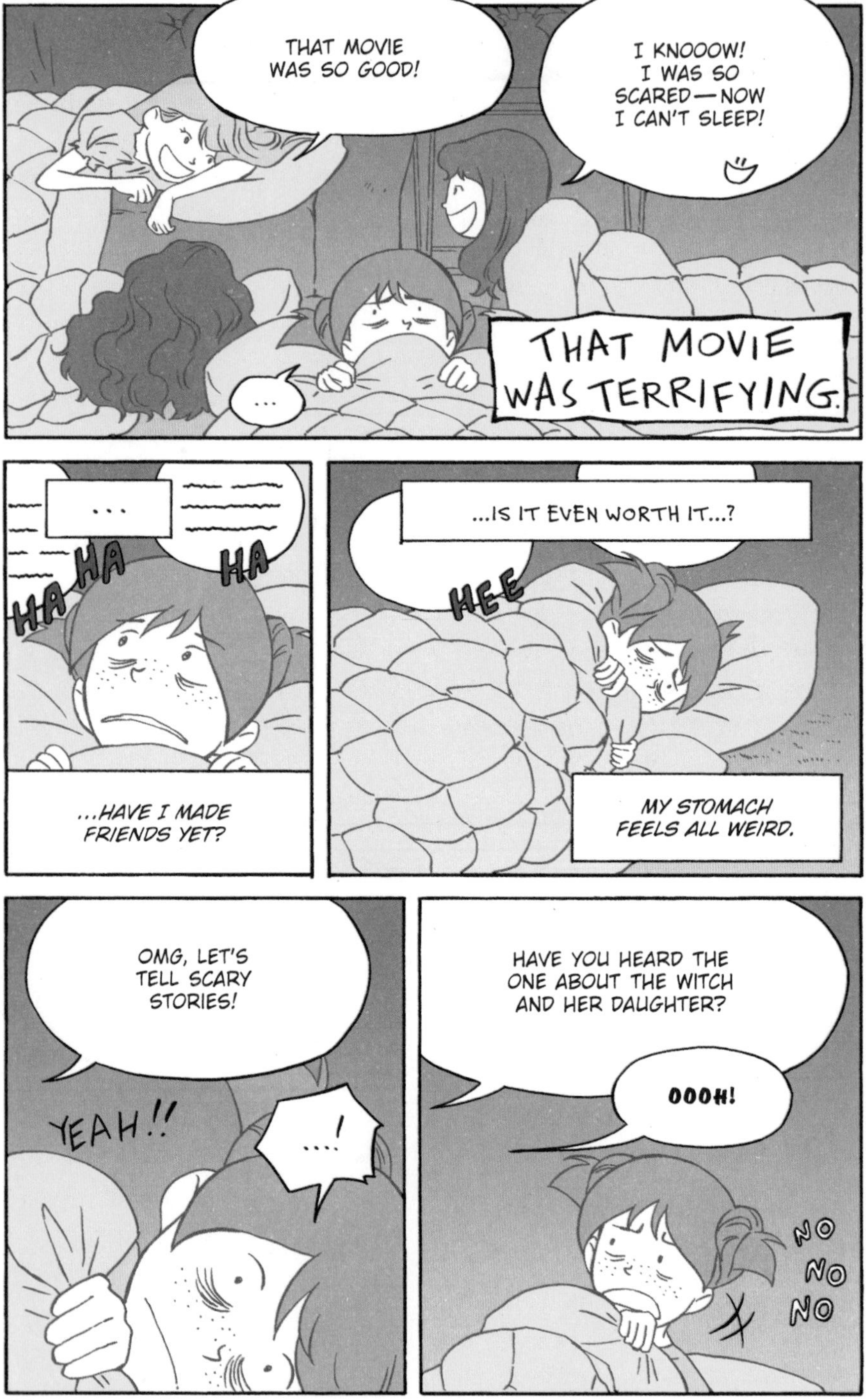
THAT MOVIE WAS SO GOOD!
I KNOOOW! I WAS SO SCARED—NOW I CAN'T SLEEP!
...
THAT MOVIE WAS TERRIFYING.
...
HA HA HA
...HAVE I MADE FRIENDS YET?
...IS IT EVEN WORTH IT...?
HEE
MY STOMACH FEELS ALL WEIRD.
OMG, LET'S TELL SCARY STORIES!
YEAH!!
...!
HAVE YOU HEARD THE ONE ABOUT THE WITCH AND HER DAUGHTER?
OOOH!
NO NO NO

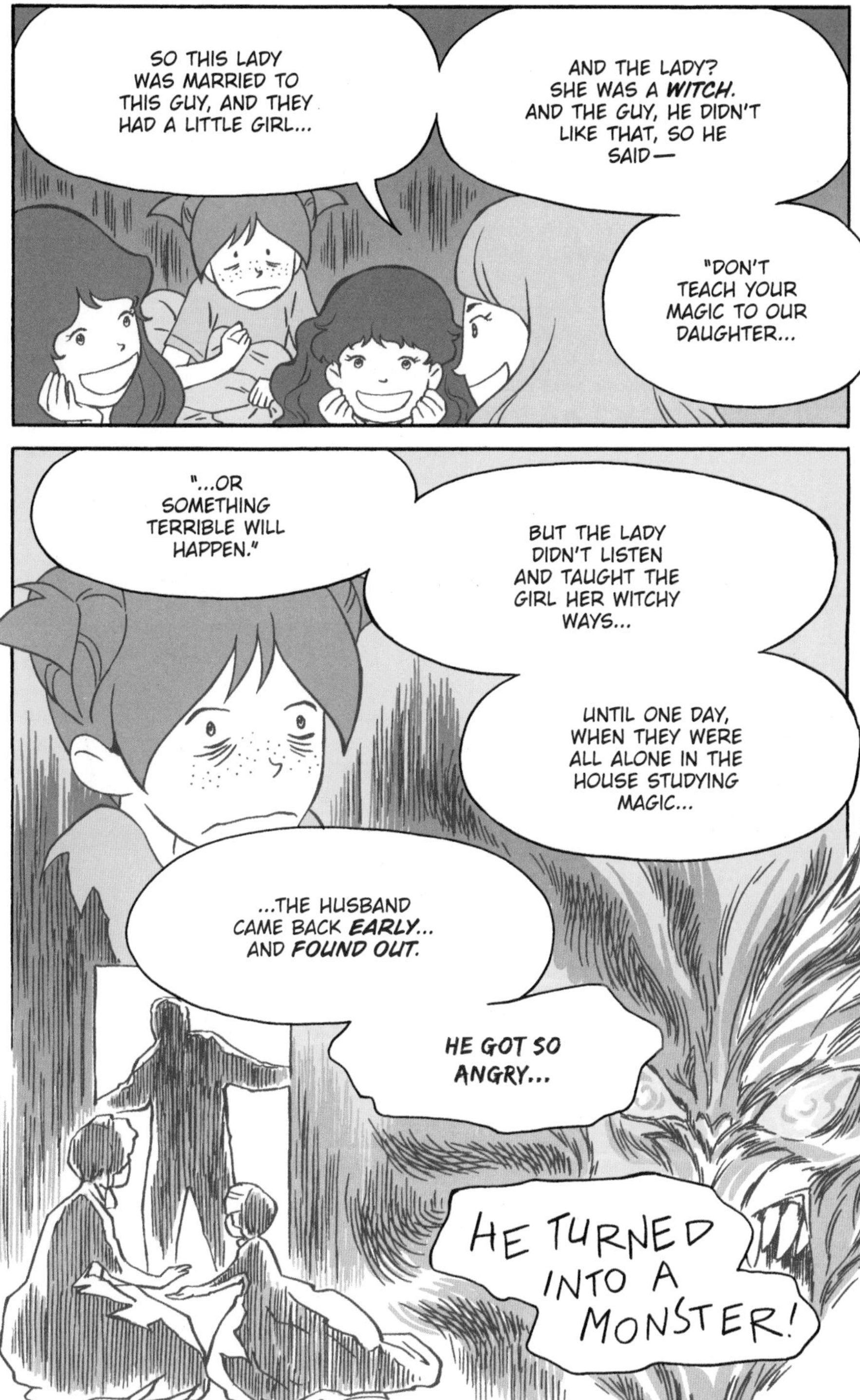
SO THIS LADY WAS MARRIED TO THIS GUY, AND THEY HAD A LITTLE GIRL...
AND THE LADY? SHE WAS A WITCH. AND THE GUY, HE DIDN'T LIKE THAT, SO HE SAID—
"DON'T TEACH YOUR MAGIC TO OUR DAUGHTER...
"...OR SOMETHING TERRIBLE WILL HAPPEN."
BUT THE LADY DIDN'T LISTEN AND TAUGHT THE GIRL HER WITCHY WAYS...
UNTIL ONE DAY, WHEN THEY WERE ALL ALONE IN THE HOUSE STUDYING MAGIC...
...THE HUSBAND CAME BACK EARLY... AND FOUND OUT.
HE GOT SO ANGRY...
HE TURNED INTO A MONSTER!

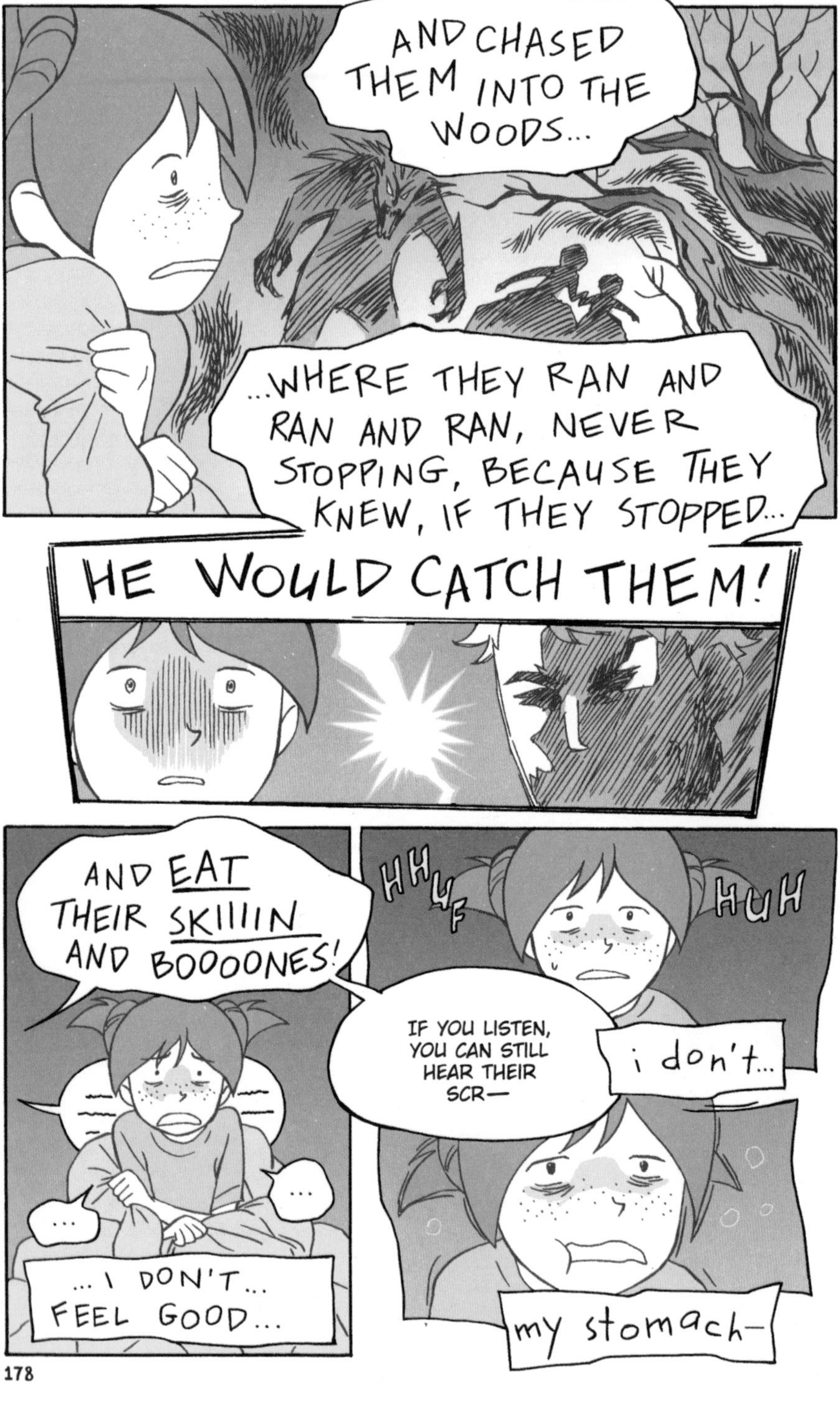
AND CHASED THEM INTO THE WOODS...
...WHERE THEY RAN AND RAN AND RAN, NEVER STOPPING, BECAUSE THEY KNEW, IF THEY STOPPED...
HE WOULD CATCH THEM!
AND EAT THEIR SKIIIIN AND BOOOONES!
HHHUF
HUH
...
...
...
IF YOU LISTEN, YOU CAN STILL HEAR THEIR SCR—
i don't...
...I DON'T... FEEL GOOD...
my stomach—

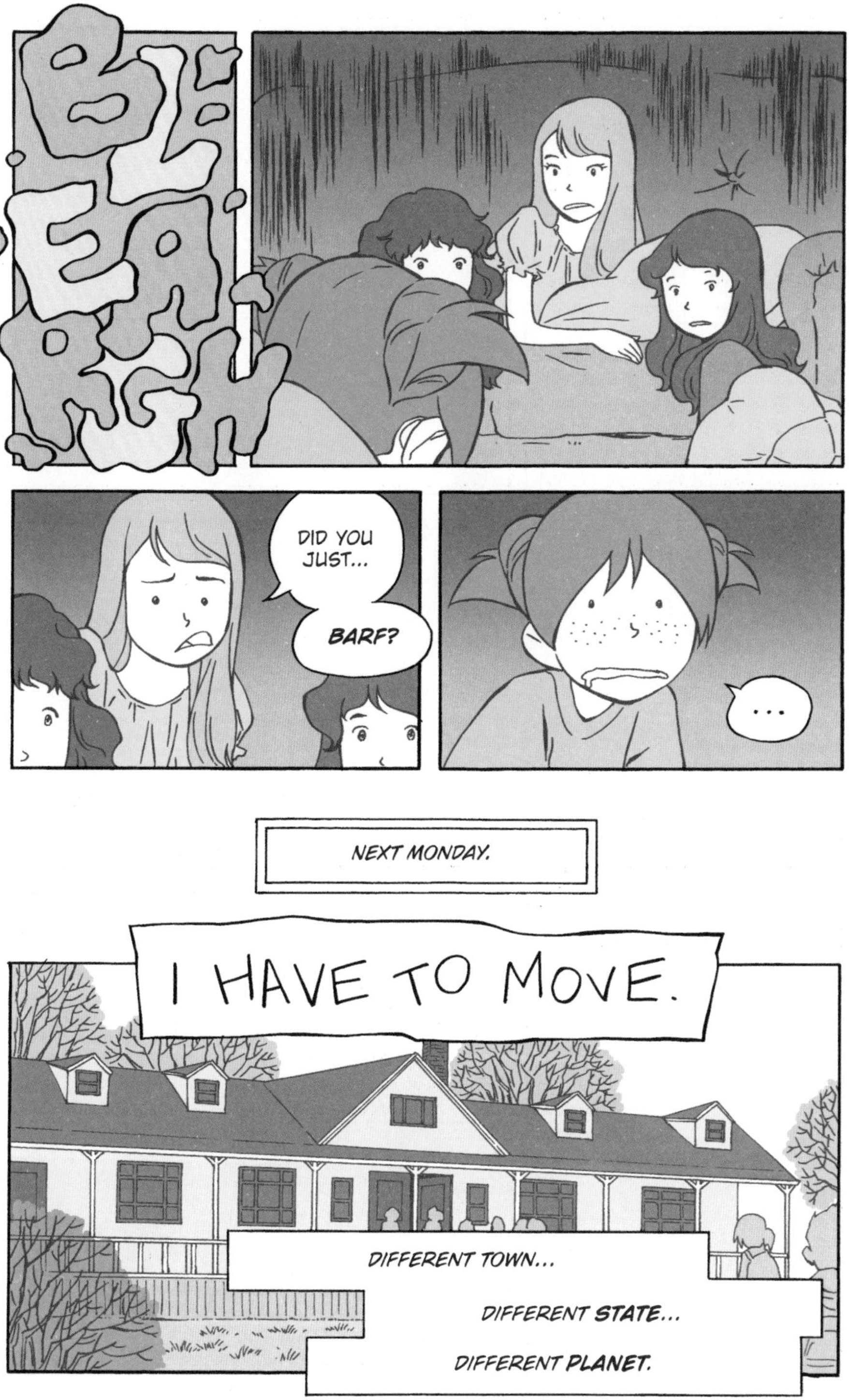
BLEAUGH
DID YOU JUST...
BARF?
...
NEXT MONDAY.
I HAVE TO MOVE.
DIFFERENT TOWN...
DIFFERENT STATE...
DIFFERENT PLANET.

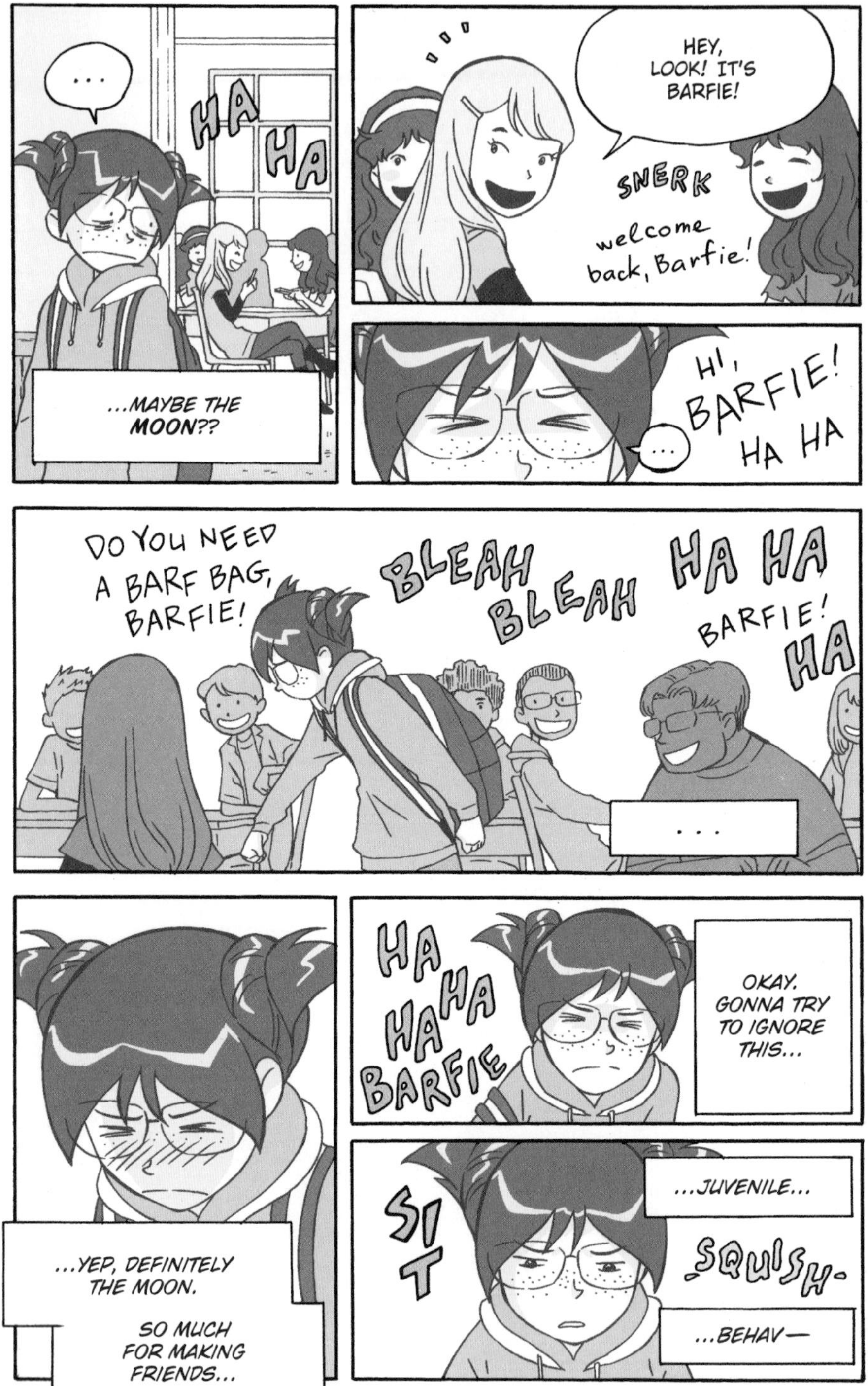
...
HA HA
...MAYBE THE **MOON**??
HEY, LOOK! IT'S BARFIE!
SNERK
welcome back, Barfie!
HI, BARFIE! HA HA
...
DO YOU NEED A BARF BAG, BARFIE!
BLEAH BLEAH HA HA
BARFIE! HA
...
...YEP, DEFINITELY THE MOON.
SO MUCH FOR MAKING FRIENDS...
HA HA HA HA BARFIE
OKAY. GONNA TRY TO IGNORE THIS...
...JUVENILE...
SIT
SQUISH
...BEHAV—

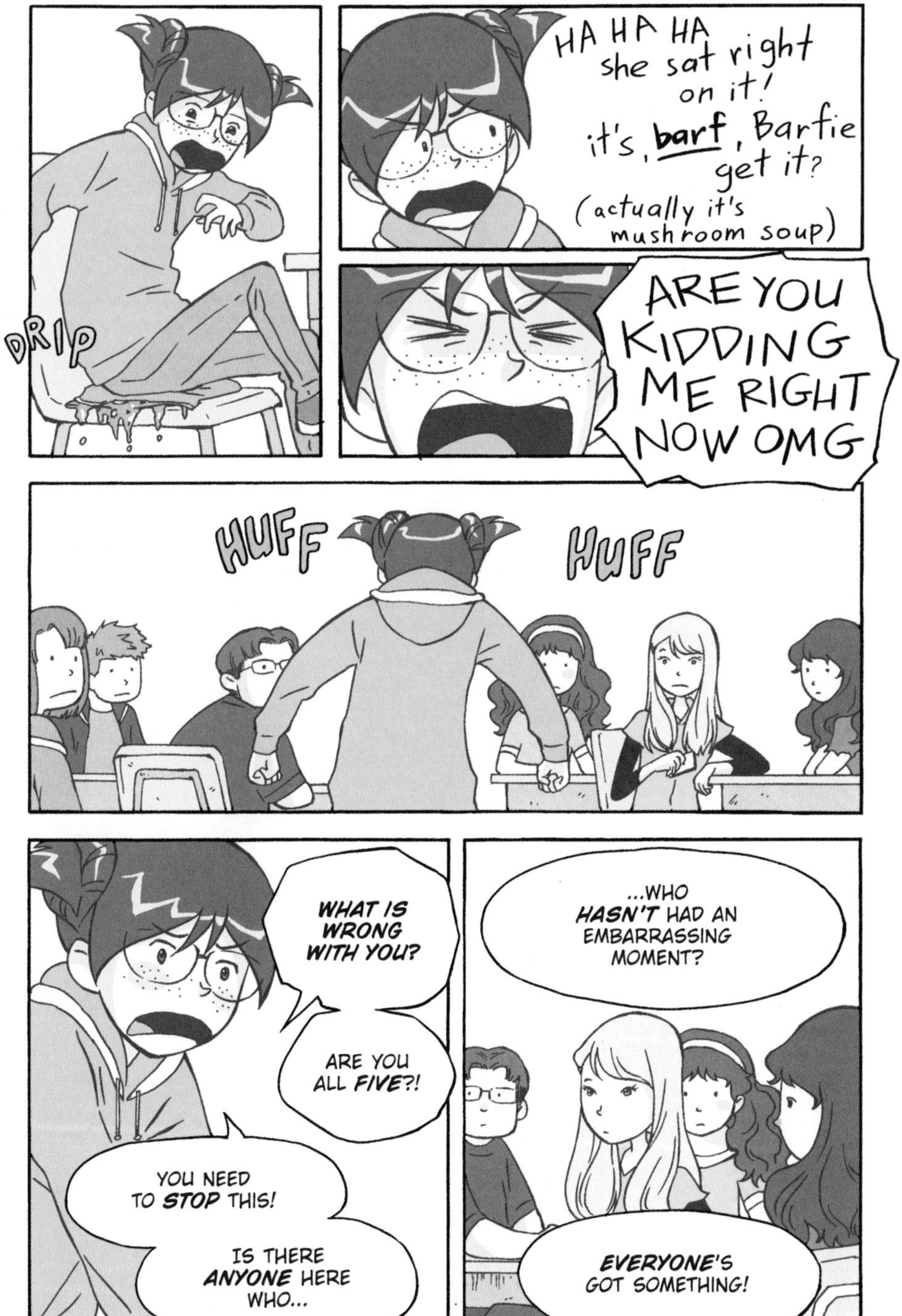
DRIP
HA HA HA
she sat right
on it!
it's, barf, Barfie
get it?
(actually it's
mushroom soup)
ARE YOU KIDDING ME RIGHT NOW OMG
HUFF HUFF
WHAT IS WRONG WITH YOU?
ARE YOU ALL FIVE?!
YOU NEED TO STOP THIS!
IS THERE ANYONE HERE WHO...
...WHO HASN'T HAD AN EMBARRASSING MOMENT?
EVERYONE'S GOT SOMETHING!

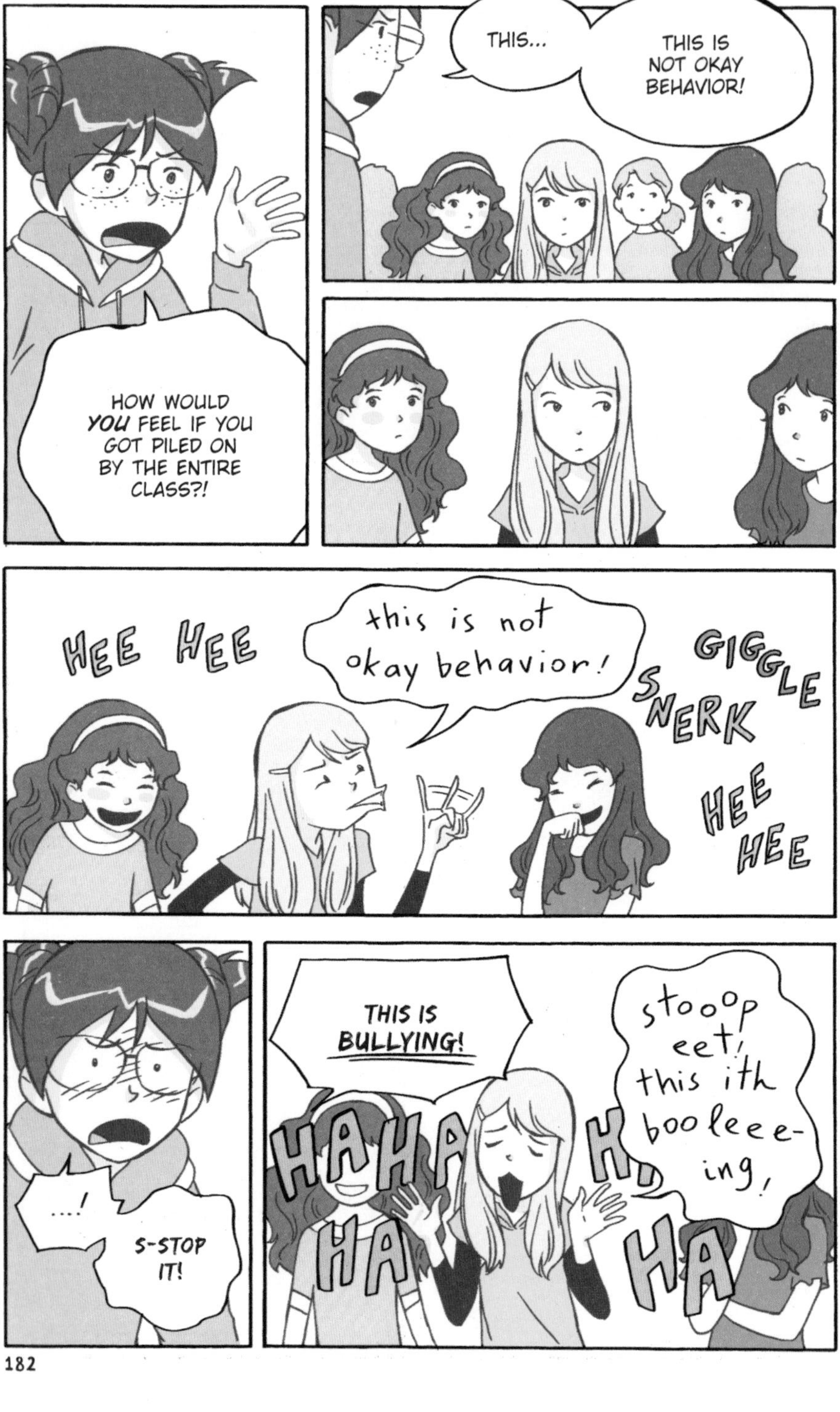

HOW WOULD *YOU* FEEL IF YOU GOT PILED ON BY THE ENTIRE CLASS?!
THIS...
THIS IS NOT OKAY BEHAVIOR!
HEE HEE
this is not okay behavior!
GIGGLE
SNERK
HEE HEE
...!
S-STOP IT!
THIS IS BULLYING!
stooop eet! this ith booleee-ing!
HAHAHA
HA
HA

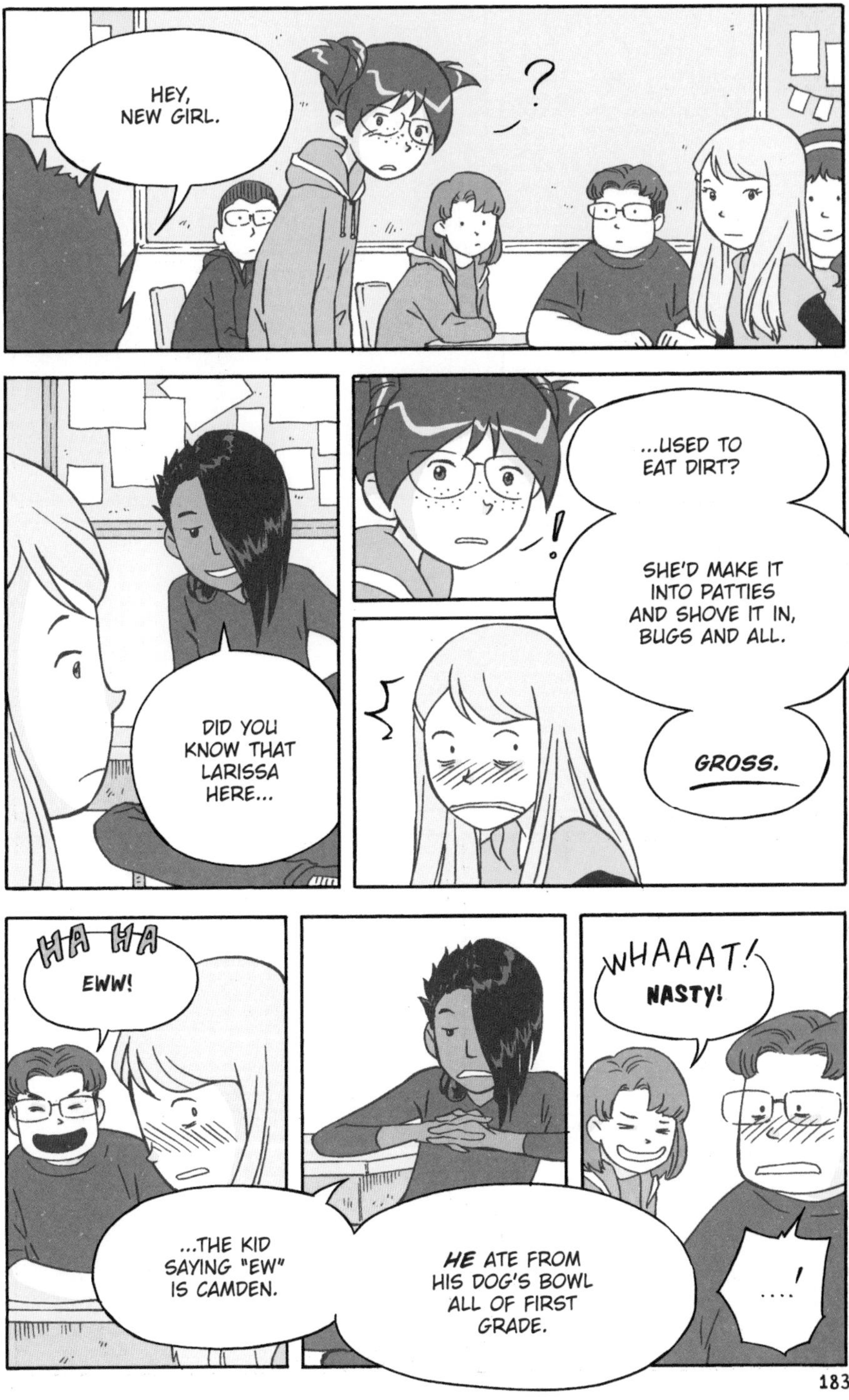
HEY, NEW GIRL.
?
DID YOU KNOW THAT LARISSA HERE...
...USED TO EAT DIRT?
!
SHE'D MAKE IT INTO PATTIES AND SHOVE IT IN, BUGS AND ALL.
GROSS.
HA HA
EWW!
WHAAAT!
NASTY!
...THE KID SAYING "EW" IS CAMDEN.
HE ATE FROM HIS DOG'S BOWL ALL OF FIRST GRADE.
...!

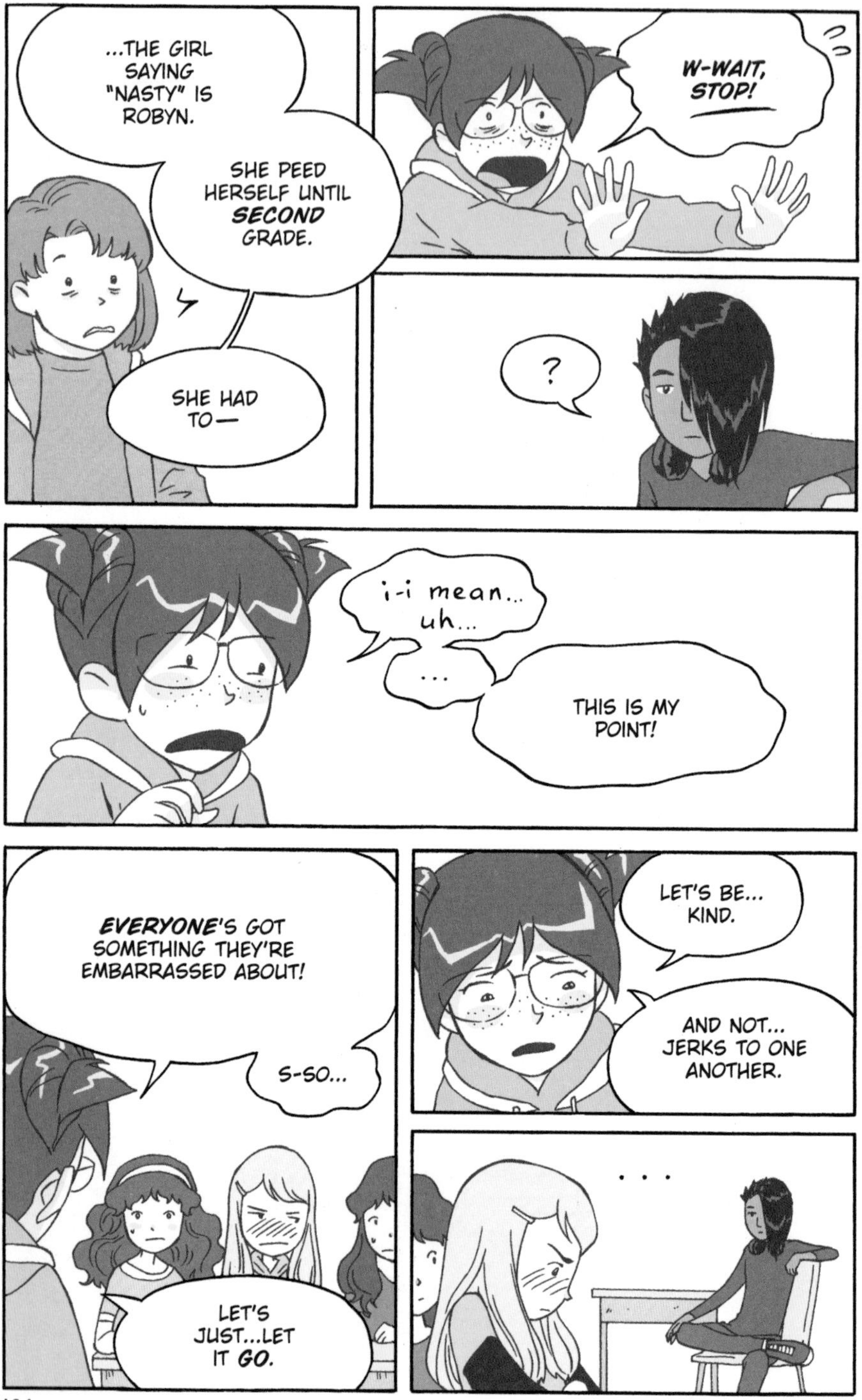

...THE GIRL SAYING "NASTY" IS ROBYN.
SHE PEED HERSELF UNTIL SECOND GRADE.
SHE HAD TO—
W-WAIT, STOP!
?
i-i mean... uh...
...
THIS IS MY POINT!
EVERYONE'S GOT SOMETHING THEY'RE EMBARRASSED ABOUT!
S-SO...
LET'S JUST...LET IT GO.
LET'S BE... KIND.
AND NOT... JERKS TO ONE ANOTHER.
. . .

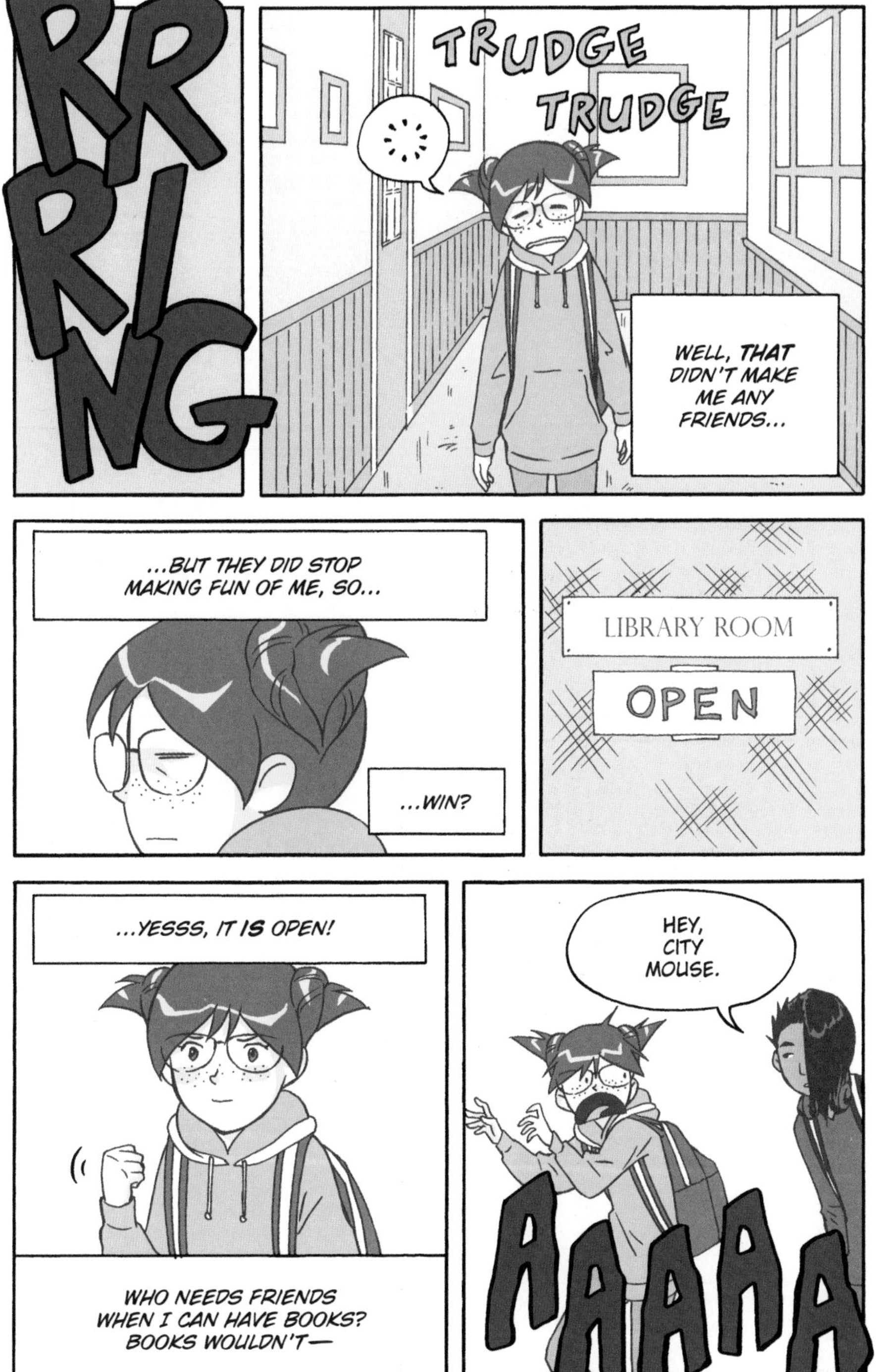
RRRRING
TRUDGE TRUDGE
...
WELL, THAT DIDN'T MAKE ME ANY FRIENDS...
...BUT THEY DID STOP MAKING FUN OF ME, SO...
...WIN?
LIBRARY ROOM
OPEN
...YESSS, IT IS OPEN!
WHO NEEDS FRIENDS WHEN I CAN HAVE BOOKS? BOOKS WOULDN'T—
HEY, CITY MOUSE.
AAAAA

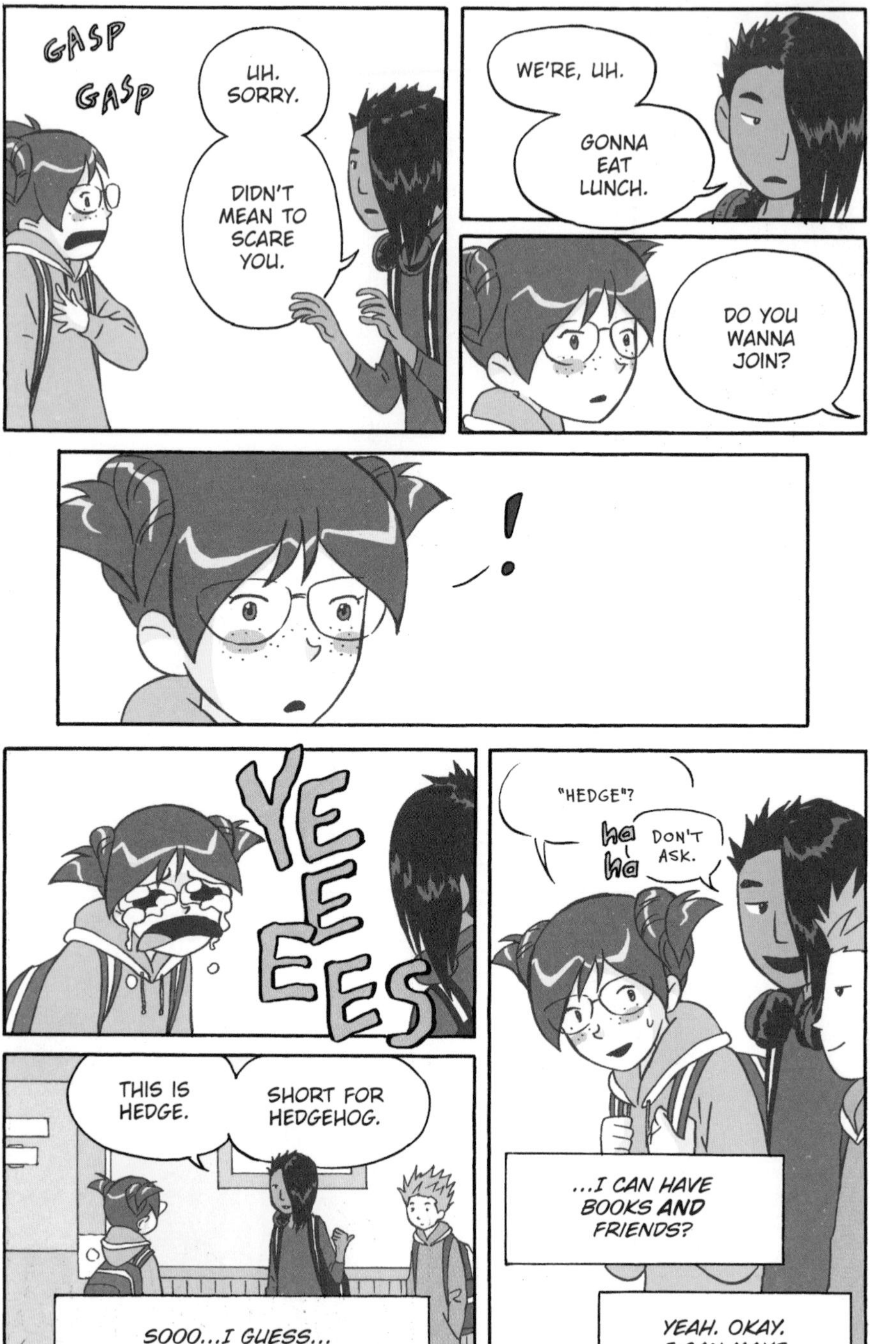
GASP
GASP
UH. SORRY.
DIDN'T MEAN TO SCARE YOU.
WE'RE, UH.
GONNA EAT LUNCH.
DO YOU WANNA JOIN?
!
YEEEES
THIS IS HEDGE.
SHORT FOR HEDGEHOG.
SOOO...I GUESS...
"HEDGE"?
ha ha
DON'T ASK.
...I CAN HAVE BOOKS AND FRIENDS?
YEAH. OKAY. I CAN MAKE THIS WORK.

NEW GIRL: THE END

Take pictures of special moments to make the memories last! You can print them out and glue them here.

FRIENDS, FAMILY, ACTORS, MUSICIANS, AUTHORS, OR FICTIONAL CHARACTERS!

• MY FAVORITE PEOPLE •

DRAW PICTURES OF YOUR FAVORITE PEOPLE IN THE BOXES!

NAME: ....

AGE: ....

FAVORITE COLOR: ....

FAVORITE FOOD: ....

FAVORITE BOOK: ....

NAME: ....

AGE: ....

FAVORITE COLOR: ....

FAVORITE FOOD: ....

FAVORITE BOOK: ....

NAME: ....

AGE: ....

FAVORITE COLOR: ....

FAVORITE FOOD: ....

FAVORITE BOOK: ....

• MY FAVORITE PEOPLE •

NAME: ....

AGE: ....

FAVORITE COLOR: ....

FAVORITE FOOD: ....

FAVORITE BOOK: ....

NAME: ....

AGE: ....

FAVORITE COLOR: ....

FAVORITE FOOD: ....

FAVORITE BOOK: ....

NAME: ....

AGE: ....

FAVORITE COLOR: ....

FAVORITE FOOD: ....

FAVORITE BOOK: ....

• MY FAVORITE PEOPLE •

NAME: ....

AGE: ....

FAVORITE COLOR: ....

FAVORITE FOOD: ....

FAVORITE BOOK: ....

NAME: ....

AGE: ....

FAVORITE COLOR: ....

FAVORITE FOOD: ....

FAVORITE BOOK: ....

NAME: ....

AGE: ....

FAVORITE COLOR: ....

FAVORITE FOOD: ....

FAVORITE BOOK: ....

• MY FAVORITE PEOPLE •

NAME: ....

AGE: ....

FAVORITE COLOR: ....

FAVORITE FOOD: ....

FAVORITE BOOK: ....

NAME: ....

AGE: ....

FAVORITE COLOR: ....

FAVORITE FOOD: ....

FAVORITE BOOK: ....

NAME: ....

AGE: ....

FAVORITE COLOR: ....

FAVORITE FOOD: ....

FAVORITE BOOK: ....

diary

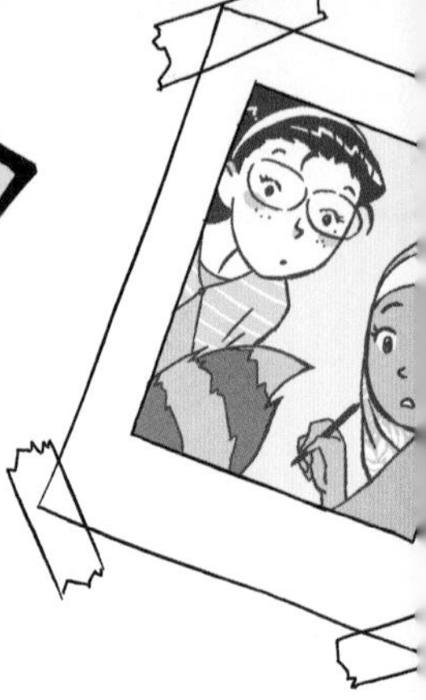

SVETLANA CHMAKOVA

Cover and interior design: Wendy Chan
Coloring assistant: Melissa McCommon
Lettering: JuYoun Lee

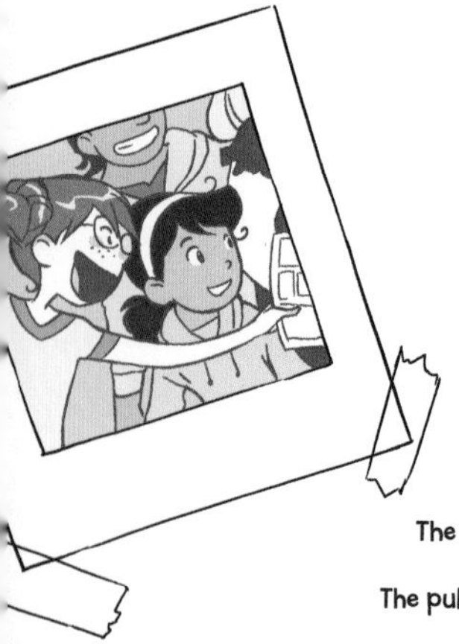

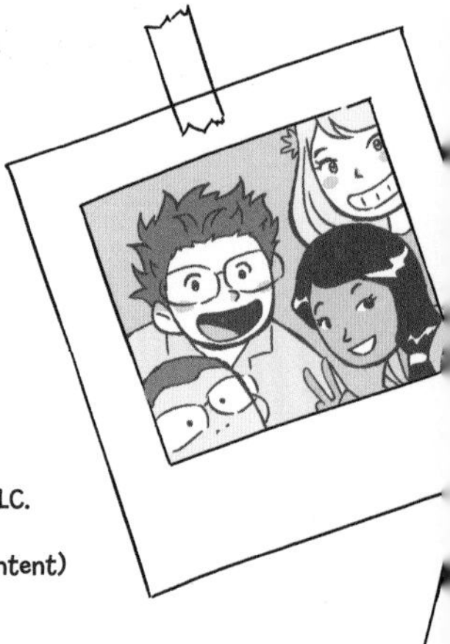

JY

150 West 30th Street, 19th Floor
New York, NY 10001

Visit us at jyforkids.com
facebook.com/jyforkids
twitter.com/jyforkids
jyforkids.tumblr.com
instagram.com/jyforkids

First JY Edition: October 2019

JY is an imprint of Yen Press, LLC.
The JY name and logo are trademarks of Yen Press, LLC.

The publisher is not responsible for websites (or their content) that are not owned by the publisher.

Library of Congress Control Number: 2019943267

ISBN: 978-1-9753-3279-2

10 9 8 7 6 5 4 3 2 1

LSC-C

Printed in China